The Kindness of Time
and other stories

*A diverse collection of tales from
a band of new writers*

Published in Great Britain in 2022 by Red Socks Publishing

Email: alexiskrite@gmail.com

The authors have asserted their right under the Copyright, Designs and Patents Act, 1988, to be identified as the authors of this work.

No part of this publication may be reproduced, stored in a retrieval system, or transmitted, in any form or by any means, electronic, mechanical, photocopying, recording or otherwise, without the prior written permission of the copyright owner.

A CIP catalogue record for this book is available from the British Library.

All the characters in this book are fictitious and any resemblance to actual persons, living or dead, is purely coincidental.

ISBN: 978-1-3999-2681-2

Printed and bound in Great Britain by Short Run Press Ltd, 25 Bittern Road, Exeter EX2 7LW

Foreword

We are delighted to donate all profits from this collection of stories to Challengers, an outstanding charity based in the South-East that provides stimulating play opportunities for disabled children and young people.

Our collection includes a wide variety of themes – including crime, mystery, humour, the supernatural and the struggles of ordinary people. We hope you will enjoy reading them as much as we did writing them.

The authors
Email address: alexiskrite@gmail.com

A message from Challengers

Founded in 1979, Challengers is a charity dedicated to breaking down the barriers of play for disabled children and young people.

Our mission is to ensure that all children, regardless of their impairments, have access to exciting and inclusive play and leisure opportunities.

Each year more than 1,400 disabled children and young people, aged 2-18, benefit from our pre-schools, playschemes and youth schemes, all based across the South East.

Challengers is a place where all disabled young people can make friends and try activities they may have never had the opportunity to before.

Play is crucial for children's development – helping them to develop key social, physical and emotional skills that are vital in later life. Significantly, the children who attend build their confidence and self-esteem, enabling them to enjoy happier and healthier lives.

Whilst their child is in our care, parents can feel confident that their son or daughter is happy and safe, and that their needs are well catered for. Parents are often in need of breaks from their care responsibilities. Our services provide respite for them and fun for their child. Families have said Challengers' lifeline of support keeps them strong.

Challengers will never turn away a child. Our non-exclusion policy ensures that everyone is included, regardless of the complexity of their care, needs and impairments. Where other providers of play and leisure say No, Challengers will always say Yes.

Web address: disability-challengers.org

Dedicated to Daniel and Sarah

Contents

Red Socks for Mondays   11
Alexis Krite

Life Sentence   25
Alexis Krite

The Face from the Past   31
David Reading

The Month of Good and Bad Things   39
David Reading

Motherhood   49
Sally Stone

Restoration   61
Alexis Krite

Aanjay Jumps from a Plane   73
David Reading

Crime in the Time of Covid   79
David Reading

The Haunting at Wellspring House   93
Alexis Krite

The Stitch-Up   103
Max Bevan

A Peculiar Sort of Friendship Alexis Krite	107
The Kindness of Time Alexis Krite	121
Aanjay Meets a Mugger David Reading	135
Conspiracy David Reading	139
Travis County Max Bevan	147
The Secret Life of Remus J Metro David Reading	163
Did He Jump? David Reading	175
Aanjay's Heroic Deed David Reading	191
Bait Alexis Krite	197
Angelina Alexis Krite	213
The Life and Death of Harvey Patton Jane Churcher	223

The Lesson for Today   233
David Reading

Thicker than Water   239
Alexis Krite

Aanjay in a Troublesome Spot   247
David Reading

The House Sitters   253
Alexis Krite

Superstition   265
David Reading

Father's Day   273
Alexis Krite

One Who Cheats Death   293
Alexis Krite

Carbon Copy   303
David Reading

Jago Stark's Christmas Gift   317
Alexis Krite

Acknowledgements   329

Red Socks for Mondays
Alexis Krite

Although she was only eighteen months older than him, Victoria Smith had decided early on that Robert was to be her vassal. Her brother was to fetch and carry her toys, wipe the dog mess from her shoes and hand over his share of the tea-time cakes and biscuits. Should he fail to respond appropriately to her demands, he would receive a punch or a kick, or worse, his beloved teddy bear would be hurled down the stairs.

To protect himself from her bullying, Robert withdrew into his own world. A world that he could control. He ordered and tidied and placed his toys with care, exactly where they belonged. He started watching and counting: his father took ten steps to get from the front door to the kitchen. Robert counted the risers on the stairs when he went up (eleven) and the number of spindles when he went down (fifteen). He learned to count long before he could write and then, when he learned how to form his letters, he wrote all the numbers down. He started making lists. He wrote and re-wrote these lists on any paper he could find.

As he grew, his parents looked on with a mixture of amusement and concern. "He'll be an accountant when he grows up," his mother said proudly one evening, just before Robert turned ten. She picked up the electricity bill from the kitchen table and looked at a list that

Robert had written on the back. It was a stock take of the contents of the larder. She walked in and began to check the shelves against the list. "Eight tins of mushy peas; three packets of self-raising flour; five jars of Marmite."

"Boring!" Victoria called out. She dipped her paintbrush in burnt umber and filled in an intricate drawing of a leaf she had just sketched.

"Five jars of Marmite?" His father looked up from his paper: "Why do we need five jars of Marmite?"

"You never know, John, when you might be thankful that we have plenty of Marmite." His wife leaned across the wide marble shelf and lined the little brown jars up in a neat row, just in front of the five tins of fruit cocktail that Robert had missed from his list.

Her husband shook his head and went back to his crossword. "Five letters, *h* something something, ending in *rd*." He glanced over to his son, sure of getting the answer.

On the other side of the kitchen table, Robert had built a tower using his father's empty cigarette packets. He had balanced them carefully, one on top of the other. He took a tape measure and dangled it from the top packet until it rested on the flowered oilcloth. Twenty-six inches exactly. He wrote it down. Without looking up, he half-whispered: "Hoard". His father smiled and filled in the blank squares. Suddenly Victoria reached across and swiped at the cigarette tower, sending the packets across the floor. "Swot!" she screamed at him.

"Now then, Vicky…" her father started.

"Don't call me that! I'm Tori, not Vicky, you're so common, Dad!"

John ruffled his son's hair and helped him pick up the packets.

***

Robert's mother thought his *little* ways, as she called them, were something he would grow out of. But his father would watch his son, sitting alone, absorbed in the intricacies of alphabetically ordering the family record collection, or perhaps tidying the books in their case, tallest to shortest and ask, "Have you got no friends to bring home, Robert?" The boy would just shake his head.

And so, to encourage him to get outside more, his father built a tree house in the branches of the oak. When it was finished, he stood back, his arm around Robert and looked up at the structure. "There you go, son, maybe ask some lads from school to play up there with you." His father knew that Victoria was far too plump and *cool,* as she would say, to haul herself up the tree.

Robert was pleased and smiled up into the branches. "Thanks, Dad."

He noticed how uniform the oak leaves were. He examined those that were nearest: some had six, some had seven lobes. But both sides were a mirror image of each other. "It's great, Dad, really great."

And every day after school, Robert would sit up there alone, high in the leaves with his pencil and notepad, and observe as the world functioned around him but never invited him in.

***

When Victoria left for art school there was no need any more for Robert to escape to the tree house. And despite his mother's prediction, he didn't become an accountant. He became a librarian. He felt comfortable with the Dewey system, with the logic of it all. Robert continued to live at home. He had no desire to move out and his mother was grateful for this when his father's arthritis affected his mobility to the point where he could no longer walk.

Victoria became an established and collectable artist. Success, however, didn't improve her attitude to her family. She still considered her father common and her younger brother dull. "And this is my little brother, the conventional one. He's a *librarian!*" is how she would introduce him to her friends, laughing.

From time to time she gave an exhibition which the family would be obliged to attend. Her chosen genre was abstract. "Can't make head nor bloody tail of it," Robert's father would say as they took in the huge canvasses that were covered with lines and dots and occasional circles. Robert's mother would tilt her head from side to side. "Mmm, yes, I see now, mmm." And then her eyes would be drawn to the price tag at the side. "Eleven thousand pounds, John!" And then to the little red dot at the top. "And somebody's bought it!"

Her husband would roll his eyes. "More money than sense."

Robert would walk around the exhibitions as quickly as he could. The complete lack of organisation, as he saw it, in the works made him dizzy. A visit to the gallery usually brought on a migraine. But as his father was in a wheelchair and his mother was too weak to push it up the sloped floors of the buildings, he was obliged to go.

Brother and sister saw little of each other and when their parents became unable to attend her exhibitions, Victoria rarely phoned and never visited. Robert became the carer for both his parents and reluctantly left his job at the library. He found some solace in organising and counting the various pills he had to administer. He wrote a weekly schedule and a menu for each day. He catalogued his parents' clothes according to days of the week and fabric. His father's string vests were folded on the top shelf: light cotton vests went on the middle shelf, thermals at the bottom. He laid out his mother's clothes each day: red socks and cardigans for Mondays, pink twinsets for Tuesdays and so on.

When they died, his mother four weeks to the day after his father, he discovered they had left the house entirely to him. He was thirty-six years old.

He took some time to sort and pack the evidence of a forty-year marriage. He listed the items under *charity shop*; *tip*; *attic* and *Victoria*. The house slowly emptied and Robert began to feel more comfortable. Work surfaces could be clear now; there was a home for everything. He smiled as he dusted and wiped and swept even miniscule crumbs from the floor. He straightened the chairs just so. The curtains hung in identical loops, the bedclothes smoothed, the pillows stroked into wrinkle-free puffs.

Six months after his mother's death, with the house silent and calm, Robert felt the need to return to work. A community library had opened a few streets away and they welcomed Robert's experience and adroit knowledge of the Dewey system.

It took him ten minutes and forty-three seconds to walk to the library. He passed thirty-two small shops on his way, an unemployment office, a primary school, two estate agents and a small veterinary surgery. He left the house each morning at eight-thirty, then returned two minutes later to check all the sockets were switched off. He left again and returned to check the window locks and the bolt on the back door. As he left the house for the final time, he tapped the inside of the letterbox three times and pulled the door behind him. Every morning. Monday to Friday.

As he walked to work, he would sometimes pause for a while outside the primary school, watching the parents dropping off their children. The mothers, it did seem to be mostly mothers, would stand by the railings as the pupils lined up and then followed their teacher through the archway into the dark Victorian building. He noticed that one or two of the women would smile at him and nod. He realised they assumed he was a parent too, watching and waiting to wave goodbye to a son or daughter, or both. He wondered what that would be like.

One morning as he neared the school, he saw a woman in a green coat with a small boy ahead of him. She seemed to be playing a game with the child, hopping and stretching one leg, then the other; sometimes twisting and then taking a jump forwards. At the gate she released the boy's hand and stood for a moment as he ran into the playground. Then she continued down the road: hopping, stretching, twisting and jumping, until she reached the corner where the paving slabs ended and the smooth tarmac began. Robert realised she had been avoiding the cracks.

His route to the library took him to the left at the traffic lights. This morning, however, he was so fascinated by the antics of the woman in the green coat that he took a deep breath and forced himself straight on, resisting the pull to the left. Once the tarmac ended, the woman continued in her strange ambulatory fashion. She stopped at a small supermarket and appeared to tap her right foot on the pavement before entering. Robert followed; he needed some biscuits for work anyway. He walked along the aisles, watching out for the woman, until he came to the biscuits. He chose a packet of custard creams and some Bourbons. He glanced briefly towards the till before touching his chin twice with the custard creams and twice with the Bourbons.

At the check-out, the woman was unloading her basket and as he stood behind her he looked at the contents. He was always fascinated by other people's shopping, trying to imagine what their lifestyles were like. The woman in the green coat had selected semi-skimmed milk, custard creams and a cheese and onion sandwich. Robert imagined she was buying her lunch. Perhaps she worked in an office nearby. As she unloaded her basket, her moving arm wafted a scent of coconut around her. She paid for her shopping, dropped it into a small bag and left the shop. When Robert went out, she had gone.

The next day was Saturday. From Monday to Friday Robert felt safe. He had his routine, nothing changed. But the weekend was dangerously unpredictable. You never knew who might decide to drop in, or who might phone. It seemed people were concerned about Robert. They worried that he was depressed, isolated, perhaps still in mourning. The day after he saw the woman in the green coat, Victoria turned up on the doorstep. Furious.

"Well, where is it then?" she demanded, planting herself heavily on the one remaining kitchen chair. She took out a packet of cigarettes, tore the cellophane off and to Robert's discomfort screwed it in a ball and threw it on the table. He picked it up and walked to the empty kitchen bin and dropped it in. When he turned around, he saw she had emptied the contents of her pocket: tissues, scraps of paper, a pound coin, on the table. She looked at his face and sneered. "Just looking for a lighter." And then finding one, she lit her cigarette and blew the smoke in Robert's face.

"Where's what?" he asked, feeling the familiar clench in his stomach that Victoria always brought on.

"The will, of course, you moron!" She drew heavily on the cigarette and, looking Robert in the eye, flicked ash onto the pristine oilcloth.

He began to sweat. Outside, the branches of the oak tapped against the window. He glanced up towards the treehouse, dilapidated now, but still offering refuge.

"It's with the solicitor, you know that." Robert shifted uneasily from one foot to the other. Behind his back he tapped the wall twice.

"I mean the *real* one, the one they wrote before you coerced them into leaving the place to you."

"I didn't coerce them. It was what they wanted. Anyway, they seemed to think you were OK financially." He wondered if he should offer her coffee, but that might encourage her to stay longer.

His sister heaved her bulk up from the chair and folded her arms across her chest. She was wearing a huge Indian print kaftan and the intensity of the colours and chaotic patterns threatened to bring on one of his headaches.

"That isn't really the point, is it, Robert? I should have been given my fair share of the estate instead of a few bits of tat that you decided to send to me."

Robert wondered at the word *estate*. It sounded rather grand to describe the post-war semi they had been brought up in.

She continued, "I'm going to contest it you know. You haven't heard the last of this." And with that she swirled out of the house, slamming the door behind her.

Robert looked at the table and slowly began to clear the detritus from it. Peace descended once more and in the silence he considered what it would mean, losing the house. He was settled now. He didn't like change. He would need to speak to the solicitor sooner or later.

On Monday he saw the woman in the green coat again, child

attached to her; both hopping and jumping from paving slab to paving slab. She saw Robert and smiled. Her hair was scraped back from her face and hung in a long ponytail. As she walked it swung from side to side. Robert followed her, fascinated by her peculiar gait, mesmerised by the swinging ponytail. Soon he found himself looking down at the cracks. He started to step more carefully. Again, she went into the same supermarket and Robert followed. He bought his biscuits, she her milk, custard creams and sandwich.

For the next two weeks, the routine didn't change, only now the woman in the green coat gave a friendly wave and sometimes called *hello*. But the following Friday, when he got to the till, he noticed the woman was agitated. She kept brushing her hand across her face and looking nervously around her. She caught his eye and smiled briefly. He looked into her basket and there, as usual, was the sandwich and milk. But no custard creams. As she went to pay, her hand was shaking. She left with a dazed look on her face.

Robert paid for his biscuits and walked out through the automatic glass doors. The woman in the green coat was still there. She seemed undecided, glancing back at the shop and then down the road. He stood for a moment and this time, when she saw him, she spoke. "Oh hello, you're one of the parents aren't you?"

Her accent suggested an expensive education. Robert was relieved. He had been afraid she was going to accuse him of stalking her, afraid she would be aggressive. Perhaps he *had* been stalking her.

"Not exactly one of the parents, I just stop and look at the school gate on my way to work," he replied.

She raised her eyebrows. In his head, Robert replayed what he had just said. Now he did sound like a stalker or even something worse.

Robert could feel himself blushing as she started to walk away. He reached out and touched her arm. She stopped and turned but didn't appear to be angry, or afraid. Just agitated.

He cleared his throat. "I'm a librarian," he said as if that explained his behaviour. She nodded an acknowledgement.

Robert held out the packet of custard creams to her. "I thought you might want these. It was the last packet on the shelf. Sorry."

The woman looked at the biscuits and then at Robert. Her shoulders dropped and instantly she became calm. Robert smiled and held his hands up. "Not a stalker."

She looked awkward. "Oh, I didn't think that, not for a moment."

Yes you did, Robert thought. He looked down at the pavement. "Not too many cracks here," he said. She looked startled and then smiled at him. "You noticed."

"I noticed."

Her face was pale with a few distinct freckles scattered across her cheeks. He started to count the freckles and then stopped himself.

She hitched up the briefcase in her hand. "I must be going. Work."

"And me. Work." He touched the bourbons to his chin twice. The woman frowned and then smiled. She walked off, her head lifted towards the horizon. He could see she felt pulled to look down at her feet. The effort showed in the stiffness of her back.

On Monday, Robert decided to avoid walking past the school. It meant adding an extra twenty minutes to his journey but he realised now that his curiosity might be misconstrued by some of the parents. With an immense effort, he left the house without tapping the letter box. He had a sense of dread all the way to the library. But as the day went on and he heard no police sirens or fire engines zipping in the direction of his house, the feeling left him. He had an appointment with the solicitor at lunchtime and arrived at the office promptly at one-thirty. The receptionist looked up at him.

"Oh hello, Mr. Smith, I'm afraid Mr Blakey is off sick today, are you happy to see another partner?"

Robert would have preferred to say *no,* and that only David Blakey would do. The man had known Robert's father and was familiar with the dynamics of the Smith family. But it seemed rude to refuse and so he smiled, said *that's fine* and sat down to wait.

At exactly one-thirty-one the phone rang on the receptionist's desk. "Miss Windsor will see you now, third door on the left."

Robert stood up and walked down the corridor and tapped, three times, on the door marked *Caroline Windsor.*

"Come in." The voice from inside sounded familiar and as Robert stepped into the office, he saw the woman in the green coat sitting behind the desk. She wasn't wearing a coat now, she had on a pale blue pullover with a matching cardigan.

"Oh, it's you," she said and reached out a hand to shake his. "I missed you at the school this morning. I mean, I didn't see you there."

Robert took her hand and shook it twice, gently, but she held it for a moment longer for a third shake. She blushed. "Sorry about that, there's something about three." She waved at the chair next to him and he sat down.

"Sometimes two is OK. But generally, three does it for me," Robert said, his voice quite serious.

She nodded and he began again to count the freckles on her face.

"Six on the left, eight on the right," she said, looking back at him. "I do it every morning when I look in the mirror."

A brown folder lay on her desk with a label that read: John and Celia Smith. He looked down at it and for a second felt a tiny wave of sadness gently rock him. He hadn't cried when his parents had died, he hadn't cried since. His grief had taken the form of organising the funeral and endless lists. And then lists of the lists.

Caroline spoke again. "I've looked through the will and your parents were quite clear in their intentions. Your sister would struggle to find a solicitor to contest it."

She closed the file and placed her hands together on it. "They obviously felt that you had cared very well for them. Had taken on all the responsibility."

"It wasn't just duty." Robert felt his voice shake. "They were good parents, they, well, put up with me. I was a bit of a puzzle." He smiled and looked at her. "If you know what I mean."

"Yes, I do know what you mean. But they loved you, Robert, that's obvious. Parents can't always work out their children but it doesn't mean they don't care."

He noticed her screensaver: a photo of the boy she took to school.

"Your son?" He asked.

She shook her head. "No, not my son. I don't have any children. He's my nephew. My sister has just got a new job in town so it's easier for me to take him to school now."

She glanced up at the clock. "Tea? We've got a little time left."

Robert rested his hands on his legs and leaned back in his chair. He felt comfortable; the desk was clear, apart from the brown folder. No pens, no notepads, no half-drunk cups of coffee. "Tea would be lovely, thanks."

He watched her as she stood by the kettle waiting for it to boil. He saw how she dropped the tea bags in the cups; how she tapped each bag gently with the spoon; how she laid out four custard creams in a perfect line on a plate and how she stood with one foot slightly raised as she poured in the hot water. She felt him looking at her and turned. "I actually meant what I said, I *did* miss you at school today."

"Tomorrow then?" Robert asked.

"Tomorrow," she replied.

Life changed that day for Robert. On his new route home, he passed a second-hand furniture shop and bought a chair. And as he put his key in the lock he realised he hadn't counted any shops, or timed how long it had taken him to get back to the house.

The other parents at the school waited now for the arrival of Robert, Caroline and Simon, her nephew. They made quite a procession as the three of them hopped, skipped and twisted along the pavement. After Simon joined his class, the mothers would watch in bewilderment as Robert and Caroline continued on their way: gyrating and jumping to the end of the road. Sometimes the couple laughed, sometimes they seemed deadly serious. The parents would smile benevolently at each other. There was, apparently, someone for everyone.

Life Sentence
Alexis Krite

Today is Friday, the day Angela comes to visit. I don't know why she comes to see me. I don't think she *likes* me. Perhaps she thinks she loves me. Perhaps she's worried about regret. It could be guilt. It could be the fine traces of Catholic duty that nestle in the ley lines of her body. Perhaps she sees herself in me, sitting here, in a care home just like this, in thirty years' time.

To be honest, I have no idea. But Friday is the best day of the week for me.

There's a knock on the door. There's no need to knock, the door is open. It's just a throw-away gesture to me. As if I have a say in who comes in, and who doesn't.

"Hi Mum." She sets her shopping bag down on the bed and walks over to me. Just three steps is all it takes. The room is so small. She leans down and brushes my cheek, the barest touch of her lips. She smells of cold air and peppermint.

"You're looking well," she lies. "Gosh it's warm in here." She pulls her coat off and folds it neatly on the bed, next to her shopping bag.

"Hello darling," I greet her. "How was the journey?"

"Oh, you know, usual mad traffic. I didn't get away till late, so I got caught in the rush."

I nod, letting her see that I appreciate she has put herself out for me.

"You could have just called, saved yourself that drive." I give her permission to elaborate on the effort she has made.

"It's not the same. Besides, I've got you a few bits and pieces." She opens the shopping bag and takes out a pack of face wipes, a bar of Yardley Rose soap, a packet of chocolate-covered crystallised ginger and a tin of white crab meat.

"Ooh lovely! I'll have that for my tea." I actually *do* like white crab meat. Sometimes she brings me smoked salmon: slivers of pink that sit like diaphanous shreds of fabric on my plate. I've seen the other residents look enviously at them. I know for a fact that Elsie, the one that discovers my room every hour or so, has slipped a piece into her hanky at least twice. But I don't begrudge her. She glances mischievously around her before lifting her hand, quick as a flash, to my plate. Sometimes I pretend to look the other way. At other times I turn my back on her so I can eat all the salmon, letting it melt on my tongue and then, one or two chews, and down it slithers. Delicious.

Angela sits on the bed. She doesn't like to use the only other chair in the room. She knows what lies hidden beneath the plastic-covered foam cushion. I tell her I don't often use it; that I still get plenty of warning when I have to go. All I need to do is ring the bell and the soft-eyed little Filipino nurse helps me gently and respectfully to the bathroom. She never compromises my dignity. I am grateful for that.

"Shall I put the telly on?" Angela picks up the remote control and switches on the BBC Celebrity Antiques Road Show. I watch her face as the images flicker on the screen.

Perhaps I should have told her the truth. Made a full confession. There is still time of course. But what good would it do? Would it make her happier? I don't think so. She manages her life very efficiently. She's good at her job, is respected by her colleagues and I'm sure she gets satisfaction from helping people find homes. People who have been on the streets for years. She does more good than I ever did.

But I don't think she has ever forgiven me.

When her father fell from that balcony and broke his neck on the crowded, heat-cracked street in Athens, no-one blamed me. The police said he had been drinking. They were sympathetic, everyone was very kind. Would they have been so kind if they had known that I had actually stepped aside and let him fall? He had lunged at me, his breath stinking of whisky, fist knotted into a ball, ready to crack my jaw again. I could have reached out and blocked his way. He might have crumpled then, onto the marble tiles. But I stepped aside and gripped the balcony door. The weight of his anger and a gentle push from me carried him on. It carried him on towards the balcony rails, on and over into oblivion. And I became a murderer and a widow with a grieving daughter who had adored her father.

It was a long time coming. This life sentence. But finally, here I am in this room that is my prison cell. With no hope of parole.

When it happened, Angela was at boarding school. I told her it was an accident. Everyone told her the same. But I saw the way she looked at me and I realised she knew. She knew because of the bruises I hid with foundation and the way I would wear long-sleeved dresses even in summer. She was always a daddy's girl. I had never taken to her. The moment she was born I looked at her little face, scrunched up and primate-like, and I felt like something had been removed from me.

I tried to love her. I dressed her in pretty clothes, bought her Sindy dolls and paid for riding lessons. But it was always the same. Each time I closed my eyes against her cheek to inhale her warm child's breath, I could feel his face pressed into mine, pinning my mouth down with his. In the dark, as I lay with her in my arms, I remembered how he had ripped into me; how he had discharged his fury and his despotism, marking me forever as his.

My parents decided we should marry. It was the right thing to do, and quickly. My mother rarely spoke to me after the wedding, my father left the room each time I entered. But their friends and neighbours were delighted for them. I had made such a good marriage.

And now, here Angela sits. She will glance at her phone from time to time and at 18.50 exactly she will say her goodbyes and leave.

"Angela," I say. She looks at me and smiles. "Yes?"

"I'm sorry I made you do it. I wish I'd done things differently back then."

She looks away. "You did what you thought was best." She is being generous with her ninety-year-old mother, generous to the woman who forced her to have an abortion.

"Darling, it's just that…"

"Yes, I know Mum. You didn't want me to make the same mistake."

I try to protest. "It wasn't a mistake, *you* weren't a mistake."

Sometimes I think I was acting out of vindictiveness. Jack would never have done to her what Richard did to me. Jack was kind, not very bright, and very young.

She stands up and looks out of the window.

"I don't suppose I would have been a very good mother anyway, but…" And she turns to me. "I never had the chance to find out."

There are tears in her eyes. Something stirs inside me. I can't identify it. I think it might be love.

Angela stuffs her shopping bag into her pocket and picks up her car keys. She bends and very lightly kisses the top of my head. "Salmon next week?"

"Yes please, darling, that would be lovely."

She walks through the door. I call after her. "And a crusty roll!"

I hear her laugh.

The Face from the Past
David Reading

I'm sitting on the Tube, travelling south from Euston to Waterloo. It's some time after ten o'clock on a Friday morning. I have no plans: I will go where the day takes me. Right now I am reading the front page headlines on someone else's paper. The headlines tell me an actor I have never heard of has died of a heart attack and a young black man in Brixton has been stabbed to death. I feel a twinge of sadness knowing what happened to the young black man but feel nothing for the dead actor. My imperfect mind will never understand why people worship film stars the way they do, although I have no strong opinions about that. Likewise I have no strong opinions about why people stab each other with knives and yet I can't help feeling a little sad – just a little – when I imagine what that young black man felt as he became aware that his blood was flowing away.

The headlines also tell me that a dead mouse was found in a pot of jam. That too strikes me as sad because drowning in jam must be a very unpleasant way to die.

People get off the train and people get on. I study the face of a young blond-haired man sitting opposite and smile. He looks away quickly, uncomfortable with my attention. A teenage girl wearing a short skirt that they used to call *the Mini* is reading a paperback book and I find that if I lower my head just a fraction I can catch a glimpse of red knickers. She looks up, sees me trying to catch my glimpse, and moves her legs to block my line of vision, so that I have to shift to the left slightly in order to get the same glimpse. She tugs at the skirt to pull enough material forward to foil my little pleasures and I look up and smile, acknowledging her as the victor. She does not smile back and therefore she does not understand the game. I want to speak, want to tell her there are no nasty thoughts going through my head, it's all innocent stuff really, but she gets off at Goodge Street before I have a chance to say that.

A young woman boards the train, sits opposite me. There is a troubled look on her face as if she has received bad news. Next to her there is that blond-haired guy who was so upset by my smile and on the other side of her a young man in a tracksuit wearing headphones. These two young men glance sideways at exactly the same moment to take a quick look at her, presumably to judge her physical qualities. I too decide to look at her. Her sleek black hair is tied back in a pony tail and her skin is golden-brown and healthy. She is holding a maroon rucksack on her lap and wearing the same light blue top that she wore when I saw her before. It looks good on her, as it did the last time we met: the only time we met. She hasn't noticed me yet because there is no reason to look. As soon as the train rumbles out of the station she dips her hand into the pocket of her jeans and takes out her mobile phone. She glances at the screen briefly and puts it back into her pocket.

While she looks down at her hands, deep in thought, I study her hair, her face and then her clothes. I notice that her nice blue top has a brown stain on the left sleeve and I wonder how it got there: spilled coffee, maybe, or perhaps dirt from the garden. She wasn't concerned about removing the stain or finding a different top to wear. She wanted to wear this one, never mind the blemish, and here she is wearing it for me now.

She looks at me and looks away quickly, looks back, keeps looking for just a little bit longer, looks away again, screws up her face, looks back, this time holds my gaze. I take a chance and smile at her, but she refuses to smile in return. She rummages inside her pocket again, but this time she isn't reaching for her phone, she is keeping her hands busy while she wonders to herself why she is feeling the discomfort she feels. She opens her mouth a little as if she's about to speak, but she shakes her head lightly and looks away again. She is staring now at a point somewhere on the left trouser leg of the man sitting next to me.

She is staring because she is thinking deeply. I know that for an absolute fact. There is a question that's troubling her. *Why does he look familiar?* She doesn't know whether the answer to that question will bring forth a memory of a happy occasion or whether it will cause her pain. Maybe she wants to escape from knowing, but she won't be able to relax until she gets an answer. I was different then, with a full beard and hair down to my shoulders. I think it's unlikely she will find her answer without help.

So I say to her, *Hello again.*

Her response confirms that she is confused. *Do I know you?*

Think hard, I reply. I speak those words in a whisper and can't be sure she has heard. As the train stops at Charing Cross, the seat beside her becomes vacant and I cross the gangway to join her.

Who are you? she says.

My name is John.

I say that like I'm a character from a children's first reading book. *My name is John.*

Do we know each other?

I realise I have a choice to make. To remind her of what happened when we met will cause her pain. To create a new story would protect her from that pain. That is a philosophical problem, but instead of searching for a philosophical solution I react spontaneously without concern for the consequences.

We met in a pub near King's Cross. You were with friends, I was on my own. We began talking. I had nowhere to stay that night. You let me sleep on your couch. Your name is Amira. It was just for one night. I had a beard then so you may not remember me clearly.

On some deep level she understood our connection the moment she saw me sitting opposite. That was why she was unable to smile. *You're that guy*, she says coldly. *But you're so…*

Different.

You could say that.

I can tell what is happening inside her. Thoughts and emotions are crowding in on her. Each one becomes foreground for an instant until another one pushes it out of the way. She appeared calm and gentle when we met before, but she's not calm right now. Right now there is another side about to show its face. The next thing she says comes from her dark side. It is spoken in an angry whisper.

I wanted to kill you, do you know that?

Do you still want to kill me?

What was it, a scam?

It wasn't planned. It was spontaneous.

But you looked so bedraggled that night. Like a….

A tramp? A down-and-out?

I wasn't going to use those words.

That's the way I liked to dress in those days. This is how I like to dress now. I cut my hair short for reasons of hygiene. Do you like it?

She brings her hand up to her face and runs her index finger down her cheek.

Was that there before?

I bring my own hand up to my own face and touch the scar that runs north to south from my right eye down to my jaw.

No, it wasn't.

What happened to you?

Nothing happened to me. I did it to myself. I did it to improve my image. I took a Stanley knife and I carved a line, top to bottom. I did it so people would see me differently. I think it worked, don't you?

She looks down at her hands and speaks quietly. *You're completely insane. I understand now.*

At that moment, the moment I took hold of the knife, perhaps I was insane. At this moment?

I think about that for a second but can't come up with an answer. I don't think I'm insane, but how are these things judged? It's true what I told her about the knife but I'm not sure I'd do the same thing again.

So let's go through this. You just took my property – stole it – without any thought for the sorrow you'd cause? I gave you a place to sleep and that's how you rewarded me?

Yes.

You abysmal bastard.

That phrase seems to me like a punctuation mark placed there to end the conversation and I allow it to be the last word. But of course it isn't the last word.

Where is it now? The necklace.

I sold it.

Of course you did. Where did you sell it?

A shop in Hampstead. Do you want me to take you there?

She shakes her head. *There'd be no point.*

She is remarkably composed considering what is happening between us. Some people would be screaming for a police officer right now or wrestling me to the ground. She turns quickly and looks out of the window. *I'm getting out at the next stop,* she says. *Just one question. Do you think there's any chance you could bring yourself to feel sorry?*

I don't know. It's possible.

So who exactly did you sell it to? Did they know it was stolen?

Do you have a pen? I'll write down the address of the shop.

It belonged to my mother, you know. She was killed by a soldier in Baghdad. It was just a little keepsake, but it's all I had left that was hers. Do you understand what it meant to me? No, how could you understand, you're a callous bastard who doesn't think about stuff like that.

Amira, I say, as if I am addressing her as a friend. *That was months ago. Come on, forgive and forget. Water under the bridge.*

How much did you sell it for?

I sold it for five hundred. They probably sold it on for double that. As soon as I saw it I knew it was valuable.

I don't care about the value. It was worth more than money.

But at the end of the day it's just a piece of metal on a chain with a stone in the middle. People get too attached to inanimate things. What have you got in the bag, by the way?

She doesn't answer. She is staring at the floor thinking. Perhaps she is wondering if she should report me to the staff at the next station.

Come on, Amira, what have you got in the bag?

It's none of your business.

Come on, don't be like that. We can still be friends.

Do you think so?

When the train pulls into Waterloo, she gets up abruptly. *Anyway, I suppose it doesn't really matter now*, she says. *Nothing matters. Not for me, anyway.* I am puzzled by that remark. Moments before we were talking about a treasured possession but now it has been dismissed in a short, curt sentence. She throws the maroon rucksack across her right shoulder and leaves the train without looking back.

I follow a few paces behind, out of the carriage, along the corridor, over the ticket barrier, up the escalator. When we reach the top she turns around and is surprised to see I have followed her.

* * *

As I arrive home I wonder what exactly happened back there, at the top of the escalator. I conclude that the catalyst was those venomous words she whispered as she saw me approach: *you're pathetic*. There are some words that cut deeply. They strike at something buried inside. *You're pathetic*. When she spoke those cruel words I wanted to hurt her and all I could think of doing to hurt her was to take something from her so I snatched the rucksack from her shoulder. She put up no resistance. The passing crowds were preoccupied with their own thoughts. Nobody noticed. I ran home with my new bag.

Here in my little flat I place the bag on the kitchen table and undo the straps. Surprisingly, the first thing I notice is a plastic wallet and through the plastic I see a photograph. The photograph shows a face, a woman's face. The features are soft but spoiled by the first lines of middle age. That woman is smiling: it is a happy picture taken by someone who's fond of her. Sitting at my kitchen table, I study her face. There is something recognisable there in the eyes. It's as if I have seen those eyes before and after a while the answer comes: It must be Amira's mother. *She was killed by a soldier in Baghdad,* Amira said. And turning the photograph over I read words written in blue Biro, strange words: *What I do today is in your honour.* I lay the photograph to one side and open up my new rucksack. At first, what I see makes no sense. I see a clock. The clock has two hands, one pointing at twelve, the other moving clockwise. The moving hand is at the four position. There is much more in the bag, but it means nothing to me: just a tangle of coloured wires, red, black and blue. The moving hand is at the six position now and when I dip my hand deep into the rucksack and bring out this mysterious clock along with its tangle of wires, a conclusion is beginning to form. The moving hand is at the eight position now, moving upwards and as it reaches the nine position, I know what I am looking at. And strangely, I see the humour in this present scenario. The hand moves from nine to ten. A futile thought: there's still time to get away. But I remain seated, looking for comfort in the eyes of the woman in the photograph.

The Month of Good and Bad Things

David Reading

Her name was October, although she'd been born at the end of June. October Jane Phillips. When she was five years old she asked her parents why they had called her October but her father simply smiled and said, *No reason. We just liked the name.* And he winked at October's mother. October didn't understand that mischievous look at the time, but a few years later a shrewd, older friend pointed out the nine-month difference between the two dates and everything fell into place.

October's father died in battle and her mother was taken from her a week later. She was only ten, but barely a month after her mother's death October found the courage to leave the home that was now just a shell. She packed a few clothes into a small suitcase, along with her toothbrush and flannel, and walked away from the house and away from the town. She had no conscious idea where she was heading but ended up at a spinney near the cliff top. It had been their favourite picnic spot. She sat on a log with her suitcase at her feet, wondering what she was going to do next.

On her first afternoon as a runaway the wind was cold and there was a light drizzle in the air. She sat there for an hour or two, realising she had probably made a terrible mistake. She should never have left home. Without warmth and shelter she would soon get sick. But going back would be worse. At her young age she didn't quite know what *being taken into care* involved, but she knew it couldn't be good. Her Aunt Olive had stayed at the house with her in the weeks after her mother's death, but October knew this could never be permanent. She'd heard her aunt speaking with the people in smart clothes who came to the house to talk it through. Her aunt said she had her own life to live.

Grief had not hit her yet. Aunt Olive commented that she was *in denial*. October felt a pain in her stomach as if the muscles had tensed up like a clenched fist, but she didn't cry. Just that dull ache. *So that's what you feel when someone dies*, she thought.

October knew it would get dark soon and she would have to find a place of safety. She got up, grabbed her suitcase and trudged through the undergrowth hoping the future would simply take care of itself. Eventually she reached the edge of the spinney and climbed over a rotting wooden stile. Ahead of her she could see the sea.

***

Through some quirk of fate, everything seemed to happen to her in October – things good and bad. It was on a sunny October afternoon that she sat on an open-top bus with her parents touring Paris: *the best day of my life*, she said. But her favourite grandfather had died on Halloween and a year later, almost to the day, she slipped on wet leaves and broke her wrist. Always in October, so it seemed. And it was on October 1st that she was told about her mother. She came home from school to find a policewoman standing on the doorstep. She said she had some very bad news. They went inside, and October heard just how bad that news was. The details were held from her at first, but it wasn't long before she overheard what people were saying. *She must have been driven to it by grief,* her aunt told the man who lived next door. And she added, *How on earth could she abandon her own flesh and blood? Killing herself like that.*

***

At the edge of the wood there was a steep downward grass slope and at the bottom of the slope was the cliff top. October still didn't have a plan. She walked slowly down the slope and stood on the edge of the cliff staring at the ocean. She was cold and hungry; she could have been enjoying dinner. Her aunt's cooking skills didn't reach far beyond Marmite soldiers, but she liked Marmite soldiers.

And yet some powerful force was keeping her from going back. It was as if she had been drawn to this place where the land met the sea. She looked behind her and saw familiar sights. The oak tree her father had climbed, half scaring her mother to death. A red and blue kite tangled in its branches. The cottage on the edge of the spinney that her father said was a gingerbread house. Yes, the sights were familiar but there was something else about the place. She felt she *had* to be here for some reason.

She stared down at the rocks at the bottom of the cliff. The earth began to crumble under the pressure of her feet. She put her suitcase down and imagined what it would be like to leap off the edge and fly. She stood there with the wind driving her from behind as if encouraging her to move even closer to the edge. She thought of her mother, and her aunt's words rang through her head. *How on earth could she abandon her own flesh and blood? Killing herself like that.* Had her mother really abandoned her?

But then something happened that pulled her back to reality. A dog was barking and someone was calling out.

"Are you all right?"

She turned to see an old man in a funny-looking hat coming down the slope, holding a large silver-coloured dog on a leash.

"You look as if you're lost," the man shouted.

She stepped back from the edge and began to walk away along the cliff path, uneasy at the attention she was getting.

"It's OK, Lady won't bite and nor will I for that matter."

So the dog's name was Lady. And come to think of it, her owner did look a bit like a tramp. The hat seemed quite respectable but the rest of his clothes were tattered and a little grubby. Looking closer, she saw his trousers had been tied up with a piece of string as a belt. She remembered where she'd seen a hat like his: in a picture, on the cover of one of her father's books. It was the kind of hat Sherlock Holmes wore.

He said it again. "Are you all right?"

Most children are taught never to talk to strangers, but October's parents were different. Her mother had said she didn't want her daughter to grow up mistrustful of the world. She should certainly be careful with anyone she didn't know, but eventually she would learn to make sound judgements about people.

The man with the Sherlock Holmes hat was untidy and maybe smelly, but that didn't make him bad. October decided she would be quite safe with him. She stopped to talk.

"That's a funny looking dog," she said, bending down to stroke it.

"She's a Weimaraner," the man replied. And then, seeing the puzzled look on her face, he explained, "It's a German breed. Some people call them grey ghosts. I've had her from a puppy."

October crouched down and ran her hand over the dog's soft coat. Instantly she felt agitated, as if the dog was about to harm her in some way. She stood up and drew back. "I'm not sure I like her," she said. "I have to go now."

The man seemed concerned. "You're rather young to be out here on your own. Is everything all right?"

October started to walk away but turned suddenly. "I've run away from home," she said.

Instantly she was sorry she'd said it. Even at ten she was mature enough to realise she shouldn't give away too much. She decided to put it another way.

"Well, not running *away* exactly. Running *to* something."

"I see."

But how could he see? She knew adults often said things they didn't quite mean.

"So what exactly are you running *to*?"

There was no answer to that question. She'd set off that day without any idea where she was heading. The place she'd arrived at – the top of a cliff – offered one possibility. There were probably others.

And then words tumbled out of her mouth that were never intended to be said. Afterwards she didn't know *where* they came from. Maybe there was someone quite daring living inside her.

"I think this is the place where my mother died. She jumped over the edge, I think."

She felt a chill inside. She didn't know why she'd said that. She didn't even know if it was true. She just had a feeling that it was.

It was an extraordinary moment. But what the man said was even more extraordinary.

"Oh my Lord! Then I know who you are."

"You know what?"

"I know who you are and I know this is the place where your mother passed over." He didn't say jumped over. He said passed over.

October stared him in the eyes wondering whether he was playing some cruel game with her. But he looked shocked. And he looked sincere.

The old man gazed down at his shoes. "I don't know how to tell you this," he said, "but I know all about you."

This couldn't be true. He was beginning to frighten her. "What are you talking about?" she asked him.

He didn't look up. She began to feel scared. His dog was sniffing round her ankles, trying to be friendly, and the man pulled her away sharply.

"Lady," he said. "Behave, old girl. And let's all get well away from the edge. It's not safe here."

"Come on," the man said. "There's a bench just over the ridge. We can sit down together and breathe in the sea air. And I'll tell you everything."

***

For a few moments they sat in silence, October trying to make sense of what was happening. As she looked towards the cliff edge she remembered what her aunt had told the postman. *It was a terrible long way down,* she'd said. *There was no way she could have survived. She would have been killed instantly.* October hadn't wanted to hear any more. She'd stuck her fingers in her ears and had run upstairs. That night she dreamed she was swallowed up by the ocean. Next morning Aunt Olive said rather casually, *You realise, don't you, that you can't stay with me. We'll have to sort something out through social services.* October wanted to ask what that meant, but was too frightened to hear the answer.

She and the old man sat watching the seagulls wheeling overhead and listened to the waves hitting the rocks below. Lady sat at the old man's feet. October was in no hurry to hear his story. She didn't think that what he had to say could be good. She had heard a lot of bad things in the past few weeks and this would be one more. And she wasn't quite sure how much she could trust the man not to tell the police about her. He hadn't yet reached for his phone, but he could still do that. And then she would have to run.

Lady looked around and barked as a woman in a woolly hat and walking boots approached. "Easy, Lady," the man said. "She's not going to hurt you." The woman stopped briefly and nodded. "Afternoon, Reverend. Bit of a chilly one isn't it." So the man was a vicar! October hoped the woman would sit down with them because this would make her feel more at ease, but after exchanging pleasantries she moved on. There was another long silence until finally the man said, "Your name's October, isn't it?"

Things were getting even more confusing. "I think I have to go," she said.

"Is that your name? I'm right aren't I? It's not a name you easily forget."

She didn't answer. She took hold of her suitcase and looked around to see if there was anyone else in view. She wanted to feel safe among people, even if those people were strangers. The woman in the woolly hat was out of sight now. She wondered if her original judgement about the old man had been wrong. She looked sideways at him and saw his eyes were closed as if he was in pain.

"I know your name," he said, "because I met your mother. I met her on the day she passed over. She told me she had a daughter and she told me she was grieving for her husband."

October said again, "I think I have to go." She got up and began to walk back towards the slope hoping to catch sight of the woman in the woolly hat.

"She didn't kill herself," the man shouted. "I swear to you it's true."

October stopped and turned. For some odd reason she was suddenly taken back to the day her grandfather died. It was a rainy lunchtime at school and she was sitting in her classroom reading Jonathan Livingstone Seagull. She liked reading but her eyes were tired and she closed them for a moment. Her friend Esme said something to her about a TV programme she'd seen but October didn't take it in. She continued to sit with her eyes closed and her mind in a kind of suspension. And suddenly she felt a shock through her body followed by a sensation of deep sadness. The teacher came into the room to find October whimpering like a sick puppy. She wouldn't stop, and so the teacher took her to the office and allowed her to lie down on the couch. At about that time the call came through that her grandfather had died. Later she heard her mother say something strange: She has a sixth sense, you know.

A sixth sense. As she stood at the cliff edge, October felt that same powerful force, the one that had drawn her here. It was something inside her, something she felt but couldn't grasp. She turned and walked back to the old man, who was still sitting on the bench.

"Are you a vicar?" she asked.

"Retired long ago," he replied. "I spend my time writing books. Books about sin and forgiveness, that kind of thing. Which is what I need now. I need forgiveness."

October sat down next to him again. The dog shuffled around at his feet.

"I know how your mother died," he said, "because I was here when it happened."

His eyes were clenched tight again and he was trembling. "She was sitting on the edge of the cliff when I saw her, exactly where you were standing. I was taking my morning walk. She looked forlorn so I asked her what was wrong. She told me what had happened to her husband and she told me about you. She was grieving but she said sitting out here watching the waves made her feel peaceful. She had come out here to connect – that was the word she used – and she said she needed to be strong for your sake. She actually thanked me for listening to her and then she stood up and she smiled. She really did look serene – you could almost say happy. And that's when it happened."

"What happened?"

"She didn't mean any harm. She was just being friendly."

"What? What did she do?"

"I'm talking about Lady. She was just showing affection like dogs do. She jumped up at your mother to lick her face and…" He could hardly bear to finish the sentence. But he had to. "And your mother fell backwards over the edge."

October gasped. She looked up at the old man and saw his pain. At that moment she knew she didn't have to run away. It seemed she had been drawn here to find the truth and now she would no longer be haunted by fears about how her mother had died. Somewhere in the mixture of emotions there was what, in later life, she would call *a release*.

"I tried to grab her but she slipped anyway," he said. "I couldn't stop her, you see. I couldn't stop her from leaving you. Can you ever forgive me?"

October thought of the sheer drop from the cliff edge and the sea smashing against the rocks fifty feet below. The old man was sobbing gently.

She didn't know what you were supposed to do when an old person cried, but that someone inside her took over. She laid her hand on his and smiled.

"Thank you," he said.

They sat together for a while, and then October stood up to go home. She walked along the coast path towards the slope that led to the woods. She turned back to wave goodbye. But the man and his dog had disappeared.

Motherhood
Sally Stone

"I'm sure you'll make a wonderful mother," Mrs Hollis said as she placed baby Maria gently into Liana's arms.

Liana sat down on the sofa and looked into the child's eyes. She held her uneasily, gripping rather than cuddling her. To Liana, Mrs Hollis's words of encouragement didn't seem genuine. They seemed part of a script, which all the agency workers were told to memorise, in order to give confidence to their new adoptive mothers. "I'm sure you're right," Frank said, but he too sounded uncertain. As Mrs Hollis left through the front door, she looked back into Liana's eyes. Liana thought she saw unease.

In her wicker crib, the little girl slept for almost three hours. While she was sleeping, Frank and Liana sat on the sofa and watched the news on their new television, checking from time to time that the baby was still peaceful. The day before, Frank had unveiled the TV with a flourish, as a kind of celebration of their new family life. "Just think – we're the first in the street to own one," he'd laughed.

As the programme ended, the baby began to cry and Liana froze, just for a moment. Frank was upstairs getting his suit ready for the office the next day. "Frank," she called out. She knew this would happen, of course, knew the baby would place demands on her but even so she was unprepared.

Liana picked up the child from her cot and rocked from side to side. This didn't come naturally but she'd seen other mothers do this to soothe their own babies and it seemed to work for them. For Liana, it didn't feel right; it felt awkward. The baby was hers but somehow it still felt like someone else's. When the child continued to cry, Liana made the sounds she'd heard other mothers make. "There, there, mummy's here, don't fret. Be a good girl for mummy." That felt awkward, too, as if she was an actress playing a part. The baby continued to cry. "Frank," she called out. "Please hurry." She heard the toilet flush.

Liana tried to remember what she'd been told to do when the baby cried and of course it was obvious. The baby needed feeding. She carried her through to the kitchen. Frank had prepared a bottle earlier and left it on the side. It was tepid now. Did that matter? She wasn't sure. "Frank," she called out. "I need your help." But there was no answer. Cradling the baby in her left arm she picked up the bottle with her free hand and leaned back against the kitchen worktop. She looked into the little girl's eyes. She hoped that one day she would see recognition and a smile, but that time wasn't now. In a forceful prodding motion she attempted to press the teat between the child's lips. It was rejected. Baby Maria turned her head to the side and carried on yelling.

"Come on," she said, "it's good for you." The woman at the agency had said that on some deep level a baby came to understand everything its mother said. "It's good for you," Liana said again, in a forced tone that she imagined was comforting. "Don't you want to grow up to be a big strong girl?" She tried again with the teat, but the baby squirmed and wriggled.

"My God, why won't you take it?" She was getting annoyed now.

She tried again but with no success. "For the love of God, what's the matter with you?"

Frank came into the kitchen at that moment drying his hands with a towel. "So she's awake at last," he said. "Let's have a look at her."

"Why won't she stop crying?" Liana asked him. "I've tried to feed her but she just turns away. Is that normal?"

Frank put down the towel and gently stroked the crown of Maria's head. "She's probably a little bit frightened. Everything is new to her. She'll settle down, don't worry."

"I do hope so. I'm absolutely exhausted. I really need a good night's sleep." She pushed the baby towards Frank. "Here, you take her."

Frank took the baby from Liana's arms and held her to him closely. "Come on," he said softly, "be a good girl and have your milk."

He took the bottle and attempted to press it into the baby's mouth but she screwed up her face. "So it's like that, is it?" he said. "Surely you don't want to go to sleep hungry."

Liana sighed loudly. "You're doing it wrong. You're pushing too hard. How did the nurse do it? Try to remember, for goodness sake."

Frank ignored her rebuke. He carried the baby into the lounge and sat down on the sofa. The television was still on and for a moment he was distracted by a man in a dark suit talking about the arrangements for the King's funeral. Again he tried to push the teat into little Maria's mouth, again she rejected it. "You're a little minx, you are," he said. "Let's hope we're not in for a rough night."

Liana was standing over him looking forlorn. "Frank, I desperately need to have a lie down. Do you mind?"

"You go ahead," he said. "I'll keep battling on. Would you like me to bring you a hot water bottle later? Or a warm drink?"

"Stop fussing," she snapped. "I just need a good night's sleep. I didn't get a wink last night. I was just too anxious."

"I must say you do look done in. I've never seen you so pale."

"I said stop fussing. I'll be all right."

***

Liana was woken just after midnight by the baby's crying. Frank's bed, next to hers, creaked as he pulled back the covers and sat up. "My God, what time is it?" she moaned. Frank turned on the lamp. "Five past twelve," he said. "I finally got her to take her bottle. Maybe she wants some more. Will you…?"

Liana knew that at some point she would have to start playing the part of a mother. She got out of bed and put on her slippers and dressing gown. As she walked across the floor the slap-slapping of her footfall on the lino irritated her. So did the tick-ticking of Frank's alarm clock. She reached the baby's bedroom and stared down at Maria's face, contorted in a look of distress. "Frank, did you make up another bottle?" she called out. "It's in the kitchen," he shouted back. "You'll need to warm it up though."

Liana remembered now what you had to do with the milk. She left the baby lying there, went downstairs to the kitchen and turned on the hotplate on the electric stove. Then she filled a pan with water and began to heat it up. When it started bubbling she took it off the stove and placed the bottle into the hot water.

The crying grew louder and more desperate. "Frank, for God's sake do something with her," she called out. "I'll go mad in a minute."

The baby stopped crying for a few blissful seconds and she could hear the padding of Frank's footsteps on the lino. Then the crying started up again, more shrill than before. A moment later she could hear Frank's silly shooshing noises: a universal but ineffectual method of quietening difficult babies. "Come on, come on," she could hear him say. "What's all this about? What on earth is the fuss?" She didn't see how that could help. *Stupid man*, she whispered to herself.

Liana took the bottle out of the pan of hot water and squirted a few drops on to the back of her hand, as she'd been instructed. It was all coming back to her now. It seemed warmish so she took it upstairs, where Frank was holding the baby, still making those silly noises. "Give her to me," she snapped. Back in her bed with the baby, things seemed calmer. When Maria had finished half a bottle she fell asleep. Liana took her to her cot and went back to bed.

***

Frank stood at the kitchen door holding his briefcase. "Are you sure you're going to be all right?" he said. "I could always phone and tell them I need more time off. This is a big event after all. First day with a new baby and all that."

It was so tempting. She'd had just three hours' sleep and with Frank home she might be able to snatch a nap during the afternoon. But his fussing was irritating her at the moment. That was almost as bad as the baby's complaining. "Just go," she said. "I'll be all right."

"Are you absolutely sure? I can get someone else to go through the Mills account."

"Just go," she said again, more forcefully. She was sitting in the kitchen with a cup of tea. Baby Maria was sleeping in her cot upstairs. She'd woken up crying at 2am, 3.20, 4.45 and just after 6am. To his credit, Frank did his share of the feeding but why shouldn't he? It was pretty much his decision to adopt. He persuaded her it would help their marriage and she went along with it. *Something to focus on*, he'd said. *We will raise a right little madam. She'll be top of the class in every subject and she'll marry a successful businessman. We'll be proud of her.* And maybe he was right. Maybe they really would raise a child they could love and be proud of. Maybe the early stages were always difficult. Things were bound to improve. She finished her tea, picked up *The Times*, glanced at the headlines and put it down again. She couldn't concentrate.

Frank looked into his briefcase to make sure he hadn't forgotten anything and headed for the front door. "Don't forget, the nurse is coming round at eleven," he said. Liana rolled her eyes. "Of course I won't forget. For goodness sake will you stop fussing?"

"I just thought you might need reminding. You look a bit washed out this morning."

"Goodbye, Frank."

Liana listened to the front door slam and his feet crunching on the gravel driveway. And then she heard Mrs Thomas's voice, *good morning Mr Hodgson, lovely morning*. She felt irritation at this. Mrs Thomas was a busybody, couldn't keep out of other people's affairs, and now she was going to make Frank late with her wittering. She thought about going outside and telling him to get a move on but didn't have the energy. After a few moments she heard his car starting up. As soon as he accelerated out of the drive, she slid off her stool and began to do the washing up. She'd only finished rinsing the first cup when baby Maria let out a wail. Liana dried her hands and went upstairs.

***

The nurse arrived 20 minutes late and Liana showed her annoyance by neglecting to offer her tea and biscuits. She said her name was Carol. She was 45 years old and said she had been caring for babies ever since she left school. She was pleasant enough, but Liana didn't warm to her. As they sat together in the lounge, with baby Maria in the nurse's arms, Liana showed her displeasure at Carol's poor timekeeping by answering her questions brusquely, in short, sharp sentences. When asked how Maria had been during the night, Liana gave an exaggerated shrug as a bad actress might do. "It was OK. She woke a few times." Did the baby take her feed without any problems? "I don't know what you mean by problems." Well, did she finish her milk? "I suppose so. I was rather tired. I didn't really notice."

Carol was patient even though she sensed the hostility. She said she was there to help if there were any problems. She said adopting a child could require a lot of patience and a lot of stamina. Most of all, it required a lot of love. Carol didn't sense very much love in that house on that morning, but she gave Liana the benefit of the doubt. She'd had children of her own and knew what it was like to get by on a few hours' sleep. She asked about Frank. Was he giving Liana a lot of support? "I suppose so," Liana said. "He's got a good job in the City so we won't go short of anything." But what about emotional support? Liana didn't know how to answer that. There were times when Frank could be rather feeble, in her eyes, but he would usually do the right thing when it mattered. "I suppose so," she answered abruptly.

The nurse examined the baby thoroughly. Liana was perplexed by this. She wondered if Carol was expecting to find signs of neglect even after one night. But she realised she was being paranoid. She took a loud, deep breath. Carol glanced at her and then returned her attention to the baby. "She seems content enough," she said. "It's bound to be a bit unsettling for a while, being taken from one environment and plunged into somewhere completely strange." And then she repeated what the woman from the agency had said. "I'm sure you'll make a wonderful mother."

***

After the nurse had left, Liana reflected on those words. *You'll make a wonderful mother.* She tried to *feel* whether she had this potential inside her but she couldn't find anything there. She felt cold and emotionless, but hoped this was simply a result of her lack of rest. There was one thing she was certain of: compared with the alternative, Maria would live a life of luxury. Here she had a future. A few months back the outlook was chaotic. Somewhere there was a 15-year-old who would be pining for her child. But the right decision had been made for her.

Liana gave the baby a bottle just after midday, changed her nappy and put her down in her cot. To her relief, Maria fell asleep immediately. She made herself a ham sandwich and ate it while she listened to the news on the radio. She had caught a few snippets of the reports from Armenia earlier that day but had missed the full story. A small demonstration of her fellow countrymen had taken to the streets to remind the world of the horrors of the Armenian genocide. Liana was five when the massacre happened. The memories were faint, but she retained images of brutality that would never leave her. When the newsreader's descriptions became too distressing, she turned off the radio and sat in contemplation. She knew she would never be whole. It was her fate.

Liana went upstairs, pulled a shoebox out from under the bed and took out a bundle of old photographs tied up with red ribbon. She did this occasionally when she'd been reminded of her past. She sat on the bed and began to sift through the photos one by one. She had looked at each one hundreds of times: pictures of her mother, her father and her brothers, all taken before the horrors that engulfed them. Happy pictures of family life. Three of these showed Liana herself: just a baby in a funny white dress. Everyone looked solemn in those old photos but she knew the truth: despite the uncertainty, family life could be joyful and nurturing. She smiled at a photo of her grandmother. *She looks like Mr Punch*, Frank had said. Frank could be irritating but he could also be funny. And kind.

She tied up the ribbon and placed the photos back in the drawer, glancing at her reflection in the mirror. *God I do look tired*, she sighed. She knew exhaustion was going to be her normal state for the coming months.

Before going downstairs, Liana took a quick look at Maria and saw she was still asleep. A chance, she thought, for her to take a nap on the sofa. But just as she reached the door to the lounge she heard a cry coming from Maria's room and gave a cry of her own, in despair. She spread out on the sofa hoping things would settle down on their own, but after ten minutes the baby was still awake and in distress. She wondered about leaving her a little longer. It was possible that indulging her – picking her up every time she cried – would spoil the child and store up problems for the future. Ear plugs seemed a good option at that point, but she chose instead to try another solution: she collected Maria from her cot, settled her in her pram and prepared to set off round the block. It was possible, she thought, that the rocking motion of the pram would calm the baby.

***

Liana was in no mood for conversation so when Mrs Thomas tried to ambush her at the end of the driveway she uttered a curt, *sorry, Mrs Thomas, must dash* and turned left towards the shops. Within minutes Maria had stopped crying, which Liana viewed as a small personal success. She paused briefly before reaching the shops and looked down at the baby, more peaceful than she had seen her so far. Wisps of dark hair fluttered in the breeze; her tiny hands were held above her head as if in a position of surrender. Through an act of will, Liana tried to summon up affection. She should have known this wasn't how human emotion works, but she felt desperate. If a bond between them failed to develop, there could be years of resentment ahead.

She considered taking a walk around the park but remembered she needed flour from Lipton's. Frank's birthday was coming up and she had promised to bake him a cake. *As if I haven't got enough to do*, she thought. But a promise was a promise. The pavement was narrow outside the shop so she parked Maria in her pram just inside the alleyway next door, put on the brake and went inside. Seeing three other women ahead of her in the queue, she sighed impatiently, prompting all three to turn and glare. She ignored them, making a pretence of searching through her bag for her purse. The woman at the head of the queue was dithering. She was frail and elderly and couldn't seem to focus. She asked for cheese but didn't know which variety she wanted. She told the shopkeeper she preferred Cheddar, but changed her mind. She asked for the price of Cheshire and then decided on Red Leicester. But no, it had to be Cheddar. This conversation with the shopkeeper carried on seemingly going nowhere. Finally Liana couldn't help herself. She found herself shouting. It wasn't that she had made a decision to shout. She just couldn't help herself. She opened her mouth and the words just tumbled out.

For goodness sake, hurry up you stupid woman.

Instantly the hostility towards her became clear. As Liana saw it, they all drew ranks. She was the foreigner, the outsider, the one with the funny accent. She was used to being labelled a Russian, or a Pole and even a Communist – she had learned to live with that – but today she was particularly vulnerable. The queue of shoppers turned on her, glowering, muttering at her, words she couldn't make out. The shopkeeper, normally a jovial sort, simply pointed to the door. "You won't get served here today, Mrs Hodgson. Take your money elsewhere."

Shocked and humiliated, Liana retreated. She slammed the shop door behind her and marched up the street. She no longer knew what it was like to cry – she was incapable of that – but her pain was physical. Her stomach cramped up and she felt a migraine coming on. Her mind was awash with the images of what had just happened: the disapproving expressions on their faces, the low grumbling, the stern command from the shopkeeper. *Take your money elsewhere.*

She had reached her driveway when she remembered the baby.

Oh my God, she murmured to herself. She had been away from Lipton's for ten whole minutes. Those distressing images from inside the store were now replaced by a different nightmare. She turned and ran back towards the shop. Arriving at the alleyway, she cried out in horror. The pram was still there but the baby had gone.

Panic-stricken, Liana looked both ways up the street. It was dotted with pedestrians but as far as she could see none of them was holding a baby. Forgetting the shopkeeper's hostility, she rushed back into Lipton's. The shop was full of customers but her attention was drawn to a man in uniform with his back to her. The sight of the uniform triggered a half-buried memory: a different place, a different time, a time of horror. When the man turned round she saw he was holding a baby. *Her* baby. Liana rushed forward and snatched Maria from his arms. "Please don't hurt her," she implored.

The policeman looked startled. "She was crying," he said, "making a right old fuss. I managed to calm her down, but she wanted her mum. She's a little angel, isn't she. You must be very proud."

Liana was shaking as she held the child close to her. She rested her cheek against the baby's downy head and breathed in the scent of talc. Something leapt deep inside her: a strange, unfamiliar feeling, in the place where a baby could never grow. The child reached up and grabbed a lock of Liana's hair. Gently cupping the tiny hand in her own, Liana whispered, "It's all right, sweetheart. Mummy's here now."

***

When Frank came home Liana was on the sofa cradling the baby. He'd never seen his wife looking so content. He put his briefcase on the floor, sat down next to them and stroked Maria's cheek gently with the back of his hand. "How did it go today?" he whispered.

Liana leaned her head against his shoulder. "It was good. We had a good day."

On the table next to the sofa, Frank saw a black and white photograph propped up against Maria's empty bottle. It showed a woman and a baby. The baby was obviously Liana.

"Frank, get your camera," Liana said. "Let's take a family photo."

That day she had made a promise to herself. The house would be full of life and colour. And there would be photos that Maria would come to cherish. Their child would never have to hide her memories away in a dirty old shoe box under the bed.

Restoration
Alexis Krite

It is cool here. The beech leaves block out the August sun and only odd fingers of light poke from between the branches. The midges dance up and down in little auras of brightness and finally there is respite from the frenzied strikes of horseflies.

Amarillo snatches at a cow parsley and I let the reins be pulled through my fingers. I lean forward and run my hand down his soaking neck. He walks along, throwing his head up and down, the white flowers dangling from his mouth as he flounces like a bride along this covered green aisle. I hold my hand to my nose and breathe in the fragrant scent of horse sweat.

The tree tunnel encompasses me and I fold my arms across my horse's withers and rest my head on them. Shaking my feet loose from the stirrups I lie slumped on his back, my legs dangling along his side. He walks rhythmically, the crushed cow parsley sweetening his breath. The ground passes under his feet, the flints jutting like dried knuckles from the soil. We walk along like this for a while and I rock with his body and close my eyes.

He has finished the cow parsley and stops, swinging his head around to nudge my leg. I push myself up on my elbows and sweep his mane to one side and kiss him. My lips taste of salt.

The tunnel empties into an open field where straw bales are stacked like golden building blocks. Amarillo pricks his ears and begins to dance. Quickly I gather the reins and slip my feet back into the stirrups.

And we are away.

We race into the hot summer currents and I feel the air pulling my sweat-soaked hair from my scalp. We gallop into the wind and soar across the yellow stubble, flints sparking from steel shoes. Too soon we reach the boundary of the field and I pull him up before he thinks we are going to jump the hedge. He snorts and bounces to a halt. I swing my leg over his neck and slide down, leaning against his heaving side for a second. Slipping the reins over his head I let him graze on the sparse grass encroaching on the stubble.

The hedge is busy, full of anxious bees, eager to draw the last of the pollen from the white bryony and honeysuckle. The blackberries are changing colour and I pull one and crush it between my fingers. I wipe it on Amarillo's neck but he is occupied with the grass and ignores me.

I sit down with my back against an ancient oak that must have somehow escaped the hedge layer's knife, finally becoming too thick to tame. There is no birdsong here, the summer heat has silenced everything. All I can hear is Amarillo, ripping at rogue tongues of grass that have crept out from the damp coolness of the hedge. The baked soil seems to creak and tick as the sun presses down on it and above me an unseen hand has scribbled the silver tails of jets across a perfect blue sky.

The sun is still high when I ride into the yard. As I watch Amarillo suck at the green bloomed water in the trough, my son comes over to me. I hear him sigh before he reaches us.

"Mum!"

I turn towards him. "Give me a minute, let me untack." He nods and I can see he is displeased with me. When was it that I first allowed him to scold me? I think we just slowly slid into these new roles and now I wait for him to berate me as I pull the leather girth straps up and let them slip through the buckles.

"Where's your hat, Mum?"

I shrug.

"For goodness sake, Mum! What if you had fallen off?"

What about it? I think. I would have lain upon the pricking stubble and the flints. Amarillo would have stayed with me. It would be good to die like that. Sandwiched between the sky and the warm rough soil. I wonder if Amarillo would know, would be sad. Eventually he would find his way home and eventually they would find me. But I would be long gone and they would tut and fuss and cry and finally they would say: "That's how she would have wanted to go."

And of course it is. They would feel better too and I hope they would feel blameless.

"Well, I didn't fall off." Do I sound disappointed? I don't mean to hurt him. "Come on, let's have a drink." And I hand him the reins and watch as he leads the horse into the cool dark stable and shuts the door with a bang, lifting it on its hinges as he heaves it into position. He snatches at a trail of ivy that has wormed its way between the stones. As he pulls it, crumbs of mortar trickle out and fall onto the yard. He shakes his head.

"There's a couple coming to view tomorrow," he says, "I had a bit of a clean-up, let's just hope they see the potential." He looks towards the barn, seeing two neat holiday cottages. I see the cockerel dancing behind the red hen, herding her towards a crack in the cement. She tugs a worm from the chasm and next they are squabbling. He wants his reward, but she is not interested and runs, wobbling from side to side, back to the barn, the fat worm swinging from her mouth.

I pour a cold lager into his glass and we sit outside, not speaking for a while. The cockerel is blustering around the bantam now but she carries on with the business of examining the muck heap, raking and pecking, chatting away to herself.

"Zeynep wants to take you shopping, to choose some curtains for the annex."

I nod. Zeynep is a sweet girl. She wants me to feel at home with them. There is no sense of duty as there might be with an English daughter-in-law. She cares for me and worries for me. She wants to encompass Ben's family with a cloak fashioned from generations of love.

The sun is balanced on the very top of the Scots pine that hangs ragged above the farmhouse. Zeynep steps carefully across the scattered cobblestones and sets a tray down on the table. Gently she lays out small pottery bowls filled with olives, tiny fried fish and sweet red peppers. She hands us each a paper napkin, neatly folded with a tiny fork laid on the top. Still standing, she refills our glasses and finally sits down, a glass of cola hissing and spitting in front of her. She leans back in her chair, eyes closed behind huge round glasses, and shakes her hair free. A mass of brown curls tumble and roll over her shoulders. Ben glances at her and smiles.

Across the yard, Amarillo looks out toward the hill. He strikes impatiently at the door and the vibration sends a tile slithering into the gutter above his stable. Ben half stands but I put my hand out and touch his arm. "I'll go."

I slip a head-collar over my arm and heave the stable door upwards on its hinges. Inside it is dark and there is a scattering of straw on the floor. The wooden beams are saturated with the smell of horses. Sometimes I can almost see their ghosts, jostling for room behind Amarillo: feathered heavy shires, tired from a day of ploughing; sensible bay cobs patiently waiting for the trip to town; stout dappled ponies nipping and barging, anxious for the hunt.

And soon this will be a self-contained holiday cottage, or a garage, or an artist's studio.

I lift the head-collar over Amarillo's nose and buckle it against his cheek. He shoves me hard with his head and unbalances me, I slip on the wet straw and grab at his mane to right myself, my ankle jars and a sharp raw shock shoots up through my leg before settling somewhere in my abdomen. Out through the half door I see that Ben and Zeynep are in conversation. They haven't seen the wince of pain on my face.

I wait a moment until I am sure my ankle can take my weight, then push the door open with my elbow and lead Amarillo out into the yard. We walk together. He is slightly ahead of me and when we reach the gate he pushes into me as I fumble with the bolt.

The rope slips from my hand and he spins away to where the top bar of the fence is split and hanging, bandaged with orange bale string.

I try to snatch the rope but he is on his hind legs and springs, from standing, over the fence.

He lands and then bucks, shooting his rear legs high above his back.

I watch as he stands on the dangling rope and jerks his head, fighting against the pull.

The head-collar snaps and falls limply into the docks and nettles. He canters away, throwing his head from side to side, adding a buck here and there as he heads towards the lusher grass that grows in patches near the stream.

I turn and realise that Ben and Zeynep have seen it all. I wander slowly back towards the table and the faded green umbrella and the chairs that will never settle on the uneven ground. Ben is going to say something but Zeynep speaks first. "You and your horse, Jill, someone should do a painting of you together, we could put it above the fireplace in your room." It is a kind thought and it has stayed the ticking off that was resting on Ben's tongue.

I wonder how much she understands. More, I believe, than her husband does. I catch her watching me sometimes as I breathe in and let the silence of this place wash over me. She sees me listening to the dark, to the branches as they creak rhythmically in the night, to the owls as they call to each other along the wooded valley. She sees me drowning in the stars and bathing in the evening scent of honeysuckle, jasmine and the wild buddleia that has seeded itself between the cracked roof tiles and in the long-empty stone troughs.

I think I remind her of home.

We stay outside until the light has been completely drawn from the sky. I wonder how many more summer evenings I will have here. And I know that Ben is right, I cannot manage this place on my own.

The ancient grey flags of the kitchen floor still keep the cold of winter. The stone walls repel the evening heat and so it is chilly now.

Zeynep has left me a pie made from filo and filled with vegetables and cheese. I turn the gas on to heat the oven, but in a few minutes the flames have flickered to nothing. Outside I shake the gas bottles but both are light and empty.

Back inside the house, I coax the Rayburn into life, little twigs popping and cracking as the flames spread. The flags become warm under my feet as I sit and eat the pie.

My new home will not have a Rayburn, it has under floor heating and an electric fire with imitation flames. The draughts won't whisper through the gaps in the window frames and sway the cobwebs that billow like tiny sails. Instead, I will be sealed from the weather. There will be no mud to walk across the floor, or pieces of hay clinging to my pullover. It will be easy to keep my new home clean. I will have plenty of time.

The darkness saturates the house and the land. It cocoons me in a soft black shawl. There are no car lights swinging from wall to wall, no yellow glow of street lamps reassuring nervous residents. I wonder if I will ever sleep again once they have moved me.

Ben arrives early the next day. He is excited about showing the house to potential buyers. He cleans around me as I make coffee and tuts when my toast leaves crumbs on the scrubbed table. And so I take my breakfast out into the yard and settle on the moss-covered well head. A cat hops up beside me and sits, watching for the tiny movements beyond human sight, listening for the scuttle of a mouse. Ben is outside now, pulling handfuls of grass and camomile from the fissures in the doorstep. He looks across at me, sitting, doing nothing. "I thought I asked you to spray these weeds!"

"You did," I reply, "but the camomile smells wonderful when you walk on it. I didn't think it was right to murder it with chemicals."

I am really in trouble now. I understand that the property is valuable and I know I have let things slip. But I am happy to let the house give up the ghost. It has housed us for centuries. Perhaps it has a right to sigh and crumble and return to the land it was created from. And so the wood rots, the stones fall from their mortar and flowers push in to fill the gaps they leave behind.

I was sure I would fall and crumble with the house and lie under the chalky soil and that the oxeye daisies and the vetch would benefit from my bones. But it seems I am not to be allowed to grow old here. I am to be maintained and kept tidy.

And I know that this is because Ben loves me.

I think about Amelia, Ben's cat, an intelligent, aloof pedigree who loved to race up the stairs and pounce on him when he was least expecting it. She would hide in cupboards and call to be found. Slowly she stopped her games and the vet diagnosed kidney disease. For a while they kept her alive with a change of diet and medication. But her joy never came back. "She has no quality of life, Mum," he explained.

And I understood. We buried her in the orchard and planted a tiny pear sapling over her.

What quality of life will I have, I wonder, at number 63 Churchill Road?

"They're late." Ben is watching the lane.

"Perhaps they've changed their minds." He hears the pleasure in my voice and turns on me. Suddenly. Angrily. "Mum!"

"I know, I know, I'm sorry. I expect they're having problems finding us."

We hear a rattle, then an explosion, or is it gunfire? A puff of smoke coughs and belches into the air as a vehicle bumps and judders down the lane. A van comes into sight. It is bright blue and has a little chimney peeking through the roof. On the side is a painting of the Green Man. Stars and suns decorate the bonnet and on the passenger door is a half-moon.

"Travellers! That's all we need! I'll get rid of them." And Ben strides out through the gate as the van wheezes to a halt.

"Hey!" he shouts as the door opens.

A child slips down from the passenger seat and stands, looking around her. Her hair is long and matted and she has the remains of some organic meal smeared across her face. She bends down and picks up a flint. She licks it and examines its shininess.

The driver's door opens and a man walks around the front of the van. He holds his hand out to Ben. There is something familiar about him. He stoops slightly as he walks, as if to apologise for his height. His hair is long and hangs in dreadlocks over his shoulders. I watch Ben's back. He suddenly seems to sag.

A woman jumps down and sweeps up the child in her arms. She leans into Ben and kisses him on the cheek. She pushes the child towards him and Ben reaches out and lifts the little girl above his head. She squeals and crows and kicks out, laughing at him.

The tall man looks up and catches my eye. He puts an arm around Ben and together they walk in through the gate, the grubby child still in Ben's arms. The woman lifts up her skirts and trots along behind, all flying red hair and laughter.

"Hello Mum." And the tall man, who is my son, holds out his arms and hugs the breath from me. Over his shoulder I see the woman spinning, her skirts flaring out around her. She stretches her arms, embracing the land and the house. "This is heaven! Pure heaven!"

And perhaps it is heaven. For here I am, with my son whom I thought was long dead. And whose blue eyes I thought I would never look into again, staring at me.

"The old man died then." There is no sadness in his voice.

I nod.

He looks down at me. He doesn't need to say anything. He doesn't need to tell me why he left and he doesn't need to say he is sorry.

"I heard the place was up for sale." Adam, and I haven't used his name for years, turns to Ben.

"Well, we thought we might buy it."

Ben looks at Adam and he looks at the van. He looks at the ruddy-faced woman who is dancing in the yard and he looks at the placid child in his arms.

"You know I couldn't stay, Ben."

I expect to see fury in Ben's face. I wonder if he is reliving the long search for Adam; hugging me while I wept; watching me mourn my child, not knowing if he was alive or dead. Does he want to lash out in anger? I wait for him to reach up and strike my youngest son. But he doesn't. I see something lift from his face, something I hadn't noticed until now.

"I made a bit of money Mum and I want to come home." I had kept the memory of his voice, playing it again and again in my head, afraid I would forget. That precious sound.

The woman trips across to me and slips her arm through mine. She smells of patchouli oil and very slightly of sweat. We watch as Amarillo rubs his head up and down against the gate post. His auburn mane flies in waves that catch the light from the morning sun. The child wriggles to be put down and squats, staring at the bantam as it pecks and gently clucks among the weeds.

Ben awakens. "We've fixed up an annex at our place for Mum." And then his face flushes as he turns towards his brother. "She can't look after the farm anymore you know!"

I open my mouth to object but Adam stays me with a smile. "She won't need to."

Well I am still here! I want to say. *I don't need to be spoon fed, or changed.*

I want to be cross but it's difficult. The woman squeezes my arm and whispers in my ear. "Please, please, teach me to ride!"

And just like that, I am restored.

Aanjay Jumps from a Plane
David Reading

When Aanjay pulled the ripcord he was confident the parachute would open as planned. A man with a moustache and three stripes on his sleeve had told him this would happen. Indeed, Aanjay had been shown how to make it happen, and was optimistic about his ability to perform what was really a very simple task: in effect just a sharp tug on a metal handle. In any case he was doing this for a good cause. This was a sponsored parachute jump in aid of the Blue-Tailed Mole Foundation and Aanjay was determined not to let them down.

But when he pulled the metal handle nothing happened. The parachute did not open as predicted. The man with the moustache had been mistaken and so now Aanjay was falling at a very high speed towards the ground. As a young fellow with a curious nature, Aanjay wondered how fast he was travelling. He had read in a magazine that the fastest skydiver ever was a man called Bjorn from Sweden, who achieved nearly 400 miles an hour. That was quite some feat, Aanjay thought, but he felt it unlikely that he was travelling quite as fast as that.

Another question that began to occupy his mind at this point was how long his descent would last. Making a quick calculation (taking into account his weight, his estimated acceleration and the height at which he began falling) he guessed the answer was somewhere around a minute. That seemed rather a lot but he made the calculation again and reached the same figure.

Reflecting on the likely outcome to this present dilemma, Aanjay wondered whether his friends who had pledged their money to the Blue-Tailed Mole Foundation would honour their pledges or whether their point of view would be: *Well, he didn't actually do what he said he would do so we cannot be expected to cough up.* That was a debatable point. It might be argued that although the parachute jump didn't go *exactly* as planned (i.e. it was an *unsuccessful* parachute jump ending with the death of the jumpee) Aanjay had kept to the spirit of the arrangement. No doubt the fine people at the Blue-Tailed Mole Foundation would make that very point.

Over the next few seconds Aanjay seemed to pick up momentum and of course that is always what happens to falling objects. They don't remain at the same speed. They accelerate. Aanjay remembered from sixth form science that something falling from a great height has an acceleration of 9.8 metres per second per second. He was under no illusion: that was not good news.

So there we have it, he thought to himself. *I really am in a bit of a pickle.*

The chances of a positive outcome were hard to establish. Those chances were probably rather small, Aanjay mused, although surely they weren't non-existent. He had read somewhere that a parachutist named Steve had escaped from a similar tight spot by falling into a blackberry bush. Aanjay's generally cheerful disposition wouldn't allow him to become downhearted. He hadn't yet reached the ground and therefore it was a case of *so far so good*. Although there was every likelihood that he would *eventually* reach the ground, nothing in this sorry mess could be clear-cut. Perhaps he too would fall into a bush like the man named Steve.

It was while pondering on these matters that Aanjay saw a large bird directly below him. For his tenth birthday his Uncle Harish had given him a handbook on how to recognise British birds from a very long way away and so Aanjay knew the bird he could see directly below him was a golden eagle. At the sight of such a splendid creature, Aanjay felt a thrill ripple through his body. He had never seen a golden eagle before, except on the television and once on a stamp. There were several good reasons why he wanted to survive and now here was one more: he would simply love to phone his Uncle Harish in Mumbai and tell him he had seen a golden eagle, and not just on the television.

But just then a troubling thought entered his mind. The laws of physics determined that as time went by, the distance between Aanjay and the golden eagle would become shorter and shorter, and this worried him because a collision between their two bodies seemed a possibility. He had never knowingly killed another creature before, unless you count ants, which are difficult to avoid when you are going about your daily business. Now here was the possibility that in his final seconds he would be responsible for taking the life of a magnificent bird of prey.

But something fortunate happened. The golden eagle, perhaps on seeing this shadowy form looming above him, growing larger by the second, had soared rapidly to the left and had thus moved out of harm's way. Aanjay was delighted.

For a very small space of time, he drew level with the eagle and as he did so, he fancied he saw a look of compassion in the bird's eyes: sympathy, perhaps, for a fellow creature living the last few seconds of its life. By now he was close enough to the ground to notice a small group of people standing in a field, who seemed to be following his progress with interest. He fancied he could see among them the man with the moustache and three stripes on his sleeve, staring upwards showing obvious concern. Aanjay hoped the poor man would not feel in any way responsible for what was happening. He wondered whether, in his final seconds, he could convey a message to the man – *you are not to blame, good sir.* But his attempt to mouth those words while travelling at speed made him feel a little ridiculous.

His minute of freefall was almost up. Aanjay had found it an interesting experience: most certainly a one-off. For the last few seconds it seemed as if he was falling in slow motion. His final thoughts were on where he would land, and whether his arrival would inconvenience anyone living in the vicinity. Directly below him he could see a large, white oblong shape. It was impossible to speculate on what the shape was exactly, but he knew this was where he was destined to fall.

He hit the large, white shape in its centre. A variety of sensations followed: a sudden halt, pain in his left shoulder, the voice of the American crooner Frank Sinatra, the smell of cooked seafood, people calling out in surprise. Then there was a hefty jolt and a tearing sound as his downward motion resumed, more gentle this time, followed by further cries of alarm as he landed on grass. He was inside what seemed to be a large tent, with a gaping hole in the top where he had arrived.

As Aanjay came to rest, he noticed a crowd of faces circling around him displaying expressions of curiosity. He was aware of an air of lavish celebration. His attention focused on a lady dressed in white and a fellow in a top hat looking rather irritated.

It had been such an eventful afternoon. Later that day, when Aanjay returned home, he was unable to contain his excitement. He telephoned his Uncle Harish in Mumbai immediately and eagerly told him the news: today he had seen a golden eagle.

Crime in the Time of Covid
David Reading

It's surprising what you'll do to make a bit of cash if you're desperate. Who'd have thought that three weeks after leaving London I'd be working for a gangster?

I met Ray in a café in a small town on the south coast just as the money was running out. I'd ordered a sandwich but found I was 50p short and the manager was starting to get stroppy. He was standing about two feet away, breathing all over me. No face mask or anything.

Ray was sitting at a nearby table, talking on the phone and finishing a cup of tea. When the call was over, he asked me what the problem was. I said I couldn't pay for my cheese sandwich. So Ray coughed up the money and asked me to do him a favour in return. His driver had phoned to say he was in A&E with a suspected heart attack. Ray described this as *bloody inconvenient*. He said he needed someone to drive him to a warehouse somewhere off the M27. Would I be that someone?

Ray was twice my age – old enough to be my dad – but he would probably have been a poor substitute for a dad and a poor role model. Then again, my real dad was a poor role model too. After he left home I saw him only twice and each time he was with a different woman. Maybe that's why I find life so confusing at times. Someone once told me I'm easily led and perhaps there's a lot of truth in that. Anyway I hardly had to think about it: I agreed to drive Ray to that warehouse somewhere off the M27.

Was Ray really a gangster? It depends on your definition of the term. If a gangster is defined as a member of a violent criminal gang, then he would have disputed the point. He said he didn't like violence and only used it as a last resort. But let's not split hairs. The thing I witnessed on Day Two of our relationship would put him right up there in the category of hardened criminal.

When I drove his white BMW for the first time, with Ray in the back, I didn't know what I was getting myself into, not at first, but it soon became clear. There were enough clues in what he said as we pulled out of the café car park.

"By the way, when we get there you will see nothing and hear nothing."

I wasn't sure what he'd said so I had to ask him to repeat it.

He didn't answer for a while. The radio was on low and he was slapping his hand against the seat. I guess he thought he was keeping time with the music, but he sounded way off beam to me. Ray was definitely not musical.

He repeated it for me nice and slowly.

"When - we - get - there - you - will - see - nothing - and - hear - nothing."

"OK," I said. "I get the point."

We arrived after a half-hour drive. The place was located in an out-of-town industrial estate. There was a print firm nearby and a used car dealer opposite. Down the far end there was a sign saying *recycling centre*. The warehouse Ray directed me to was off the road, behind a nondescript building that didn't seem to serve any purpose. There was no name on the door and little sign of life, apart from three heavies outside unloading stuff from a truck. One was wearing a face covering.

The three men were taking cardboard boxes off the back of the truck and stacking them up just inside the building. There was also a wooden crate. It took all three of them to shift that. Ray didn't help. He stood there with his hands in his pockets watching. He was Mister Big with his long mac and cocky attitude. When the three guys had finished the job, Ray handed over a brown envelope and got back in the car. I wasn't sure what to do next. I was waiting for instructions.

"You seem to be able to drive OK," he said at last. "I take it you have a licence."

"It's about all I do have," I said.

"Then how would you like to come and work for me?"

"To do what exactly?"

"Driving. That's all. No heavy lifting, and nothing that will get you into trouble. So long as you're careful, that is. All I ask is that you make yourself available twenty-four seven. You'll be paid OK. In cash."

"But you don't know anything about me," I said. "I could be an undercover cop for all you know."

He scoffed at that. "Do me a favour. If you're a cop then I'm Boris bloody Johnson."

I thought about it. I was out of money. I needed a job. But did I want to work for someone who did his business outside a warehouse and handed over brown envelopes to men who looked like bare-knuckle fighters?

"Why me?" I said. "What about your regular driver?"

"He's unreliable. Anyway he's probably dead. You look like you'll do as you're told and you drive OK. The fact is, I need someone ASAP and I haven't got time to piss about. As it happens, I need someone tomorrow. After that you can make up your own mind."

"What's happening tomorrow?" I asked. If he'd answered that question truthfully I like to think I would have got out of the car and walked away. But all he said was, "Nothing much. We've just got to pick up a few bits and pieces from the town." I should have been careful, I really should, but I made a snap decision. "I'll give it a shot. Let's see how it pans out."

"Good," he said. "We'll go back to my place and you can tell me all about yourself."

And so that was where my brief stint as a gangster began.

***

I took a down payment without giving it a lot of thought. *Dirty* money, some people would call it. There wasn't a lot of it: just enough for a takeaway and a bottle of wine. But the amount of money was irrelevant. Every last penny was tainted because its origins were somehow tied in with unscrupulous deeds. That much was obvious and I make no excuses: I am wholly responsible for my actions.

When I met Ray's wife in the lounge of their home I thought at first she was his daughter. Jo looked 20 years younger than him and there was a look of innocence in her eyes, as if she had only just ventured out into the world. I wondered why she was with Ray; why she had chosen the life of gangster's moll.

"This is Sam, my new driver," he said. "Colin – how should I put it? – is indisposed."

She gave me a light wave from across the room where she was sitting. "Pleased to meet you, Sam," she said. "You can take off the mask, I'm sure we're all perfectly safe. Can I get you a drink?" She was wearing a blue dressing gown but didn't seem self-conscious about it even though it was seven in the evening.

I took off the mask, asked for a beer and sat down. The place was tastefully decorated: oak parquet flooring, Persian style rugs, framed Monet prints on the wall, that kind of thing. I'd expected nouveau riche.

"Do you want a glass?" she said.

"A can will do."

As she left to fetch the drinks, Ray asked me what I'd been doing for the last couple of years. It wasn't a very happy tale but I told him the truth. I'd lived in West London with my mum and my step-dad Kevin, but Kevin threw me out on the streets. He was a drunk. He accused me of taking fifty pounds from his wallet. The accusation was false – I only took thirty – but I was sick of being pushed around so I said goodbye to my mum, we hugged and I took off. Someone said I should go south because the air was cleaner, so I did just that. I told Ray I lived in a caravan five miles up the coast. That too was true. It wasn't actually *my* caravan but so far no one had turned up to claim it.

When Jo came back into the room Ray was telling me the rules – *get smartened up, keep the car clean inside and out, check the oil once a week*, that kind of thing. "It's German lager," she said. "Hope that's OK."

As she handed me the can she smiled and stared into my eyes for a few seconds. There was vulnerability in that look, as if she was silently pleading with me. Or did I imagine that? And there was a slight tremor in her hands. I'm sure I didn't imagine that.

Ray told her to put on a CD and the music she chose was one of those swing numbers, Dean Martin, I think. My dad – my real dad – used to listen to that kind of stuff all the time. She sat down and began tapping her hand on the arm of the sofa in time with the music.

"Sam," she said. "Look after him, won't you."

"I'm sorry?"

Ray sighed heavily.

"Watch him for me, Sam. Don't let him get into too much trouble. I know he goes close to the line sometimes. Don't let him cross it."

"Don't listen to her, Sam," Ray said. "You answer to me, not her. She seems to think I'm bloody Al Capone. I can never seem to convince her that I'm just a businessman and everything I do is for her benefit."

"I'm only the hired hand," I said. "I'm not sure I have any influence over what your husband does with his life."

"Well, do your best," she said.

Ray opened another can of beer for me, then another, and then he brought out the Scotch. He didn't seem to be going anywhere so we drank and he talked. I asked him what he thought about the latest stats – nearly 120,000 deaths in the UK alone – and he shrugged.

"Doesn't bother me. I'm fit and healthy, no medical problems, so I don't expect to get it bad, if I get it at all. It won't affect my business either, because I know how to manage risk. There are businesses that are in deep shit because they've been caught wrong-footed but if you ask me people should have seen it coming and made plans. Anyone who knows what they're doing will sail through this. You've got to do your research, see. Think ahead."

Jo kept quiet at this point. I got the impression that she didn't share Ray's views but knew better than to argue with him.

When Ray left the room to get more ice, Jo leaned forward and began to whisper.

"Don't let him bully you," she said. "From day one he'll try to intimidate you. Stand up to him, otherwise he'll walk all over you."

"OK," I said. "I'll try to remember that. Does he walk all over *you*?"

She evaded the question. "He's worse when he's had a drink. When he has a drink he argues about the most stupid things as I'm sure you've noticed. Politics is one. He was a great fan of Margaret Thatcher. Don't ever say anything rude about Margaret Thatcher. He'll really go off on one."

"OK. I'll steer clear of that one," I said. Actually I had no opinions about Margaret Thatcher. I used to find my mind was awash with opinions: opinions about anything and everything. I soon found that they serve little purpose and no one really wants to hear them. Over-sharing of opinions is a great way to get you into trouble. So I try not to have them.

"And most important of all," she was saying. "Don't ask too many questions about his private business or else…"

She didn't finish the sentence. Ray was standing in the doorway holding the ice bucket. "Or else what?" he shouted.

"Nothing, I was just…"

Ray leaned against the door jamb. If he hadn't he would have fallen over. By now he was obviously drunk.

"I think you'd better get to bed," he snarled.

He looked towards me. "Ignore her," he said. "I don't know why I put up with this crap. Sometimes I think she's stark raving mad."

Jo got up, took a book from the shelf, and slipped out of the room. Thankfully Ray passed out in his armchair soon afterwards. He woke up about midnight and, as it was too late for me to get a bus, he told me to sleep on the sofa. At about one o' clock I thought I heard a shout followed by someone whimpering. I should have left at that moment, I really should. Maybe I was weak or maybe I was curious. Something was about to happen and a part of me wanted to know what it was.

***

Next morning Ray told me he was meeting people at that same warehouse a few miles off the M27. But first he wanted me to smarten myself up, as he put it. We drove into town and parked at a multi-storey. "Here's a couple of hundred quid," he said. "I'll grab a coffee. You go and get yourself a makeover. Now this is important: don't get anything too flashy, just get jeans and a dark jacket, that kind of thing. And buy yourself a deodorant. You could do with it." So I got myself a dark jacket and jeans and threw my scruffy old hoodie into a waste bin. And do you know what, people started to notice me. Women started to notice me. The barber called me *Sir*. That too was a new experience. Ray seemed happy enough with the way I looked when I got back to the car. I even had thirty quid change.

Ray was due at the warehouse at two. On the way he sat in the back seat messing around with his phone. He made a couple of calls, speaking secretively, using guarded language. I imagine it was designed to keep me in the dark.

When he'd finished his calls he opened a bag of something – sweets, I suppose – and began chewing noisily. He also began humming a tune. He could chew and hum at the same time. I thought that was quite impressive.

"Do you play chess?" he said suddenly.

"I used to. I'm a bit out of practice."

"Maybe we could have a game sometime. I'm crap at it. I need to find someone I can beat. Are you a good loser?"

"It depends what you mean by good?"

"You know what I mean. Are you OK with losing or do you throw a tantrum?"

Here's something I once read. I once read that winning and losing are illusions. The person who said it was some ancient Chinese mystic. He said that winning and losing are both neutral but the mind makes winning feel good and makes losing feel bad. But it's all a delusion: something created by the mind. When I read that, I kind of understood. I tried to explain it to Ray but he didn't get it so I gave up.

"One thing you'll learn about me," he said, "is that I always win. It's a tough world. You can't just roll over every time you come up against a problem. I like to think there isn't a problem in the world I can't solve."

We stopped for coffee on the way and arrived at the warehouse just before ten. There were three different men there this time, all wearing overalls, standing near a black Transit. Ray told me to get out of the car and into the Transit and wait there while they went inside. They were in there for about half an hour.

When they came out they were all wearing black face masks and Ray was also dressed in overalls. They got in the Transit: Ray in the front, his three mates in the back.

"Right," Ray said, "this is where you really start earning your money."

***

The place he told me to drive to was at the end of a row of shops in a quiet street at right angles to the seafront. The name of the place was Diamonds Are Forever. As we approached he told me to drive past the shop, turn left around the corner and stop but keep the engine running. I did as I was told.

Ray took out his mobile and dialled. I could hear a phone ringing in the back of the van. "It's me," he said. "Two minutes. I'm just filling in our young friend here."

"Right, Sam," he said. "I guess you know by now what business you're in. This particular job is important to me, you understand? I lost a lot of money last month – we won't say how that happened – and I have to make it up today. If I don't, someone you don't want to know about is going to be seriously annoyed. A lot of planning has gone into this and I don't want it to go wrong. If you do exactly as I say everything will be fine and you'll make me very happy. Do you understand?"

I didn't answer. I was mulling over what he'd just said. In truth, I knew we weren't here to pick up a pizza order from the local takeaway. It was something well outside my normal sphere. But the aggressive tone in his voice wasn't the real problem. It was what happened next that was the real problem. He reached into the glove compartment and pulled out a gun. It was the first one I'd seen close up, unless you count those you come across when you walk past sports goods shops. He stuffed it into the pocket of his overalls.

"I said do you understand?"

I could have said this wasn't the life for me. I could have opened the van door and done a runner. But I did neither of those things. It may have been fear of crossing him, or it may have been that I needed a touch of excitement in my life. It was a bit of both probably.

"I understand, Ray."

"OK, let's hope you do," he said. "Now just wait here. We'll be five minutes. If anyone asks what you're doing here, just say you're delivering a parcel to someone over the road. These days every other van is a delivery van so no one will suspect anything dodgy. When we get back in the van just drive away slowly and carefully. And keep your face mask on. That's one advantage with what's going on at the moment. You can be masked up like you're one of Ronnie Kray's boys and no one will bat an eyelid."

Ray got out of the van and banged on the side. I heard the back doors crash open and then slam shut. I looked in the wing mirror. All four of them disappeared up the street and around the corner towards the front of the jeweller's shop. Two of them were holding what looked like baseball bats. I turned on the radio and one of Ray's CDs came on automatically. It was Frank Sinatra singing New York, New York. Frank got as far as the second line when the door opened and Ray got back in. He was muttering through his face mask. I could tell he was seriously upset.

"Drive," he said.

"What's wrong, Ray?"

"Don't ask questions, just drive."

The back doors slammed shut and I set off down the street.

We dropped off his accomplices at the station and headed towards the warehouse, where his BMW was parked. Frank was still singing away.

I've got the world on a string, sittin' on a rainbow
Got the string around my finger
What a world, what a life…

Throughout the half-hour journey Ray didn't say a word. Frank carried on singing but Ray didn't seem to feel like joining in. We dropped off the Transit and went back to his place in the BMW.

After we got out I thought about the gun. "Ray," I said, "I'm not sure what happened back there but there is one thing I am sure about. This probably isn't the right line of work for me – I need something a bit more routine. Do you get what I mean?"

He didn't reply at first. I thought that was the end of it and I was about to turn and head off up the street. But he reached out suddenly and grabbed my collar. "If you are ever tempted to breathe a word of this to anyone, just remember one thing," he said. "I have a very long reach."

***

I thought it was time to move on but I just had to know. Next day I hopped on a bus and went back to the scene of the aborted crime. The bus stopped right outside the place. As I got off I saw a sign on the door and security bars covering the front windows. But there was nothing inside for them to guard. The windows were bare. The job had obviously been meticulously scripted but one tiny detail eluded them. They had looked terrifying with their masks and their baseball bats and their Mafioso attitude. But their bravado must have faded as they came to a halt at the front door and read the sign.

Sorry. Closed Due to the Pandemic.

The Haunting at Wellspring House

Alexis Krite

After a sleepless night, it became clear to Robin that he did, in fact, need Jack Turner's help. For hours, the house had been trembling, its restless vibrations constantly reminding Robin that he now had no choice in the matter.

During the day, the July sun had baked the clay roof tiles and even at this moment, at the edge of dawn, they retained their heat. The roof seemed to throb and pulse as it squeezed and stretched its ribs of ancient Sussex timbers. Fine cracks had begun to appear in the newly-plastered ceiling. Soon he would have to get up and reluctantly make the phone call.

Through the open window, a warm breeze drifted in and lapped across his body, setting the sweat tingling and prickling where it had pooled on his chest. He could feel the sheet, damp beneath him. He turned gently, trying not to wake Annette. The moon was still full and he could see her body clearly outlined beneath her fragile satin nightdress. Tiny beads of moisture sat like freshwater pearls on her forehead. She slept on. Was it only him, then, who heard the house sighing in the darkness? Behind the wainscot, a mouse skittered up some secret tunnel in the cob walls.

And then, from the room below, a sob. Gentle, hardly audible.

***

It was three weeks earlier that Annette had first contacted Doctor Jack Turner. He had arrived in a well-worn Morris Traveller just as the weather was breaking. A crack of thunder tore through the thick air and the clouds hurled heavy pellets of rain at the unfortunate figure who stumbled hastily across the gravel towards the front entrance. Annette was holding the door open and beckoned to him, her voice almost unheard in the turbulence of the storm. "Come in, come in. Oh never mind the floor," she said, slamming the door behind him. He stood, dripping, on the Persian rug. His boots, Robin observed, were mercifully free of mud.

Robin held out his hand. "Doctor Turner, I'm Robin Hardacre. It's very kind of you to come at such short notice, although I'm not sure how you can help."

Jack Turner pulled his fisherman's hat from his head and wrung it out onto the floor. His hair, now liberated, dropped down to his shoulders in grey, matted clods. He took Robin's hand and shook it vigorously. "Nonsense! Delighted to come. A very interesting case from what your wife has told me." He smiled at Annette. His glasses had steamed up making eye contact temporarily impossible.

"I'm not sure you would call it a *case* exactly," Annette said. "Anyway, let's go through and I'll pop some coffee on." She led the way down the hall and into the kitchen.

Turner rubbed his hands together impatiently. "Actually, do you think I could have a look at the room while the coffee brews? I really am most anxious to start my investigation."

Robin frowned. "Investigation? Look, I hope you haven't got the wrong impression. To be honest I think we're more in need of a plumber or a builder than a psychical researcher, or whatever it is you call yourself."

Annette gave her husband a reproachful look. "Follow me Doctor Turner," she said and led him towards the stairs." *Doctor* Turner indeed, Robin thought.

She led the way cautiously up the stairs and into the room. "We bought the place six months ago," she said. "Robin was hooked from the moment he saw it. Felt drawn to it, he said. This used to be the owner's bedroom but we converted it into a guest room for our B&B visitors."

Robin joined them on the landing and Turner, his glasses un-fogged now, looked at him intently.

"So I'm assuming you've noticed some unusual activity in the room. Strange sounds, vibrations, smells, that kind of thing," he said.

Robin shifted uneasily.

"No, *we* haven't," Annette said, "but we've had a few comments from our guests, that's why we felt we had to do something. You were recommended." Annette smiled awkwardly.

"By another disbeliever?"

"Well, no actually. By our local vicar."

Turner raised his eyebrows. "Interesting."

In the brief silence that followed, the three of them stared into the bedroom. Of all the guest rooms, this was the prettiest. It had windows on two sides with views across the Sussex Weald. The house had been built into the hillside and despite being on the first floor, a door from the bedroom opened out on to a small terrace.

Annette led the way cautiously into the room. "This used to be the owner's bedroom." She walked towards the French windows and lifted the latch. "And here's the little terrace." Steam was rising now from the paving slabs and the scent of honeysuckle drifted in through the open door.

Turner smiled. "Beautiful, beautiful. Yes, I can see why it could be popular with visitors." He stepped out on to the terrace and turned, looking back into the room. He ran his hand down the wooden door frame. "I should think this was some kind of way out into a yard originally." He stamped his feet on the paving slabs. "It sounds hollow under here." He peered at Robin over his glasses. "Was this terrace here when you bought the place?"

"Yes, we did a lot of redecorating, but nothing structural really."

Turner nodded. "Mmm. Do you mind if I have a look around on my own? I'll just be a few minutes."

"Of course, we'll be in the kitchen." Annette took her husband's hand and pulled him firmly from the room.

"How do you know he's not casing the joint?" Robin hissed as they went downstairs.

"Oh for goodness sake, Rob! We're losing business! Look at the last two reviews we've had. We've got to try something… *anything!*"

The previous guests had left after one night. At breakfast the next morning, they had both seemed exhausted. Annette had plied them with coffee but they wouldn't wait for the full English breakfast that had been included in the deal. Instead, they asked Robin to bring down their suitcases, reluctant, it seemed, to return to their room.

As they were leaving, the man turned and asked, "Has anyone lost a puppy round here? Something was whimpering all night."

His wife glanced at him. "Well, it sort of *sounded* like a puppy. But then, not really. I thought it was a baby crying. But you don't take children, do you?"

Annette smiled. "No, no children and we haven't got any of our own. I expect it was a fox cub, or a badger."

"Or a seagull," Robin added lamely. The door closed behind the guests and Robin and Annette stared at each other. Not again.

And now here was Doctor Jack Turner. At the vicar's suggestion they had brought up his website. Sussex.psychicsolutions.co.uk certainly had some impressive reviews.

Turner joined them in the kitchen and Annette passed him a coffee. He shovelled in three spoons of sugar and stirred it noisily. "So it seems to be your guests say the same thing, something crying, weeping perhaps. *Whimpering.*"

Annette nodded. "We've checked all the gaps round the windows. We thought maybe it was the wind or a breeze catching on something. Robin's oiled all the door hinges and we've even had the floor boards up in our room. We sleep right above. Nothing."

"I think," Turner spoke slowly, "what we have here is a spirit remnant."

A sudden shaft of pain shot through Robin's head. "A *what*?"

"A remnant. Part of a soul that has been left behind. Abandoned."

"Is that why it's crying? Because it's been left?" Annette asked, gripping her cup.

Turner nodded. "And it's interesting because it's a whimper, not a wail, just a whimper."

Robin lifted his hand to his head. A migraine was beginning to burrow into his brain. He knew that soon his vision would be filled with kaleidoscopic images. "Oh come on, Turner, you can't be serious," he said with an attempt at a snigger. And then he heard it – a faint cry from the first-floor bedroom. "Listen! There it is!"

Annette stared at him. "There what is?"

"Well can't you hear it? That's what the guests must have heard. A seagull crying or a bird of some sort." The whimpering rose and fell as if something were reaching out to him.

"What are you talking about, Robin? You're scaring me, I didn't hear anything. Did you, Doctor Turner?"

Turner slowly shook his head. Robin started up from the table. "There it is again! That noise! I don't know… a feral cat. Air in the pipes?"

He was agitated now, running his hands up and down his thighs. "Right, well. So tell us, how much do we owe you for your analysis?" He needed to lie down.

Turner slurped his coffee. "I charge nothing for this initial assessment. If, however, you wish to resolve the issue, my fee depends on the amount of work needed to liberate the spirit. This could entail structural exploration, re-location of artefacts; the introduction of other artefacts. It's all on a case-by-case basis."

Annette didn't hesitate. "Well Rob, don't you think we should book Doctor Turner in?"

Robin tipped his head from side to side, pressing his fingers into his temples. "I can't deal with this now, Annie. Doctor Turner, thanks again for your time. Give us a week or so to think about this."

"Well, you have my number, I'm happy to come back at your convenience." Turner stood up.

"I think we know, don't we, Mr Hardacre, that this is a little too complex for a plumber."

"I'll see you out," said Annette. As he stepped out onto the gravel, Jack Turner hesitated.

"I don't really do this for the clients who call me, Mrs Hardacre. I do it for the ones who can't."

***

In the three weeks since Turner's visit, they'd had four cancelled bookings and one early check-out. And now, as the sky began to peel back the darkness and the first tentative light slipped through the dormer window, Robin's chest heaved with a stifled sob. The grief was becoming all-consuming. It pervaded the entire house.

The bed rocked gently, yet Annette lay still. He stretched a leg out and stood up slowly. As far as he knew, she hadn't been affected by the sorrow in the fabric of their home. He picked up his clothes from the floor and his phone from the bedside table and made his way down to the kitchen. Turner's card was still propped up on the dresser, where Annette had left it after his visit. Reluctantly, Robin dialled the number.

He was surprised by the speed of Turner's response. He arrived later that morning, the Morris loaded with tools. *He looks more like a builder than an exorcist,* Robin thought.

Turner was dressed this time in cut-off denim shorts and a sleeveless vest that had once sported the tour dates of a long-retired band. He wasted no time. "Right, you grab that pickaxe, Robin. I can call you Robin now, can't I? And you, Annette, if you look under that blanket, you'll find a crowbar." Turner himself carried a wooden box with indecipherable writing carved into the top.

The house was humming in the late morning heat. "Hear that?" Turner asked, cocking his head at Annette. "Bees?" she ventured. Turner shook his head: "Not bees. Excitement!"

He walked straight up to the bedroom and out on to the terrace. To Robin's horror he took hold of the pickaxe and swung it up, bringing it down on to the paving slabs. A crack shot across the first slab and a fissure opened in the second, sending part of the slab down into what appeared to be a deep empty space. Turner straightened up. "Aha! I thought so! A well." Robin peered over the edge of the slabs; the well was dry and didn't seem particularly deep.

Turner stood, his hands on his hips, sweat starting to leach through the armpits of his vest. "I took the liberty of looking in the old deeds. There were a few plans available and this used to be the main water supply to the house until they excavated a new well higher up. The water to this one was diverted to the new well and bit by bit this has started to fill with rubble. I'm going down." With surprising agility Turner leapt down into the pit and squatted at the bottom. He called up, "Can you drop my torch, shovel and that hessian bag down to me?" Soon he was scrabbling in the semi darkness. Every now and then he threw up a rock. "Watch it! One coming over!"

Annette moved over to Robin and whispered. "He's actually *enjoying* this!" A few moments later they both became aware of the silence. Robin walked across to the edge of the hole. "Jack, are you all right down there?"

"Yes, yes." They heard him sigh. "Yes, very sad, very sad. Poor little mite."

Annette and Robin glanced at each other in alarm. "Turner?" Robin crouched on the broken paving slabs, looking down into the darkness. Turner's head appeared above the edge of the hole. "Here, take this, gently please." He handed up the parcel of hessian to Robin's outstretched arms. It weighed nothing. For a moment Robin thought he had been presented with an empty bag. But then in his hands the sack became heavier, warm, moving. He leapt up, ready to drop the squirming bundle. But then it lay still again and from behind him he heard the house catch its breath.

"What is it, Rob?" Annette reached out to touch it. But Robin shook his head and drew the bag tightly into his chest.

***

They buried the infant next to his twin brother in the churchyard. The lichen-covered headstone read: Mathew Hardacre 1835 to 1930.

"It was quite common," the Reverend Sarah Gladwish explained, "for a second birth to be concealed, especially when the sibling was so much smaller and weaker than the first. It was believed the mother should give all her milk to the one child that could survive." She scattered a few grains of soil onto the tiny wooden box.

"And Mathew *did* survive," she said. "Thanks to my grandfather we know who this other child was. If he hadn't recorded the deathbed confession of the midwife, this would have remained a mystery forever."

Jack Turner stood with his hands clasped together and spoke: "A little while, a moment of rest upon the wind, and another woman shall bear me."

The vicar frowned at him. "You're quoting Khalil Gibran. Reincarnation?" She clutched her Bible to her chest, "I'm not sure if…"

Turner cut in. "It is my belief that for some reason, part of this little soul remained buried with the child. But I don't expect your Christian orthodoxy will allow you to accept that."

The vicar smiled. "And the other part?"

"Well, I believe someone else is that soul incarnate. And whoever that person is will find their peace now." And he laid his hand on Robin's shoulder.

The Stitch-Up
Max Bevan

Their plan was infallible. Everything had gone just right. *Rio here we come*, Leo thought.

It was a warm, sunny afternoon in late autumn. He'd chosen the pub by the river and sat outside on the patio with a large glass of red to toast their success. He sipped his wine and watched the ducks.

"Started already?"

Leo looked up. "Yeah, you bet," he laughed.

Paddy placed another large glass of wine and a pint of lager on the table and sat down laughing.

They clinked glasses. "All sorted?" Leo asked.

"Yeah, nothing to worry about. Just a minor hiccup."

"What do you mean?" Leo's eyes narrowed.

"It's OK, don't worry. I moved everything into the Singapore account. I was just shutting everything down when the phone went. It was that surgeon bloke, Parker. You dealt with him didn't you? I think he's smelled a rat. I told him you weren't back 'til Monday. We'll be on the other side of the world by then."

Leo sighed. "Trouble is, those medical people are smart. The last time I saw him he was asking some awkward questions. I thought he was going to pull out."

"Well, you stitched him up like a kipper mate." Paddy looked at Leo's serious face. "Come on, cheer up. We cracked it. This is it." He leaned across the table and smacked Leo on the shoulder.

Leo responded with a weak smile. He stared across the fields beyond the river. He wouldn't feel completely relaxed until he was on the plane and taking off.

By the time he'd finished his third glass his mood had improved considerably. And when he finished his fifth he was positively euphoric. They sat hunched together, hardly noticed by the early evening crowd filling the other tables. Anyone watching would have seen them grinning gleefully at each other and then roaring with laughter. What the observer wouldn't have known was they were revelling over how gullible their victims were and how convincing they'd been in fooling even their smarter subjects like Parker, the surgeon.

They had planned to travel to Rio separately, by different routes and by different airlines. They would meet up the following week. Beyond that their plans were a little unclear. They'd talked about trying their scam in Australia or the States or maybe South Africa, but not until they'd had a great time in Rio blowing some of the spoils.

The autumn air began to cool as they left the pub and approached the car park. Across to the west the angry red of the sunset against a black and blue horizon began to dominate the evening sky.

They exchanged manly hugs and got into their separate cars. Leo pulled out of the car park and sped off down the lane.

Leo wasn't thinking much about his driving – he was thinking about

Rio. He lowered his window and sucked in the cool evening air. He put his foot down. He felt exhilarated thinking of his new life stretching out in front of him. They'd be wealthy, international playboys, conning their way around the world. Hitting the highlife. Staying in the best hotels – the best food – best clothes – the best of everything. Their scam was infallible and so were they.

Leo didn't see the *MUD ON ROAD* sign just before the bend. He hit the brakes too late and the car skidded on the slurry. It almost turned a full 180 degrees before hitting the oak tree embedded in the hedgerow.

***

Awareness returned slowly to Leo. First a dim light, then a metallic tinkle and then a vague murmur of someone's voice. Nothing made sense. Eventually he felt someone next to him. He managed to open his eyes a little. A woman came into soft focus, a nurse. She was saying something he didn't understand, but he managed a small nod. He drifted off again.

Later the light returned and this time he became aware of a form at the foot of his bed. Gradually the form took shape – a voice – then a face. Leo's eyes opened wider.

"Hello Leo, remember me? We've met before, haven't we? Geoff Parker remember? I'm going to be your surgeon. I'm about to stitch you up."

A Peculiar Sort of Friendship
Alexis Krite

"This used to be a decent place to live until *they* moved in!" Nan nodded her head towards the netted window above the sink. Her elbows were deep in suds as she scrubbed the grease from the breakfast plates. "Tinkers!" She spat out the word. "Breeding like rabbits. Seventeen! Why would anyone have *seventeen* children?"

I looked up from the table. Nan's shape blocked out the light and sent a lumpish shadow onto my jotter. I thought breeding was an odd word to use about people. I had two white rabbits. The man in the pet shop told us they were both boys. But they were always "breeding". My cousin Joan, who worked in the veterinary laboratory, came every couple of months and took the babies away to give to good homes. She paid me a shilling a rabbit. I used the money to buy the Bunty and sometimes a jamboree bag from Mr. Burgess at the corner shop.

Nan was still going on about the family who'd moved in across the road. "You mind you keep away from those Flanagans. God knows what you'd catch if you got too close." And she tipped the washing up bowl, sending the slimy water spinning down the plughole. She shook the foam from her hands and wiped them on her apron.

I nodded and sucked the end of my pencil. Sister Monica had asked us to write a story about someone we admired. Janet Pike said she was going to write about Saint Francis. But I'd started writing in my jotter: *I admire Ringo Starr. He can play the drums really well. His hair is very tidy. He is a handsome man.*

I didn't think it was a good idea to tell Nan that I sat next to Orla Flanagan in class. Sister Marina had put the girl at my desk, in the empty half of the double seat. All the other desks were full. On the first day of term the rest of my class had run into our new classroom, fighting over who got to sit together. The teacher started to tell everyone where to sit but no one wanted to sit next to me.

"There's no room next to fatso!"

"Sister Marina, please don't make me sit next to Sharon – she'll squish me to pieces!"

"Her fat bum takes up all the room. I'm not sitting next to her!"

And it's true, I do take up more than half of the double seat. But that day my face burned and I looked down at the desk, running my finger along the groove for the pencils. Trying not to hear. In the end Sister gave in and so for weeks I'd had the desk all to myself. Until, that was, the Flanagans moved in to Nan's estate.

Orla Flanagan smelled. She smelled of wet knickers and frying. Her red hair hung in two greasy plaits, tied with tattered ribbons. As she concentrated on the books in front of her, she sucked and chewed the end of the ribbons. When she looked up, the ribbons would fall from her mouth, hanging, soaked in spit. I tried to sit turned away from her, my right shoulder hunched up like a barrier. She didn't seem to notice.

At playtime on the day Orla arrived, there was the usual choosing of teams for games like British Bulldog and Off-Ground He. I knew no one would pick me and I sat down on the grassy bank by the tennis court, watching the other kids play. I pulled up a handful of daisies and flicked off each head with a pinch.

Orla came over and plonked herself down beside me. Her bony knees stuck out from her skirt and she scratched at a scab on her leg. "Why aren't you playing then?" she asked, pointing to where Sandra Walsh and her gang were turning on the metal bars. Spinning like cogs, their skirts flipped over their heads, showing the big blue regulation knickers we all had to wear.

I shrugged and moved away from her.

"Is it because you're so fat?" she asked.

I was used to the other kids in my class calling me fat. But this new girl with her disgusting smell and dress that was far too short for her had no right to.

"I'm not fat!" I growled.

"You are so."

"And *you* stink!"

"I do not!"

"You do too! You stink worse than a toilet!"

"And you're fatter than my Granda's old pig!"

We were silent for a while. We watched the kids playing Off-Ground He. One of the boys leapt for the low concrete wall that bordered the playground. He missed and caught his shin on the edge. He fell and as he clutched his leg, a satisfying amount of blood oozed out between his fingers. Sister Marina lifted her skirt and ran over to him as he lay on the tarmac crying.

"That's Clayton Miller," I said. "He's from America."

"He looks like a bit of an eejit, snivelling away like a girl." Orla wiped her nose with the back of her hand.

No one had ever called Clayton Miller an eejit. He's popular with the girls because of the way he speaks. All the boys follow him, because if they didn't, they'd get a thump. He's the one who calls me fatso. I suppose that's American for fatty.

I smiled. He did look like a bit of an eejit.

"I've got two rabbits," I volunteered.

"I've got a dog. He catches rabbits."

I turned to look at her. "*Catches* them? Why does he do that?"

"So my Mam can cook them." Orla was very matter of fact.

"He'd better not catch *my* rabbits!" And I told her how my cousin Joan gave me a shilling for every baby rabbit.

Orla sneered. "Oh, so my Mam shouldn't cook the little darlings, but it's OK for your cousin to cut them up and do vivianesection on them is it?"

I was furious. "She gives them to good homes! She told me!" I didn't know what vivianesection was, but it didn't sound like a very nice thing to do to a rabbit.

"Yeah, well believe it if you want."

The bell for the end of playtime rang and we wandered back to class. I tried to keep ahead of her, but Orla managed to stay in step with me.

The other kids started up. "Oh will you look at that? Fatty Sharon has a new best friend. Stinky Orla!"

Orla turned to me. "Who's that kid? The one what said that?" She nodded towards a skinny blond girl who was dancing in through the door.

I looked up. "Janet Pike. She lives up the road from my Nan."

"Does she now?" And Orla put the end of her plait in her mouth and sucked hard on it.

***

"Come on now Sharon, or you'll be late for school." Nan took my blazer down from the hook on the back of the door and held it out for me. I struggled to push my arms into the sleeves. "You're getting a bit big for this blazer now. I'll tell your Mum you'll need a new one before next term."

Most days I call in to Nan's on my way to school. Mum never has time to make me breakfast. She's always in a rush to get to the hospital, and Dad leaves long before I wake up in the mornings. Nan does a fry-up: bacon, eggs, fried bread and a few tomatoes.

According to Mum and Nan, I am *well covered*. But I heard Dad tell them that I was fat and that they should stop me eating so much. He said if I carried on the way I am, I'd never get a boyfriend. Mum told him I was only eleven and it was just puppy fat. Dad said good job I don't wear glasses or I'd look like Billy Bunter. I still eat whatever I want, but now I don't let Dad see me eating if I can help it.

Nan gave my blazer a good yank and squeezed the buttons together. "Now, remember what I said about those Flanagans and stay well away from them. Someone pushed dog muck through the Pikes' front door yesterday. You can guess who that was can't you?"

And I could, of course. I smiled into my blue felt hat as I pulled it over my face and snapped the elastic under my chin.

Orla was standing in the playground when I got to school. The other kids had started to line up and she stood a head taller than them. She looked up. "All right?" I nodded. We both looked over to Janet Pike and smiled.

In class, Orla lifted up the lid of her desk and, using it as a shield, whispered to me. "Look at these." She pointed to a bag of five jacks, still with the price label on. "We can play after lunch."

I didn't know how to play five jacks and I wasn't sure if playing with Orla was a good idea. Clayton Miller was mouthing "Fatso" at me, so I wrote OK on the bottom of my jotter and pushed it towards Orla.

At playtime Orla showed me how to play the game. She shook out the metal jacks and the ball and we squatted over them. Orla threw up the jacks and caught two of them expertly on the back of her hand. I had a go, but only managed to catch one. "I start," she said and threw the ball up, picking up three jacks before the ball hit the ground.

Some of the kids came over to watch. "Give us a go then," one of them said, but Orla grabbed the jacks and waved them in her fist. Her cheeks were bright red and she leapt up, rushing at the others. She looked really fierce and the kids stepped back, scared. "Ger away from us!" she snarled. Sandra Walsh shrugged. "You smell anyway, I don't want to touch your germy old jacks," she said, but she stayed anyway, watching at a distance.

As we walked back to the building, Orla slid her hand into her pocket and drew out a bar of Five Boys chocolate. "Here you are, only don't let no one see," she whispered. I took it from her and held it in my hand until we got to the cloakroom. I slipped the chocolate into my satchel as I changed my outdoor shoes for my indoor ones.

After that, Orla always had some new game to play with and every day there was a bar of chocolate or bag of sweets. She knew I liked Jamboree bags and so sometimes she would give me one of those. We started to walk home together but I was careful to go my own way before we got to the estate.

My cousin Joan came to buy the new baby rabbits, six this time, but I wouldn't let her have them. "That's *six shillings* Sharon!" Mum said. "And what are you going to do with them? We're not keeping any more rabbits." But I stood in front of the rabbit hutch, my hand over the latch. Joan laughed and said not to worry and gave me two shillings anyway.

"Orla," I asked the day after this, "do you do jobs for pocket money?" If I stopped selling the baby rabbits, I wouldn't be able to buy the Bunty anymore. I wondered how she could afford to buy the games and sweets she brought into school each week. Maybe I could do some jobs too.

She made a pig noise with her nose. "Jobs? No, why?"

"Do your parents *give* you pocket money then?"

She snorted again. "What do I need money for?"

"To buy all the sweets and stuff." It seemed obvious to me.

She looked at me as though I was an idiot and shook her head. "You don't need to buy things. Sure, you just *take* what you need."

"But that's stealing. That's a sin, Orla!" I was horrified. "You'll go to hell."

Orla gave me a strange look and took the end of her plait in her mouth. For a few seconds she sucked silently on her hair. And then she spoke:

"I've got 16 brothers and sisters and my Granda lives with us too. My Da tumps my Ma most nights and we've an outhouse at the end of the garden. Last night we had bread soaked in milk for dinner. If I died and went to hell, sure I wouldn't be moving anywhere."

I thought about Orla on the way home that day. She felt so much older than me and knew words I'd never heard of, even though she could hardly read. But that was our secret. I wondered if my Dad ever *tumped* Mum. I went into the garden and looked at my rabbits. There were eight now, all squashed in a hutch meant for two. The two big rabbits had been fighting and one of them had a cut on its ear. There were rabbit marbles all over the floor and I realised I hadn't cleaned them out for days. I put fresh water in their bowl.

Dad was in the kitchen when I went in, polishing his shoes. His friend Terry was leaning against the wall, smoking.

"Dad?" He looked up and smiled. "Yes Shaz?"

"Are you going out?"

"I am. Your Mum phoned to say she'd be a bit late. You'll be all right on your own, won't you? You're a big girl now."

I nodded.

"Will you make me another hutch for my rabbits, Dad, a bigger one?" I asked.

He shook his head. "No, they'll have to go, Shaz, they'll just keep on having more babies, you know."

Terry came over and looked at me. "You're growing fast, Sharon, you're almost popping out of your blazer." He put his hands on my shoulders and squeezed me hard. "And don't you worry about those rabbits." I saw him wink at Dad. "We'll find some good homes for them." And he and Dad laughed as they went out of the back door.

When I heard Dad's car go away up the road, I went out to the shed and found a cardboard box. I opened the door of the rabbit hutch and carefully took out all the rabbits one by one and stuffed them in the box.

I got Mum's shopping trolley and dropped the box into the bottom of the bag. I went down the side passage and out onto the road. I knew Nan was at the bingo and so when I got to her house, I looked across the road to where the Flanagans lived. There was a privet hedge in the front and a broken gate hung from one hinge on a wooden post. Because of the hedge you couldn't see the front garden, or the downstairs windows. I crossed the road and pushed the gate open a little so I could get through. The grass in the front garden was waist high. There was an old pushchair stuffed with dolls, mostly without any clothes and a couple with no hair. One didn't even have a head.

I walked up to the door, dragging the shopping trolley and stood under the concrete porch. The door was wedged open with a rusty tricycle. A warm smell of damp clothes and cooked meat drifted down the hallway. I knocked on the door. I could hear shouting and words that Nan said were *dirty* coming from inside.

I called out. "Orla! Orla! It's me, Sharon!"

Suddenly a boy with a filthy face popped his head around the door. He looked at me and at the trolley I was pulling. "What d'you want?" he asked and then he stuck his tongue out at me.

I felt a bit sick. I didn't know if it was because I was afraid, or because of the smell and the dirt everywhere.

"I want to see Orla. I'm a friend of hers." Until I said it, I didn't know that Orla *was* my friend. But now I'd said it, I realised it was true.

The boy yelled up the stairs. "Orla! There's some fat girl here for you." And with that he pulled the tricycle out of the doorway and scooted off down the hall on it, making mee-maw noises as he went.

Orla came down the stairs with a dirty bundle in her arms. She looked really surprised to see me.

"Sharon! What are you doing here? And what's that?" she asked, looking at the trolley. "Maeve! Get down here and take this baby off of me."

I looked at the bundle and as it moved I saw it wasn't just a bunch of rags, it actually *was* a baby.

A girl just a bit younger than us came down the stairs and Orla shoved the baby towards her. "She's soaking wet, give her back to Mammy. Come on Sharon, let's get out of here." And she grabbed my arm and pushed me down the path. I was still hanging on to the trolley and it bumped over the holes in the concrete.

"Does your Granny know you're here?" I suppose Orla knew Nan wouldn't be happy if she saw us together. I felt a bit ashamed. I'd seen Nan giving Mrs Flanagan filthy looks when she passed us in the street.

"She's gone out. I've brought you a present, it's in the trolley."

Orla hurried me through the gate and into the road. We ran to the end and sat down on the verge outside the vicarage.

"Come on then, show us what you got."

I dragged out the box with the rabbits and lifted a corner of the cardboard. A pink nose pushed through the gap, sniffing the air.

Orla reached down and pulled the rabbit out by its ears. She sat it on her lap and stroked it. Then she brushed her cheek against its fur. It gave a little twist and thumped its back feet.

She looked up at me. "It's so warm and soft. I've never seen one alive before, not held one anyway."

I was pleased. "There's seven more in the box. You can have them all."

Suddenly she pushed the rabbit back into the box and pressed the lid down. "What am I supposed to do with eight rabbits?" She seemed cross and I got a bit upset.

"It's a present, Orla, you take them home and your Dad can make a hutch for them. You can share them with your brothers and sisters."

She made that nasty sneering noise she made sometimes. "A hutch? The only hutch they'd have is Mam's big old stockpot."

She stormed off up the road and I called after her. "But they're pets."

She shouted back over her shoulder. "Rich people have *pets*, not people like us!"

I puffed as I tried to keep up with her. "Tinkers can have pets too, can't they?"

She stopped and looked at me. The freckles on her face stood out like little brown full stops and her cheeks were bright red. She put her hands on her hips.

"Tinkers? Tinkers? Is that what your Nan calls us, so?"

I nodded. It was true. I didn't know why she was so angry.

Then just as suddenly, she laughed. "Come on, I want to show you something."

She took hold of the trolley handle and together we pulled it up the hill. After a while we got to a path that led off into the woods that everyone called Gypsy Copse. It was more difficult pulling the trolley here; the wheels got caught in the ruts and nettles stung my legs. Orla dived into the bushes on the side of the path and turned around, reaching her arms out to help me and the trolley in.

Brambles pulled at my hair and twigs flicked me in the face, but Orla moved through the bushes like a snake. We came to a clearing and she threw herself down on the grass. She rolled on her back and looked up at the sky. From the trolley I could hear the rabbits scrabbling in the box.

"This is my place," Orla said. "No one knows about this, only me and *you* now."

"And the rabbits," I added.

She sat up. The ribbons on the end of her plaits had pulled undone and her face was covered in scratches.

"And the rabbits. Give them here."

I pulled the trolley over to her and she heaved out the box and sat it on the grass. To my horror she lifted the lid and took the rabbits out one by one. They started to eat the grass. I thought they'd run away but they seemed happy. They seemed as if they'd come home.

She stroked the one nearest to her and spoke to it. "There y'are now. Better than some pokey old hutch isn't it?"

"What are we going to do with them?" I asked. I didn't have a watch but the woods were getting gloomy and I knew I'd be late home.

Orla sprung up and brushed a few dead leaves from her skirt. "Leave them, they can stay here."

"Will they be safe?" I looked around the clearing and wondered if Orla's dog would find them.

"Safer than they'd be at mine or yours."

So we left the rabbits there and tramped back down the path to the road. Orla was very quiet but just before we turned into the estate she stopped and looked at me. "Tell us, Sharon, do I really stink?"

I knew it was a sin to lie. "Yes. You do."

She nodded. I thought she was going to cry, though I really couldn't imagine it. Instead, she looked straight ahead and said, "And *you're* really fat." Then she looped her arm through mine.

It was nearly dark when we got to the estate. Nan was waiting outside her gate. Mum was there too. Mum looked as if she had been crying. She hugged me and then belted me across the backside.

Nan was furious. "You!" she shouted at Orla. "You get away now!" And then she turned to me. "I told you to keep away from that lot!" she yelled. I could smell her tea-breath in my face. As she dragged me into the house, I tried to appeal to her. "But she's my *friend* Nan." But that just got me another whack. "A peculiar sort of friendship if you ask me!" she said and pulled me through the front door.

No one seemed worried about Orla. She just skipped across the road and went in through the broken gate.

After that I wasn't allowed to talk to her at school. Mum asked the

Reverend Mother to put her in another class and she got to sit with the little ones in form two. For a while we left notes by the statue of the Virgin Mary. Mum started doing night duty at the hospital and so sometimes I had to stay with Nan. Orla and I would turn our lights on and off, signalling to each other. Then one night the lights never came on.

"Those Flanagans did a moonlight." Nan was talking to Mum in the kitchen. "And good riddance too!"

So they had gone. As I lay in bed that night, I thought about the family doing a moonlight. It sounded lovely. I imagined Orla and her rabbits dancing in the moonlight in the clearing.

I reached under my bed and pulled out a shoebox. Inside were all the chocolate bars Orla had given me. I pulled the wrapper off one and ate the whole bar. Then I took out another and another.

The Kindness of Time
Alexis Krite

Perhaps it's time to close the shop, Nicki thought as she stood outside looking at the faded window displays. *Close it for good.* Some of the stock had been there for over a year: the earthenware bed warmer, the lemonade bottles, still with their marble stoppers, the floral chamber pot she had bought in the sale at Exeter. She ran her finger along the sash window frame. It was thick with dust. While she stood there, a car whipped past, gusting her dress. It billowed around her as she stared at her reflection in the window. *I look just like a giant puffball with legs,* she thought. *Ah well.*

The shop clung to a sharp bend in the road, only a two-minute walk from the town centre. But two minutes made the difference between profit and loss in this picturesque fishing village. The popular gift shops and little cafes were clustered together in the high street, between the beach and the gentle Dorset hills. There was no pull for visitors to stroll away from the centre and so Sea Maiden Antiques got very little passing trade. That was why the rent was so cheap.

Only the serious walkers ventured out of the town and past the shop, heading along the Coast Path. They might glance in through the windows but, with their rucksacks and walking poles, they would never cross the threshold. Maybe one day a couple of celebrities from the Antiques Road Trip would call by in their classic sports cars and root about in the shop. But that was wishful thinking. The fact was, she wouldn't ever be able to rely on the income from the shop to subsidise her pension.

She tucked her towel up under her arm and made her way down the hill towards the sea front. Where the street became level, a stone bridge crossed the mouth of the river. Underneath, the water hurled itself over the rocks in a mad dash to get to the sea. She leaned on the parapet for a moment, watching the water tugging at the thongweed below. Behind her, further up the river, the town mill would be working, grinding artisan flour for the tourists.

She dropped her towel and bag on the pebbled beach and pulled her dress off over her head. Although it was September, the water would still be carrying some of the warmth of the summer. She put on her swim shoes and walked confidently across the stones and stood at the edge of the water. She let the sea lick around her ankles and then strode in. It was always a shock when the water reached her crotch and for a second she stood on tiptoes. The next moment she launched herself into a wave, swam three strokes and then flipped onto her back.

Being in the sea was never about exercise. She floated on the surface with her arms stretched out and head tipped back. The water crept across her scalp and tapped her nerves, sending a sensuous tingle throughout her body. Even in the sea she could feel herself shivering. Above her, a few herring gulls were spinning gently on the thermals. She let the waves rock her and then, quite suddenly, the sun broke through the clouds. She could feel the warmth on her face and closed her eyes against the brightness. She reached down with her feet and touched the seabed. With her arms resting on the water, she stood up and watched the millions of tiny sun stars dancing and shimmering on the surface.

The town clock chimed five and she realised she was hungry. Half swimming, half walking, she made her way back to the shore. Heavier now, with her costume wet, she stumbled over to her towel and wrapped it around her shoulders. The water dripped from her breasts and travelled over her belly, dropping onto the stones. She looked down, but standing upright now, she couldn't see her feet. *This is what it must be like to be pregnant*, she thought. The weight had just crept up, slowly, sneakily. The food here was relentless. There was no closing of pasty or chip shops during the low season. The town tempted visitors throughout the year. The lure of fossils, the sheer beauty of the coast and the network of footpaths ensured a stable trade even in the winter months. Except for Sea Maiden Antiques.

The aroma of fish and chips drifted towards her and sighing, she knew she would be seduced again.

She sat on a bench by the sea wall and looked at the fishing boats bobbing in the harbour. The wall formed almost a complete circle, with only a narrow gap allowing access to the protection of the little sanctuary. The tide was nearly fully in now and one or two sailing boats were motoring in through the breach in the stone enclosure.

The chips were still warm and she dipped each one in a blob of ketchup before savouring their oily fatness. The cod lay blanketed in batter, steaming a little. She tore off small pieces and followed each chip with a chunk of fish. When she had finished her meal, Nicki gave the finger to the herring gulls who had been eyeing her up. She screwed up the paper and put it on the bench beside her. A huge bird hopped down from the wall above and began pulling at the paper. The next moment six more were screaming and tearing at the wrapping and each other.

She waved them away and watched as one flew off, the paper in its beak. Soon there was a flock of twenty or more, fighting over the greasy remains of Nicki's supper.

In the harbour, a small yacht puttered up to an orange buoy. A grey-haired man reached out with a long aluminium hook and hauled the buoy near enough to tether the boat. He seemed to be on his own but moored up easily and efficiently. *Obviously used to sailing alone,* Nicki thought, as he winched a tender down into the sea. At one stage he stood up, as if stretching a stiff back, but once the boat was in the water, he stepped down into it and rowed to the harbour beach. The tender must have been light because he pulled it out onto the land with ease. Again, he stretched and this time bent over to rub his right knee. He stood for a moment, looking along the sea front and then, apparently having made a decision, walked over to the chip shop and queued up outside.

Something about him was familiar. His shoulder-length grey hair fell in tired curls down his neck. When he walked, he stooped forwards slightly, as if he were about to launch himself in a race. *Where have I seen him?* she wondered. She didn't mix with any of the yachty types in the town. Maybe he had been a customer at some time. As he waited to be served, he folded his arms across his chest and rested his weight on his left leg. The casual posture annoyed her: *too confident, too cocky.*

But then she lost interest and leaned back against the wall, her eyes half-closed. She found these warm evenings difficult. The sun was still holding out until about eight o'clock. In the old days, she would have been sitting outside at a bar with her mates, drinking lager and smoking. She still felt the urge for a cigarette and probably, if she had the money, she'd have a packet of Camels in her bag right now. It wasn't that she didn't have friends here, it's just they weren't really the drinking and smoking types. Certainly not the sort to listen to the kind of music she used to rock to. No, they were nice enough, but a bit dull. She would often look at them and think *there but for the grace of God go I*. And actually, would that have been so bad? At least they had family, kids and sometimes an old man still on the go.

"Mind if I sit down?" Nicki frowned at the interruption and turned to see the lone sailor, as she thought of him, gesturing to the empty space on the bench next to her.

"Yeah, I'm just going anyway." And she started to heave herself up from the seat.

"No, no, don't go. I'll go somewhere else." A London accent, a bit Eastenderish. So not the usual yachty type then.

Nicky shaded her eyes from the setting sun and looked up at him. She had been halfway up but now plumped herself back on the bench. "Bloody hell! Johnnie Roadie!"

He looked surprised, then pleased and finally confused. "Sorry love, do I know you?"

"It's Nicki, Nicki Walsh."

He shook his head. "Sorry, sweetheart. Doesn't ring any bells."

"Come on, Johnnie, you *must* remember! I used to do the backing vocals for Lenny's band. There was me, Jackie and Mo – Maureen."

He stopped, a chip half-way to his mouth. "Blimey! It *is* you! Knickerless Nicki!" And he dropped to the seat beside her.

His eyes still twinkled, but now they were rheumy and the twinkling was mostly due to blocked tear ducts. He blinked and looked Nicki up and down. "You haven't, well..." And he coughed. "You haven't changed at all."

Nicki roared with laughter and her long earrings jiggled against her chins. "And neither have you. Still the bullshitter!"

Johnnie methodically ate one chip after another as they sat next to each other. Neither knew what to say next. And then Nicki nodded towards his boat, squinted and read the name. "Your boat's called Nicki Two. What happened to Nicki One?"

"That's Lenny Hutchinson's yacht. Sixty-four footer. Flash git."

"What, he named his boat after *me*?" Nicki asked in astonishment.

"Well, yeah, sign of respect. Jim Bailey even changed his dog's name to Nicki after you disappeared. We all thought you was dead."

"I went to bloody Ireland. I didn't die! My Dad was sick."

Thinking about it, that was when her old life had sort of come to an end. She'd intended to go for a couple of days, but the days had turned into weeks and then months. It was three years before he died and she could finally leave.

"Anyway," she went on, "I came back in '84 and the pub had been turned into a wine bar. I went looking for you and the others, but no-one had heard of you. The Two Farmers up the road was full of students. It was weird, like you'd all been wiped off the face of the earth." She remembered how she'd gone round to their old flats and knocked on the doors. Some people had been polite and told her the old tenants had moved out, others just shut the door in her face.

"London," Johnnie said. "After the band got the recording contract, we all moved up to town." He turned towards her. "Why'd you go off like that – so sudden? Seems one minute you were up on the stage with Jackie and Mo, next minute you were gone. You let us down, you know. Just after you left, some bloke from Island Records came to the pub. We had to get Squeaky Sheila to take your place."

"My Dad's next-door neighbour rang me, said it was an emergency. Dad didn't have anyone else. I thought I'd be back in time for the next gig."

"We got everyone out looking for you, even got the police involved. Why didn't you tell someone where you were?"

Nicki thought about Belfast in the 70's and her Dad's affiliation to the IRA. "I didn't think it was a good idea."

Johnnie shrugged. "Whatever. So what was up with your old man then? Cancer?"

"No, he was shot in the kidneys."

"Bloody hell!"

They were silent again for a while. Then Nicki nodded towards the boat again. "So, the band made it big, eh? Looks like you did all right."

But Johnnie shook his head. "Lenny hired professional roadies after a month or two, what with the European tours and so on. He thought it was too much for me to handle."

"That was a bit rough, after all the humping about you used to do. Did you get work with another band then?"

"No. I trained as a central heating engineer. I never bore Lenny a grudge, he was right and anyway I was pretty useless with the sound." He'd been a jack of all trades then, sound engineer, roadie, general dogsbody.

"In fact, that's what I'm doing here. Lenny lives up on the hill and I've come to service his boiler. He says I'm the only central heating bloke he trusts."

"What, he lives *here*? I can't believe it!" She remembered Lenny with his long dark hair and his Burt Reynolds' moustache. "I don't suppose I'd recognise him now."

"He's faded a bit, like the rest of us. Still skinny though. You don't follow him on Facebook then?"

"Nah." She'd tried to block out the Surrey days, wipe them from her memory. She was tempted once to Google the old band, but by the time her wi-fi had come to life, she decided it was a bad idea.

"You always go to jobs by sea then? Wouldn't it be quicker in a van?" she asked.

Johnnie laughed. "You think so? I'm not really interested in quick these days. Anyway, it gives me an excuse to give the old boat a run. I'm in Southampton now." He finished his chips and folded the paper neatly, looking for the nearest bin.

"What time you off up to Lenny's?" It seemed a shame, after all these years, just to let him sail away. Maybe it wouldn't hurt to reconnect with the past.

"Not till tomorrow morning."

"Well, why don't you come back to mine? Get some wine on the way, a few snacks."

Johnnie stretched his legs out and winced. "*What a drag it is getting old*, to quote Mr. Jagger. Yeah, OK. That'll be good."

They called in at Tesco on the way and Johnnie insisted, to Nicki's relief, on paying for the wine and crisps. They both had to stop to get their breath as they shuffled slowly up the hill.

Nicki unlocked the shop door and Johnnie followed her up the stairs. The lounge was gloomy and smelled of joss sticks. A throw with Ganesha printed on it, had been hung in the window and around the room were various pieces of furniture that Nicki either hadn't sold or had taken a fancy to and didn't want to sell. "I'm not much of a business woman," she explained as she unscrewed the lid from a bottle of Merlot. Johnnie eased himself down onto a plush purple sofa that had pieces of horsehair sprouting from the arms. A few dust motes rose and fell as he settled his back into the surprisingly comfortable seat.

"How *is* business?" he asked as he watched her pour the wine into two gold rimmed goblets.

"Rubbish," she replied. "The only reason I keep the shop on is because of the flat."

Johnnie looked around at the peeling wallpaper and damp patches on the ceiling and raised his eyebrows.

"Yes, I know. It's a bit of a dump, but you try renting somewhere in this place. And I like it here. The natives are friendly and well, the sea's just down the road." She found herself defending the grubby little flat. Of course, if she'd been expecting visitors, she'd have cleaned it up a bit. Probably.

"And you never knew Lenny was here all the time?" Johnnie sounded disbelieving.

"No idea at all. He could at least have put a gig on at the local theatre."

"Too big for that, sweetheart."

Too arrogant, Nicki thought.

"So what've you been doing since the glory days? You got kids?"

Nicki shook her head. "No, never appealed to me." She often wondered if she actually *could* have children. There had been a lot of carelessness back then. "You?"

"Yep. Two girls, Livvy and Sam. Got four grandkids now, all boys and not one of them interested in sailing. Sod's law."

"So you married that girl?" He'd had some long-term girlfriend, not that that had stopped him trying it on with all the groupies.

"Lynne? Yeah. We moved to Southampton to be near Livvy. She spends a lot of time helping out with the lads now."

"Got any music handy?" he asked, pouring himself another glass of wine. Nicki got up and picked up a CD. "I'm no good at all that streaming nonsense, how about this?"

Johnnie reached into a pocket and brought out a pair of glasses and squinted at the CD. "Fleetwood Mac, Rumours. Yeah, that'll do." He opened the second bottle of wine. "They were mad days, weren't they?" He spoke affectionately, his face reflecting the nostalgia he was feeling.

"What about Rick? You still in touch?" Nicki was thinking of the bass player she once thought she was in love with.

"Dead. Overdose."

"Tommy Hudson?"

"Dead. Car crash, drink driving."

"Angie Piper?"

Johnnie took a moment to think. "Dead. Cirrhosis."

"Don't tell me Mick the drums has gone too?" This was getting depressing.

"No, no. He's still alive. Dementia."

He looked at Nicki. "You know, you came close a few times."

She remembered the ambulances, the stomach pumping. The shame that was so short lived.

"Bit of a blessing really, your Dad getting shot."

"That's a bit brutal. Wonder what would have happened if I'd stuck with the band and made a load of money?" But they both knew the answer to that. They were beginning to get maudlin. Johnnie changed the subject. "So what *did* you do after you left?"

"When Dad died, I realised I was pretty good at doing personal care, so I just carried on. I worked in care homes on and off, home visits, you know. And eventually I got a job here, two weeks on, two weeks off, looking after a woman who'd been in a car accident. She drove her Mercedes into a tree, pissed. She was only forty, so that went on for years."

"Terrible waste," Johnnie nodded dolefully.

"Yeah, lucky for her and me that she had enough money to pay for live-in carers. When she died I stayed on here. The family gave me some money so I opened up the shop. Being a heating engineer must pay pretty well then, that's a fancy little yacht you've got."

Johnnie shifted uncomfortably. "Just had a bit of luck, long time back, made a few good investments." He changed the subject abruptly. "So, you going to come up to Lenny's with me tomorrow?"

"What and hold your spanner for you?" Nicki laughed.

"Seriously Nick, he'd be knocked out to see you again."

"No, better not say anything to him. Let him think I'm dead." She slapped her belly. "He might regret calling his boat after me!"

"You still look good." And there it was, that twinkle in his eye. *Blimey he must be desperate*, she thought.

In the end he stayed the night. At first it felt good having a warm body next to her after so many years, but eventually the snoring and frequent flushing of the toilet irritated her and she moved out of the bedroom and spent the night on the sofa.

The next morning, they had breakfast together. "Sorry about the lack of action last night, Nick. I'm booked in for a hip replacement next month."

"Ah, so after that I'd better watch out, had I?" Nicki laughed in between mouthfuls of scrambled eggs.

As Johnnie was leaving, the postman dropped a brown envelope through the front door. Nicki picked it up and put it on the hallstand with a pile of other unopened letters. "They can go straight in the recycling."

"Money's tight then?" Johnnie asked.

Nicki nodded. "Shop's been a bit of a disaster to be honest." She stood on the step and watched Johnnie walk down the hill. Before he got to the corner, he turned and hesitated for a moment as if he were going to come back. It seemed to her that he was going to say something but then he waved and shouted. "See ya, Nick"

"Keep in touch!" She called, thinking *fat chance*.

A week later she found a white envelope on the doormat. *Well that's a change*, she thought. She put it on the kitchen bench and forgot about it until the evening. She finally got round to opening it while she waited for the microwave to ping. Inside was a card with a picture of a yacht. She smiled, realising it must be from Johnnie. A piece of paper fell to the floor and she left it there as she read the message on the card:

Dear Nicki, It was really good to see you again. Remember the pools syndicate we had back in the day? (Me, you, Rick, Tommy and Angie) We kept it going after you left and in '86 we had a big win. Over a million would you believe? The others blew their money but I put your share and mine into property. Sentimental really, seeing as we all thought you were dead. Well me and Lynne think you're entitled to some of the profit from the houses - we've got more than enough and the kids have got their own places too. So here's something for you, I don't want no thanks. Maybe you can get yourself a better flat but I'd steer clear of starting up another business, not sure you've got the right head for that. Take care, Johnnie x

She turned the envelope over, but there was no address written on the back. She glanced down and with some effort, picked up the paper that was lying on the lino. It was a cheque made out to Nicola Walsh for £35,000. She slid to the floor and leaning against the cupboard, held the cheque to her cheek. *Thirty-five thousand pounds!*

A thousand pounds for every year since that last ambulance ride to A and E, Johnnie clasping her hand as she passed in and out of consciousness.

A thousand pounds for every year since she'd slammed the phone down and rushed over to Belfast, to find her father barely alive.

A thousand pounds for every year that she had survived. *Oh*, she thought, *the kindness of time.*

Aanjay Meets a Mugger
David Reading

Aanjay blamed James Bond of the British Secret Service for his latest predicament. If Bond had been a tiresome character rather than a fellow caught up regularly in acts of heroism, then Aanjay would never have become absorbed in his paperback novel and would never have missed his station on the London Underground. As it was, he was captivated by a rousing tale about an evil chap called Dr Julius No and failed to notice the signs clearly stating he had arrived at Baker Street, his proposed destination. He looked across the carriage at a young lady in a blue jacket, smiled and shook his head, amused by his own folly. She smiled back, apparently empathising with Aanjay even though she knew nothing about his quandary.

At Swiss Cottage he said goodbye to his short-term friend in blue and got off the train, facing a choice of two options: whether to cross over to the opposite platform for the return journey to Baker Street, or whether to take the half-hour walk via Regent's Park. He decided to walk. It was an overcast morning but Aanjay liked all manner of weather conditions, and a little shower of rain wouldn't spoil the enjoyable stroll that lay before him. So he found his way to the escalator and headed for the exit, where his senses were assailed by the customary hustle and bustle and the sound of sirens.

As he approached the gates to the park, Aanjay met a young man who proposed to steal his money. Under normal circumstances he wouldn't have batted an eyelid. The poor fellow had an emaciated appearance and was clearly in need of a good meal and Aanjay would have been happy to treat him to one. But today he was planning to spend his money on Lucy. He had promised to take Lucy to the cinema to watch a fellow named Johnny Depp playing the part of a pirate. For that reason Aanjay was determined that the young man standing before him should not have access to his wallet; it would be better, he thought, if they met on another occasion when Aanjay had no commitments; under those circumstances, he would be delighted to fork out for a cheese sandwich for his would-be robber.

But the young man had an opposing point of view: he felt it imperative that Aanjay should hand over his wallet at that very moment and as a way of reinforcing his argument he held a knife in his right hand and the other hand was clenched in a fist. His belligerent manner suggested persistence. Aanjay was baffled by some of the language the young fellow used – he had never before heard the words *cocksucker* or *knobhead* – but he got the drift of what was being proposed.

Aanjay explained carefully that at 2.30 that afternoon he planned to accompany a young lady named Lucy to the cinema. This would not be achievable if he, Aanjay, had no money to pay the cost of admission. Under those circumstances neither he nor his lady friend would be allowed to gain entry to the building. He thought it might be possible to persuade the cashier to forego the need for payment on this occasion, but he could not guarantee this would be permitted.

Unconvinced by this argument, the young man lunged out with his knife and Aanjay was compelled to take a step back, or else feel the blade penetrate his chest. Although he realised it is not always possible in life to have one's preferences met, he felt this particular preference (i.e. not to be stabbed) was a reasonable one.

The young man lunged out again; Aanjay took another step backwards. This merry dance continued: there was something poetic, Aanjay thought, about the way the two of them obeyed the laws of motion with a skill reminiscent of two duelling swordsmen.

It was then that something rather miraculous happened. It has to be said that Aanjay did not believe in miracles as "acts of God" but he conceded that the timing of what occurred next was fortunate.

Looking over the young man's shoulder, Aanjay saw an astonishing sight. Bounding towards them, looking rather pleased with itself (or so Aanjay thought), was a magnificent Sumatran tiger. Aanjay's first concern was for the fellow with the knife, who was unaware of the surprise that awaited him within the next few seconds. But hard on the heels of the runaway beast were two men wearing rather fine green shirts: clearly both keepers from the nearby zoo, and both carrying guns. They fired together. One shot a dart into the thigh of the tiger. The other dart found its way into the shoulder of Aanjay's young would-be assailant, sending him into a deep, satisfying sleep.

Aanjay went on his way, remarking to himself that even the secret agent James Bond would be hard-pressed to find an afternoon in London so absorbing.

Conspiracy
David Reading

Mark didn't have any friends. There was a time, years ago, when people found his eccentricities entertaining and the social scene would light up when he walked into the pub. People were fascinated by his theories about the world, 'facts' that were kept secret from ordinary members of the public: Prime Minister Harold Wilson had spied for the Soviets; JFK was killed by aliens; Paul McCartney had been kidnapped and replaced by a double; the 1969 Moon landing was faked in a studio; the Earth was flat; and so on. He claimed to have proof that all these things were true and he was popular for a while, but his friends drifted away as they grew up, got married and joined what some would call *the real world*. When the Internet came along he found a more gullible audience, but nobody among his old set of friends wanted to spend any time with him. His 'friends' were all faces on Zoom.

It was because he lived in a lonely world that he had no one to confide in when he encountered the nurse with the pale skin and thin purple lips. There was an oddness about her that was difficult to define: she was both comical and sinister at the same time. In a certain light, she was almost translucent. But it was the words she spoke, and the way she said them, that upset Mark's equilibrium. Since the moment he'd met her he'd felt different. He had tried and failed to understand what had changed, but it was almost as if his very self – the character known to the outside world as *Mark* – was no longer a clear-cut thing. Back home, as he sat in the armchair watching TV, he had an impression of dissolving into nothingness. A close friend or a partner (if he'd had one) would have been there as a sounding board and might have diffused his anxiety. But he had no one. And so his imagination took over and the terrors flooded in.

The night after his encounter with the nurse, as he lay awake unable to sleep, he reached the conclusion that the only person he could talk to was Dr Bartlett, head GP at the local surgery, where the woman worked. Although Bartlett sometimes got tetchy with him, he was generally restrained enough to give Mark a fair hearing. As it started to get light, Mark lay on his back staring at the ceiling, planning what he'd say. Just after seven he pulled back the sheets, sat up and took a mouthful of water from the glass on the bedside table. It was stale and tepid, but he carried on drinking. He felt hung over and dehydrated.

A pack of diazepam lay unopened on the floor. He'd grappled with the plastic bubbles during the night while at his lowest ebb but had changed his mind about taking one. He remembered an article he'd read in the Express the week before: something about tranquillisers causing gradual mental decline. There were enough risks in life without adding one more to the list.

He showered, got dressed and sat by the phone in the study. The surgery opened at 8.30 so he had an agonising half hour to wait. At 8.30 exactly he would dial the number and then there would be that usual tussle with the receptionist. He always managed to get the same one on the line: Marge, the one who put on a posh voice, the one who insisted on knowing the reason for the patient's call before she would deign to book them in. It seemed to Mark that her job was to do the vetting: to separate the sheep from the goats, so to speak, or the wheat from the chaff. The only solution was to lie. He decided to tell her he was suffering from a severe pain in the abdomen. His description would suggest appendicitis. There was no way she would be able to put him off.

He had a crack at a crossword while he was sitting by the phone but couldn't concentrate. Today the words on the page looked unfamiliar. He made a coffee, buttered a slice of toast and spread it with marmalade. This morning the marmalade tasted different – in fact it tasted of nothing at all. He studied it closely for spoilage but it looked the way marmalade is supposed to look. He went back to the phone and dialled the surgery's number. He was four minutes early but what the hell.

She answered at the fourth ring. Sure enough it was Marge, the one with the plummy accent. She asked for his name and it was odd, but for a second he couldn't remember what it was. When it finally came to him he laughed it off and waited for those probing questions about his inner medical life, but this time she was remarkably co-operative. They had a cancellation. Dr Bartlett could see him at 9.40. He thanked her and hung up.

Mark decided to walk to the surgery rather than drive. If he took in deep breaths and let his muscles go loose, he would be relaxed by the time he got there. On the way he rehearsed exactly what he was going to say, word for word, and how he would say it. He didn't want to sound paranoid. He just had to be factual. He had a question that needed answering. His question related to the woman with the translucent skin and thin purple lips: the nurse who'd given him his flu jab the day before. There might be a rational explanation for what she'd said and how he was feeling now, and Bartlett might know what it was.

In the waiting room there was the usual mix: old people with typical old people's medical complaints and young malingerers who were there to be signed off. He picked up a copy of Heat and read that an actress he'd never heard of was about to marry a footballer he'd never heard of. He read that two celebrities were involved in a spat on Twitter. As he turned over the pages, he could not shake off the sensation that he was somehow not there.

He read a spoiler revealing exactly what was about to happen in a TV soap; he read that an American singer had got engaged. And then he heard a name called over the Tannoy. It took a few seconds for him to realise it was *his* name. There was something *other* about it. That was odd, but he put it down to stress and tiredness.

In the long walk down the corridor to Bartlett's office he thought again about his introductory words. *Dr Bartlett, what I am about to say may sound strange…* But as he stepped through the door, he was thrown off balance by the doctor's attitude. Bartlett seemed cold towards him, or did he imagine that? Mark smiled faintly, said good morning and sat down.

"So hello again," Bartlett said. "What can I do for you this time?"

"Well…"

Mark hesitated. He had the script worked out in his head, but when it came to the moment of delivery he lost his confidence.

"Yes?"

"This is difficult," Mark said. "Something happened last time I was here and I was wondering if you could explain it."

Bartlett slumped back in his seat. "Was that the time you thought you had testicular cancer? Or the time you thought your headaches might be the first symptoms of ebola?"

Mark laughed thinking the doctor was joking with him, but it was clear Bartlett was exasperated.

"Mr Fawcett, I must say you are a rather unusual patient. Do you know how many times you have sat in that chair during the last six months?"

Mark shook his head weakly.

"Well I'll tell you. It's 27 times. I've just been looking at your record. That's more than once a week. And I've told you time and time again. There is nothing wrong with you. For a 45 year old you are astonishingly fit and healthy. I have listened to your chest, examined your glands, taken your blood, felt under your armpits, yes even played around with your testicles, and I have never ever found anything wrong with you. There are people out there with real medical problems and you are taking up the time that I could be using to do some real good."

Bartlett looked at the computer and clicked away at the mouse. "In fact I see you were here yesterday. Having a flu jab. I have no idea why a man of 45 in excellent health should feel he needs to be protected against a virus that presents him with no significant risk."

"I have asthma."

"You don't have asthma, Mr Fawcett. Nor do you have…"

Bartlett scrawled through Mark's record.

"Nor do you have gallstones, rabies, hepatitis, angina, rheumatoid arthritis, type two diabetes, or gangrene."

Mark hadn't expected a lecture. He wondered if Bartlett was breaching some sort of ethical code, talking to him like that. He wondered whether he should report him to the GMC. He gripped the side of his seat and carried on. "The nurse said it was OK. To have the flu jab, I mean. And that's why I want to talk to you. It's about the nurse who gave me the flu jab. And how it's made me feel."

"Right," Bartlett said sharply. "You have exactly one minute. One minute to convince me that you're here for a good reason. And then I'm going to ask you to leave. He looked at his watch. One minute starting…now."

Finding himself centre stage, Mark felt flustered. He wondered whether to give the whole thing a miss. But he knew that if he didn't say his piece he would have another sleepless night. He began to speak but found himself stammering incoherently. "It's something the nurse said. The one with the see-through skin who gave me the flu jab. The one who looks like she's stepped out of an old horror movie. There's something strange going on. Right under your nose. You know, it's the old nurse with the black hair. She's about sixty. The one who gives the flu jabs."

"Thirty seconds."

Mark stopped, closed his eyes, let his shoulders sag and breathed deeply. "The one who gave me the flu jab," he said again, regaining his composure. "She's the one I'm talking about. While she was drawing up the injection she didn't look at what she was doing, she looked me straight between the eyes. It was a strange, creepy look that seemed to be saying…"

Mark sighed heavily. "I don't know what it seemed to be saying. I just know she didn't take her eyes off mine. Just kept me locked in a fixed stare. It was like something weird was going on. She jabbed the needle into me and smiled. But it wasn't a friendly smile, it was cold and sinister. When it was all over she pulled out the needle and dabbed the site of the injection with a piece of cotton wool. I asked her if that was it, was it over? She didn't reply. I got up to leave. As I got to the door and turned the door handle, I looked behind me. She was still smiling, still staring. And that's when she said it."

Clearly the minute was up, but Dr Bartlett had let the scene roll on. It seemed to Mark that he had genuinely caught the doctor's attention.

"So, what did she say, Mr Fawcett?"

"She looked down at the syringe which was still in her hand, looked back at me, and spoke five words."

"YOU'RE ONE OF US NOW."

Bartlett sat back in his chair and stared at the ceiling. It was a clear sign of frustration.

But Mark hadn't finished. "The real reason I'm here is because of how it's made me feel. She's done something to me. It's difficult to put into words but it's almost like I don't actually exist. I need you to explain what's happening to me."

Bartlett said something. Mark wasn't sure what it was but he knew he wasn't going to get the answers he needed. On a normal day this would have made him feel angry. But at that moment he was devoid of emotion.

Bartlett began tapping away at his keyboard. "I think I know how I can get you the help you need," he said coldly.

***

As he walked back along the corridor towards the waiting room, Mark experienced something unfamiliar. It was as if, for the first time in his life, he had achieved something significant. But that wasn't quite it. Certainly something significant had been achieved, but he wasn't sure who the achiever was. The character known as *Mark* couldn't really take the credit because Mark was not really there.

He thought about Bartlett's reaction to his problem. Bartlett had shown none of the understanding you'd expect from a GP. Instead of taking Mark seriously, he had suggested he needed psychiatric help. He had begun searching through his files, looking, he said, for someone with special expertise.

But Mark knew he didn't need help any longer. He was fine.

Reaching the waiting room, he felt the muscles in his legs weaken. He sat down, closed his eyes and let himself drift.

He had no idea how long he was in the state of drifting. He just knew that when he came to, he felt energised. He knew there was more he had to do, although he wasn't sure what it was. Not yet.

He was walking out through the automatic doors, when he saw a woman in a nurse's uniform, coming towards him. Her black hair and purple lipstick seemed familiar. She stopped in front of him, blocking his way. Lifting her face, she held his eyes with hers for what seemed an age. As they both stood there, facing each other, she laid her hand on his arm, the finger nails digging into his skin.

Behind him he heard the sound of running feet and a woman screaming hysterically. *Blood! There's blood everywhere! It's Doctor Bartlett! Help me, someone! Help!*

The woman with the pale skin and thin purple lips smiled menacingly. "And so it begins," she hissed.

Travis County
Max Bevan

Jack was a bully, a lazy bully. No question about it. Billy was almost five years younger: small, skinny, timid and very quiet. Jack was big, fat and loud. Trouble was their Pa, Claud Cummings, favoured Jack over Billy . It was nothing to do with love or affection. Billy was a kindly kid who loved nature and animals as opposed to his cruel, blunt-faced older brother. No, dirt farming and endless poverty made necessity the king. Love and affection had been left in the coffin with the boys' mother. Jack's one redeeming feature was he could fix the truck and the machinery.

Billy's chores centred on the farmhouse, the yard and the kitchen along with whatever work the seasons brought. Though not much of a cook he usually managed to put something edible on the table. Usual fare would be chicken and beans, sometimes pork depending on what was around and what season it was. He'd made some very poor attempts at apple pie but had given it up, deciding it wasn't worth the abuse from Jack and Pa. What with cleaning, cooking, messing out the pigs and chickens and staying out of Jack's way he was kept pretty busy.

Market day was the highlight of the week. This particular week there were two litters of piglets to sell along with the usual produce. Most of the time Billy wouldn't be invited along but he helped load up the truck and hung back hopefully. A slight twitch of his father's head towards the truck door was enough and he scrambled up into the cab. He was allowed to sit on the engine housing between the driver's and passenger seats. A couple of folded sacks helped protect his backside from burning. Whatever the discomfort, a trip to the market was worth it.

On arriving Billy helped unload. After that he set off alone to explore. He knew he could find his Pa and brother later in the beer tent. As he wandered around he might have seen one or two folks he knew but he never said much, maybe just an occasional "Hi". He walked among the pens admiring the variety of animals. He found the cacophony of noises and smells both brutal and exciting. He watched the auctioneering for a while, then towards the end of the morning he ambled around the periphery of the market inspecting the various vegetables and fruits.

Eventually Billy came to a large tent and went inside. He stared down into a crate of white rabbits, then moved on to a litter of kittens. He watched and smiled as three tabbies and two gingers scuffled and gambolled about. Further along six puppies really caught his attention. Billy watched a little fat brown one look directly at him, sit down and raise its paws towards him. That was all it took. Billy rushed out and ran towards the beer tent. He felt as brave and determined as he'd ever felt in his life. If he was right, if his father had got a good price for the piglets, if he hadn't got past his third beer, it was possible, just possible he would find him in just about as magnanimous a mood as you were ever likely to. He ran into the tent and found him at the bar. He grabbed him by the hand. His father turned and looked at him in surprise.

"What is it, boy?"

"Pa, I wanna show you something. Pa, you gotta come with me, I wanna show something."

"Show me what?"

"Please Pa. Please Pa."

Claud Cummings had never seen Billy as excited or as agitated since his wife had died and so let himself be led outside towards the pet tent. Billy pulled him through the entrance and up to the puppies.

"Can I have one Pa? Please Pa? Can I have one Pa?" Billy begged.

"The last thing we need around the farm is a goddamn dog," his father replied.

Billy had never wanted anything as much in his life and was not going to let this opportunity slip. Careful not to sour his father's good mood he said, "Please Pa I'll do anything you want. I'll look after it. It won't be no trouble. I'll feed it on the scraps and when it grows up it'll be a guard dog. Please Pa."

Out of the corner of his eye Billy noticed the lady who owned the puppies smiling at his father. His father smiled back. Billy stopped begging. He knew a magic moment when he saw one. His father reached into his pocket and peeled off a couple of bills from his wad, he handed them to the lady and Billy chose his puppy. He held the soft, brown bundle close to him as they walked around the market. They met Jack coming out of the beer tent.

"What the hell you got there?" Jack indicated the puppy. "Aw Pa, you haven't let him have a mutt have you?" He pointed his finger straight at Billy and said, "All I'll say is, you keep that mangy critter away from me."

They climbed back into the truck and headed home. Billy sat in the middle with the pup on his lap. He stared straight ahead with a smile fixed on his face. It didn't even waiver when he felt a warm trickle of liquid down his leg.

***

As far back as Billy could remember there had always been talk about oil drilling. Recently a corn trader had pulled into the yard and told Billy's Pa about two real gushers that had been found less than ten miles away. The talk between Pa and Jack was more animated than usual that evening.

"What's a gusher Pa?" Jack asked.

"It's where the oil comes out under its own pressure, doesn't need to be pumped. The bigger the gush the more oil there is."

"D'ya think they'll find a gusher here Pa?" Jack asked.

"Who knows," Claud answered and spooned in another mouthful of beans.

Claud had taken the farm over from his father and it was all he knew. Work and hardship had dulled his senses. He'd heard of other farmers who'd got payment for their land and had turned to drink. That frightened him. Life on the farm might be hard but he couldn't see himself doing anything different.

***

Jack's great joy was the truck and he would take off in it at any opportunity, often disappearing for hours, hardly bothering with an excuse when he returned. Occasionally he would take Billy with him if he needed something loading or unloading. Any excuse and he would take a detour and head for the White Dove Corral, which was just over the ridge from their farm. Here he would seek out the Shaughnessy girl. Any attempt at wooing the buxom redhead just seemed to annoy her. One day after a particularly pathetic effort she said, "Why don't you take your fat, spotty face and that wimp of a brother of yours and feck off!"

Back in the truck Jack tried to laugh it off and said to Billy, "Don't pay no heed to that, they're Irish, that's just the way they talk."

Billy named his dog Bessie and as she grew up she became his constant companion and followed him everywhere. Having her around made every day just so much better. Her company was such a sweet alternative to his brother's abuse and his father's indifference. Any time Billy could find they would take off together and explore the land around their farm or take the track along the riverside. Bessie would bark at any passing boats and Billy would wave.

Jack seemed to hate the dog and wouldn't allow it in the truck and kicked out at it if it got anywhere near him. The thing that alarmed Billy most was Bessie's fascination with the chickens. If he was busy he would have to tie her to the barn. Even then, she would try to chew through the rope or slip her collar. Sometimes she would howl and bark constantly much to the annoyance of his brother or Pa. Nothing Billy could do could cure her obsession with the chickens. One day Billy was in the kitchen when he heard a commotion out in the yard. Next thing the kitchen door burst open and Jack stormed in holding Bessie by the collar yelping and kicking. He threw her clean across the kitchen hitting the range. The terrified dog crouched on the hearth and whimpered.

"If I catch that goddamned mutt near them chickens again I'll kill it!" Jack roared and stormed out.

Billy found Bessie had managed to chew through the rope and later he found a half dug hole under the chicken fence. He rummaged around in the barn and found a thicker rope.

***

The contrast in the seasons in that part of the country was dramatic: the long, hot, dry summer days followed by winter's relentless cold and snow dominating the landscape. For a couple of months the nights hardly seemed to give way to daylight and a spell of gloom hung over the farm.

Meanwhile, Billy grew taller and Jack grew meaner. The previous fall Claud had slipped lifting a pig into the trailer and cracked his hip. He refused to go for medical help saying they couldn't afford the bills. He resorted to the only medication he knew: tobacco and alcohol. With Claud pretty much out of action things soon fell into disrepair and neglect. Jack reluctantly took on more responsibility and made Billy his scapegoat.

The long periods of darkness and Jack's constant and intimidating presence would have pushed Billy into a state of melancholy and despair but for Bessie. She too was afraid of Jack and stayed close to Billy, sleeping on his bed and shadowing him during the day. Their bond was the singular saving grace in their dismal household.

The invitation to Thanksgiving from the Shaughnessy farm came as a surprise. Jack accepted immediately, noting an opportunity to get close to Rosie. Billy would come too, but not the mutt. Claud declined because of the pain in his hip. Thanksgiving arrived and Jack and Billy, dressed in their Sunday best, set off together in the truck. Billy felt uncomfortable with his brother's newfound bonhomie and pressed himself against the passenger door and answered Jack's bluster in monosyllables.

The day went pretty well. Jack drank too much, but he had the sense to not run off at the mouth in front of Rosie's two brothers. He had little luck with Rosie, who managed to remain polite on account of the occasion but kept her distance. However Billy drew the most attention. Everyone seemed to want to talk to him. Rosie's mother even commented on how tall he'd grown and how handsome he was. Billy noticed Rosie's kid sister Riona. He was surprised how grown-up she'd become and admired her flaming red hair. At one stage they bumped into each other at the cake table. They didn't speak but exchanged smiles. Rosie noticed the exchange and also smiled. Jack noticed too.

The journey home was in complete contrast to the journey out. Jack started off by mimicking Rosie's mother in a bad Irish accent. "Oooow, how tall you've grown Billy and how handsome you are Billy. That girl wouldn't be interested in a stupid kid like you so you can get that idea outta your head." Billy ignored him and stared out of the passenger window into the darkness.

The following days were pretty intolerable for Billy. Jack's spitefulness was extreme even for him. Once, when Bessie inadvertently crossed his path, he kicked her viciously in the ribs causing her to yelp in pain. When Billy protested Jack punched him in the face giving him a black eye.

Worse was to come – a lot worse.

The sound of gunshot and the brief silence that followed was all Billy needed to know what had happened. The tin bowl and knife clattered on the stone floor as he flew through the door, out into the yard.

As he looked across the yard to the chicken run he cried out in anguish.

A half dead chicken scuttled around the run. There was a hole under the fence. Bessie lay dead in the dust. He looked towards his brother standing close by, staring right back at him, his rifle in one hand pointing to the ground.

"I told you. I warned you," Jack shouted.

Billy rushed towards him but Jack's fist met him full on. Billy fell to the ground. He wiped the blood and snot from his nose, got up and charged again, only to be felled by the same punch. Groggy this time Billy tried to rise again only this time he was pulled to his feet by the scruff of his shirt collar. He felt his father's hand smack him across the back of the head and then push him, stumbling, towards the house. He fell again.

"God knows why I bought you that dog, it's been trouble ever since it's been here. Now get in the house and don't come out." He pointed at Jack. "And you, wring that chicken's neck and get that dog buried. Now!"

That night Billy lay in his bed. He stared at the ceiling, his bedsheet clutched to his mouth as he bit down on it as if to ease the pain. His face was wet with tears and his chin quivered as he sobbed almost silently. The hatred for his brother overwhelmed even the loss of Bessie. Sometime after midnight he stole out of the house and crept towards the barn. In the darkness he felt around the work bench until he found a small hacksaw. He then went outside to the truck and crawled underneath.

In the morning Billy watched as his brother climbed into the truck. To his horror he saw his father climbing in the other side. That almost never happened unless they were going to market. He made to run outside, but hesitated. What could he say? By the time he'd opened the door they were making off down the track.

Billy had done a bad thing. No doubt about it. And if procedures and justice had run their course he'd be waiting on a date with Ol' Sparky.

***

He heard the sheriff talking to a couple of his men. "Damn fool kid, he drove that truck like a lunatic. Obvious what happened. He took that bend too fast and skidded, then broadsided through the barrier and over the edge."

A good detective would have noticed there were no skid marks before the broadside and closer inspection would find a pool of brake fluid that had recently soaked into the ground under where the truck was always parked. An even closer inspection of the mangled wreck at the bottom of the ravine would have shown the brake pipes cut straight through with a hacksaw blade.

First appraisals were a firm favourite with Sheriff Dawson – he had great faith in his own judgement, and anyway, it sure saved on the paperwork. Apart from a lot of neighbourhood talk, an article in the local news and a funeral, things soon settled back to pretty much normal.

Neighbours had called round with offerings and condolences and they had all mistaken Billy's white face and tears for the sudden and shocking loss of his family, when he was, in fact, still mourning the loss of his dog. He didn't give a hoot for his brother and what he felt for his father was, well – just indifference.

Early one evening a couple of days after the funeral there was a knock at the door. Billy opened up to find Rosie Shaughnessy on the doorstep carrying a basket. She put the basket down and hugged him to her breast.

"I'm sorry for your loss Billy. Can I come in? I need to talk to you."

They sat across the table from one another, Billy finding it hard to reconcile this kind and warm-hearted young women with the Shaughnessy girl shouting abuse at his brother. The aroma from the basket was making his mouth water. What with neighbourly kindness after the incident he'd never eaten so well since his mother died.

"Billy listen to me. Those oil people are moving into this area right now, and this plot of land is the most valuable around here. Not only are you sitting on a load of oil, they need your south east corner to link to the highway to get all the other oil out. Do you understand what I'm saying Billy?"

"Yeah, sure. How'd you know all this?" Billy asked.

"My Pa knows a lot of people and he overheard a meeting over at county hall between the oil people and some of the local shysters who run things around here. They know about all what's happened here and they're saying you're just a dumb-arse kid, Billy, and they'll have no trouble getting you out. This got my Pa mad and when he told me it got me mad too. Billy, you own this land and you gotta hold out for the best price. Don't let them scare you, and whatever you do, do not accept their first offer."

"You reckon they'll be coming soon?" Billy asked.

"Yeah, real soon Billy. A guy called Wallace will call round. Now he's as nice and as smooth as velvet, but don't trust him. If you hold out he'll try to push you around. Billy, you've got to stand your ground."

Billy thanked her and thanked her for the food and promised to return the dishes.

She hugged him again at the door and said, "Billy, you know where we are."

* * *

Here in Travis County people knew how to make a deal. Billy had watched his father and he'd watched the other farmers haggle at market. He knew you never accepted a first offer or even the second.

He watched as the sedan pulled into the yard. A tall man got out and put on a black Stetson. He wore a grey suit, black cowboy boots and a bootlace tie. He retrieved his briefcase from the back seat and as he walked across the yard he seemed to shine in the midday sun. Watching from the window Billy had never seen quite such an apparition before and as he waited for the knock at the door he remembered what Rosie had said.

"Hi, I'm Luke Wallace from the Osprey Oil Company. Are you Billy?" He shook Billy manfully by the hand. "Can I come in? Can we talk?"

They sat opposite each other at the table.

"Now Billy, first of all I'd like to offer you our condolences for what happened over here. We were all very sad when we heard, and the chairman, especially, asked me to say how sorry he was. Can I ask you Billy, I know it's early days, but have you got any plans for what you want to do?"

Billy frowned. "Whaddya mean?"

"Well this is a reasonable size spread, that's a lot of work for a kid. How old are you, seventeen?"

Billy nodded.

"Well it won't be long before everything goes to wrack and ruin. A boy your age doesn't want be stuck out here on your own. It must've been hard enough with the three of you. What you need, son, is to make a new start."

Billy said nothing.

"Now considering what's happened out here we're willing to make you a very special offer for the land and all the buildings and we'll take care of the paperwork. All you need to do is sign a couple copies of paper that I have right here in my briefcase. Billy, we can offer you two thousand dollars for everything – lock, stock and barrel."

Billy didn't respond.

"Billy, listen to me. Two thousand dollars will buy you a new pickup, a new suit of clothes, a year's rent over in the town and enough cash to get you started in something else. Now ain't that a great offer?"

Billy stared back at him, pursed his lips and shook his head.

"Billy, perhaps you ain't hearing me right. We can't keep a deal like this on the table for long. We've got other options."

Billy stood up, walked over to the door. He opened it and turned and looked at Wallace. "Get out," He said quietly.

"You what?" Wallace stood up. "What's the matter with you, boy. That's a perfectly good offer. Why you turning it down?"

"I said get out." Louder this time.

Wallace walked towards him. "Billy, I have the authority to offer you another five hundred dollars if we can just sit down and sign the papers right now."

There was something unnerving about Billy's fixed stare. And although a bully, Wallace wasn't a brave man. Dealing with a crazy kid wasn't on his wage scale. Billy gestured with the door.

Wallace turned to him on the doorstep and said, "Billy, just…"

Billy slammed the door.

***

Two days later Billy watched as another sedan, a larger one this time, pull into the yard.

Another man got out, not as tall but heavier and older. He wore a black suit, a dark blue tie and a black trilby. He hadn't seen Billy standing in the shadows of the barn, and headed for the front door.

"Waddaya want?" Billy called out.

"You Billy?"

Billy didn't answer.

The man altered his direction and made his way over. "Hi, I'm Chester Perkins and I'm chairman of the Osprey Oil Company." He pushed out his right hand. Billy ignored it

"Young man I haven't got time for messing around. Now, I'm here today to tell you we've gotta close this deal real quick. I'm here to offer you a once in a life opportunity. You won't ever get another opportunity like it. Now listen to me Billy, if we can close this deal today I can give you five thousand bucks for this here farm and land."

Billy squared his shoulders and spread his legs. "Get off my land," he growled.

"Billy, you gotta listen to sense."

Billy remembered Rosie's words. *They're saying you're just a dumb-arse kid, Billy, and they'll have no trouble getting you out.* He fixed Perkins with the same stare, and took a shovel leaning against the barn. He held it with both hands ready to swing. "I said get off my land." And he took a step forward.

Chester Perkins rushed back to his car, opened the driver's door, stood behind it as if for protection, and shouted. "You're beginning to annoy me Billy." He quickly got behind the wheel and disappeared in a cloud of dust.

***

The young man parked the Buick in the yard next to the church. He got out and took a bunch of flowers and a white Stetson off the back seat. "Come on boy," he called. Charlie, his golden Labrador, jumped out of the car to join him. He leaned through the open passenger window and smiled at the pretty, red-haired young woman smiling back at him.

"I'll see you soon, baby," he said.

"You take your time, honey."

She touched his arm, raised her head and they kissed.

She sat and watched as her husband in his white suit and Stetson strolled towards the churchyard with Charlie at his heels.

He stood before the three graves: his mother's in the centre, his father's on the left and his brother's on the right. He stepped forward and placed the flowers at the foot of his mother's headstone. He stepped back, removed his hat, bowed his head and said a private prayer. He replaced his Stetson and moved to walk away. Then suddenly he stopped, turned around and spoke.

"You know Pa, Jack? I wish things could've been different." He paused, shook his head once, then moved off.

As he walked along the path he stopped and looked to where he thought the old farm might have been. All the old buildings had disappeared and it was hard to make it out amongst the derricks and pumps. He looked further south and he could see the highway where it must have cut across what had been the bottom corner of his land. He carried on walking out of the churchyard and back towards his car.

The Secret Life of Remus J Metro

David Reading

"Have you got time to listen to a story?" I said.

"What kind of a story?" he asked.

"The story of my unusual name. The story of why I look so weird. And the story of why I'm going to kill myself tonight."

If I hadn't drunk the best part of a bottle of vodka I would never have made such a ridiculously dramatic statement. Vodka always does this to me. But I guess he was used to hearing people say things like that. He is, after all, a psychiatrist.

His name is Carl. I'd only met him half an hour before. He'd been watching me from the corner of the room and had bought me a drink. I guess he was hoping I'd go home with him later that night. He wasn't expecting to have to summon up the skills of his day job.

"So two questions," he said. "What's your name and why are you going to kill yourself tonight?"

"You need the full story. The short version won't do. Have you got time for that?"

"Are you hoping I'll talk you out of it?"

"Do you really think you could?" I didn't know what I expected from this conversation. I didn't know why I was about to tell my story to a stranger who was trying to pick me up in a bar.

"Don't take this as idle flattery," he said. "But what's wrong with the way you look? You don't look weird to me."

"You like the way I look?" I said. "You've got to be kidding."

No one could seriously say I look anything other than a joke. My hair is oiled and swept back like crows' feathers in the rain and my face is rough and stubbly. I wear shades, even at night, like I'm one of those guys who protects the President of the United States. I look ridiculous, but it's a disguise that works a treat. I wear a suit too. Ashley never saw me in a suit. They say a mother would know her son anywhere. But if Ashley saw me now she'd walk straight past me. That's the whole point of the revamp.

I don't know why I trusted this stranger called Carl, but I think he caught me when my defences were down. When I told him my name was Remus J. Metro, he said immediately, "You're hiding something. The image that's on the outside is a lie. You're not a Remus. I knew a boxer called Remus. His father was Jamaican and his mother was French. He really was a Remus. But when I look in your eyes I don't see a Remus. You're concealing something. You're living a double life."

"I'm impressed," I said. "What are you really? A private eye?"

"An interesting thought, but no. I'm just good at reading people. It's my job."

In truth, I wasn't living a double life. The old life no longer existed. The new one had replaced it. Anyone calling out my old name in the street wouldn't have got a reaction. The new life began when I walked out on Ashley without explanation. I abandoned the mother who'd cared for me since I was three years old – stepmother if you want to be precise. I left a cruel note propped up against a mug on the kitchen worktop. It contained a few measly lines, *I'm truly sorry, don't come looking for me, get on with your life,* that kind of thing.

At this point Carl was moving in close. It was just after seven and the place was almost empty. There weren't likely to be any distractions. A couple of skinny young men in T-shirts were getting to know each other in the corner and only had eyes for each other. The manager was reading a Harry Potter book at the far end of the bar.

Carl put his hand on mine, just like a lover would do. "Come on," he said. "I've got all night." I let him keep his hand there even though it's not really my scene. Who cares what people think? He's a nice guy.

"OK," I said. "Where to start?"

The story began with Ashley. She's 48 years old now with short hair turning grey, unless she's had it dyed. She has beautiful clear skin, unless she's had it covered in tattoos like she once threatened to do. And she speaks in a soft, calm voice, unless what I did twisted her soul and drove her insane.

I still hear that voice when I'm lying in bed trying to sleep. When I was little, scared of monsters hiding in the cupboard, she'd come into my bedroom and sing gently to settle me. She wasn't religious in the conventional sense but her favourite song was Amazing Grace. *Amazing Grace, how sweet the sound.* She defended me fiercely against the school bullies: both kids and teachers. And then in the evenings, curled up on the sofa, watching TV, she'd let me plait her hair. Sometimes, while she was asleep, an empty bottle on the carpet, I'd paint her toenails different colours. When she woke up, she'd laugh and call me her little beautician.

Ashley doesn't know the story of why I disappeared. She is only four hours away by rail, but she might as well be living the other side of the world. And the reason for this is the Topolski family.

So here's the story I related that night: the story of how I came to be Remus J Metro, why I look the way I do and why, when I have a few drinks, I end up wanting to throw myself off a cliff.

* * *

For me, it began with a ring on the doorbell and a hushed conversation. When I recall what happened that day, I always get a sense of context: the sounds and the smells. I was in my bedroom listening to The Clash. It was one of Ashley's albums, recorded on a cassette tape that I'd found in a box under the stairs. The air in the room was rich with the scent of the daffodils that she'd placed in a vase in the corner.

The doorbell rang during the space between tracks and when she went to answer it, I put the music on pause and listened to muffled voices speaking in serious tones. That was when I first heard the name *Topolski*. After that, only random sounds came through. I heard the word *driver* and I heard the word *station*. I opened the bedroom door and stood at the top of the stairs. "Noel," she said, looking up at me, "something really terrible has happened. I have to go out for a while." From somewhere in the hallway, a man said, "Come on, we need to go," and she turned to leave. It was the last time we were together in that house. Whenever I smell daffodils or hear Rock the Casbah I get a flashback of that afternoon.

Something really terrible has happened.

For Ashley, the story had begun the previous night as she sat in the back garden watching the stars. Picture the scene: It's a clear night and there's a power cut in the street, so she can clearly make out the constellations. She listens to the late trains running by, taking lovers to their homes, and she reaches for the bottle of gin on the grass at her feet. This is a universal love story. Ashley is besotted with a younger man who has tired of her. Her heart is bleeding and her capacity for logical thought is on hold. She is about to drink herself to a state of forgetfulness.

At this moment Ashley has never heard of Ben and Andrea Topolski or their eight-year-old boy Sammy. They are in their home five miles away with a smaller crisis to deal with. Sammy has been suffering with toothache for two days and has had two sleepless nights. Ben has booked him a visit to the dentist early the following day. These trivial details were drawn from the Topolskis by reporters, as if the event itself had insufficient meaning without them.

Early next morning Andrea Topolski emerges from Kentish Town tube station with Sammy. It's a cool day in July and the schools are about to break up for the summer, but Sammy isn't thinking about the holidays, not this morning. Despite the painkillers he is still suffering. His mother is holding his hand to comfort him.

Andrea is distracted by the notice of a half-price sale in the window of a shoe shop and she stops to take a look. As he feels her grip loosen, Sammy breaks free and runs ahead to press the button at a pelican crossing.

And further up the road we have Ashley, racing along in her new yellow car after a sleepless night, with an empty gin bottle lying on the passenger seat. On some level she seems to have made a decision and is driving at about 40 miles per hour towards the spot where Sammy

Topolski is stepping into the road. Who knows where she was heading? Maybe to see the man who had jilted her so she could beg him for a change of heart. It hardly matters.

The lights are at red but dear, sweet Ashley doesn't stop. I can picture her demented features, her hands gripping the steering wheel, little tufts of her hair standing up like devil's horns; her eyes crimson with the tears she has cried. I can picture the horror of this next part of the story: the car hitting Sammy full on, Sammy tossed casually into the air like he is a Tesco carrier bag caught in a strong gust of wind, Andrea Topolski locked into this mini-second of horror that will haunt her for the rest of her life. By the time Andrea is kneeling beside Sammy he is stone cold dead.

A greengrocer named Arthur Rainbird saw what happened and took the registration number of the little yellow car but he remembered nothing else. He saw the driver's face, but said he would not be able to recognise her again. Other people in the street shared his confusion. Someone said it was an old woman at the wheel; someone said she was black; someone said it was a man with a pony tail.

When the police turned up to arrest Ashley, they thought the case was straightforward: she'd crack under a few basic questions. But the memory of little Sammy Topolski being tossed on to the bonnet of her car was inaccessible to Ashley's conscious mind. Her loss of recall had begun in the garden somewhere around the time that the gin bottle was three-quarters empty. Her life was a blank until some point during the following afternoon when she woke up in the chair at home, feeling sick and with a sense that something was wrong. When the police arrived later that day she knew how bad that something was. Terrified at the notion of what she might have done, she told the police her car had been stolen.

But Andrea Topolski will never forget the face she saw inside the little yellow car that stole her son's life. The moment she was shown a picture of Ashley, she let out a scream.

That's her.

And then she collapsed in a heap on the floor of the police station.

* * *

"Carl," I said. "Is your mother still alive?"

"Yes, she's 85. She lives in Cheltenham."

"OK," I said. "Imagine this. Imagine she's about to be taken away from you. What would you feel about that?"

"Well, it's going to happen one day but I don't want to think about it," he said. "It will demolish me."

"Well that's what I had to face. Ashley was about to be taken away from me. The defence lawyer said it could be fourteen years. I've got no idea what goes on inside a women's prison and I don't want to guess. She wouldn't have survived it. She's tough on the outside but her inside is like marshmallow."

"Remus," he said, "can I ask you a personal question?"

"I thought that's what you guys did. Doesn't it always get personal when someone lies on the couch telling you their problems?"

"I still have to respect their privacy," he said. "And I have to assume there are things they'd rather not talk about."

"So what's the question?"

"It's very unusual for a son to talk about his mother with the use of her first name. It's traditional to use words like mum or mother."

I'd hardly given that a thought. "I guess it started after Dad left us," I said. "She needed a friend as well as a son. It was a spontaneous thing. I called her Ashley one day and she didn't question it, didn't even react. She's the only person I've ever been close to. I feel desolate without her."

"So your father abandoned her?" he said.

"Yep. Just like I did."

"Just like you did?"

"Dad left because he couldn't bear to live with her anymore. My reason for leaving was different, but how could she have known that? All I did was leave a stupid little note that told her nothing. She reached an obvious conclusion – that I couldn't stomach living in the same house as her after what had happened to little Sammy Topolski."

He gave my hand another squeeze. I glanced across at the manager, a little self-consciously, I admit, and he smiled. Maybe he wanted to be next in line.

"So why exactly did you abandon her?" he asked.

"I'm getting to that part," I said.

* * *

It was Ben Topolski who had answered the door. They live in a large Georgian house in a cul-de-sac in the heart of Highgate Village. I had to ring twice before I got an answer. I'd seen him at the police station but he hadn't noticed me so when he saw me on his doorstep he must have thought I was selling something. When I told him my name he knew instantly who I was. But he didn't react, didn't say anything at first. The expression on his face was vacant. "Can I please come in?" I said. "I'd like to talk to you and Mrs Topolski." He didn't say no, he didn't insult me, he didn't shout or slam the door. He didn't even hesitate. He stood aside and invited me in.

Andrea hadn't seen me either but she knew who I was. Maybe it was instinct. Or maybe the look on my face told her I was somehow connected to her tragedy. She offered me a drink but I said it wasn't right for me to stay too long. And then I proceeded to plead for leniency. I asked Andrea Topolski to stand up in the witness box and tell the judge she did not wish Ashley to have a long sentence. I asked her to tell the judge that she would understand if he showed mercy.

Andrea answered slowly in a cold, calm voice. "But we do want her to have a long sentence. Why would you think otherwise?"

That's all she said. There was no emotional monologue, *we've lost our only son, he was all we had to live for,* that kind of thing. Just those few words that could not be challenged.

"I understand," I said. "I just thought I'd try." I stood up to go. But then Andrea said *wait*. I thought she was wavering. But she had a new proposition. I don't know whether she'd discussed it with her husband or whether she'd come up with it spontaneously during those few minutes we sat together. Either way, it makes no difference. She asked her husband to join her in the kitchen. They talked for five minutes or so. When they'd finished, they told me what they wanted to happen. I agreed immediately. There wasn't anything to consider.

* * *

So before all this I was Noel and now I'm Remus J Metro. I thought that was pretty smart. It's an anagram of Joe Strummer, Ashley's favourite singer. Before all this I wore T-shirts, jeans and sneakers. And like

I said, today my hair is oiled and swept back, and my face is rough and stubbly. I put on shades, even at night, and I wear a suit. I look ridiculous, I know, but my disguise works a treat.

Ashley is suffering, but not the way the law demands. She is suffering in a way that is appropriate to the crime. She has lost what Andrea Topolski lost – her son. The deal was this: I had to disappear without explanation, never to reappear in Ashley's life. That was what would give the Topolskis their sense of justice. And if I break my bond, I know Ashley will be made to suffer. When I made that promise – when I agreed to abandon Ashley with just a short, curt note – the Topolskis agreed to waver in their testimony. Andrea Topolski went back to the police and said she was mistaken. She said there may have been a much younger woman at the wheel of the car that took Sammy away from her.

The pledge I made is that I will forsake Ashley forever. I will not see her, telephone, write or contact her through a third person. If I break this promise they will return to the police with the true story. Ashley will spend years in jail. And so I gave them my promise. The way out they gave me is clean. Ashley is left without her only son but she has her freedom.

Carl stared hard at me for a long time. I asked him if he found the whole thing barbaric. It took a while for him to answer. The manager asked if we wanted another drink but Carl waved him away rather curtly. He'd let go of my hand and was staring at a pool of liquid on the bar, as if mesmerized.

"Barbaric?" he said at last. "No, it's not barbaric, it's beautiful. Locking someone away in a prison cell is what's barbaric. This is perfect justice."

It wasn't the answer I'd expected, but then I had no expectations. This was the first time I'd told the story.

"So are you going to throw yourself off a cliff?" he said.

Living with the knowledge of Ashley's suffering had brought me to the edge many times but this time I had someone to talk to. And so a safety valve had been opened. "Not tonight," I said. "I don't need to tonight. But tomorrow night? Who knows?"

Did He Jump?
David Reading

It's a well-known fact that smoking can kill you but for Matt Crosby all it took was one cigarette. He was standing in the street outside his workplace taking a break when he was hit from above by 95 kilos of flesh and bone going under the name of Stephen Covaci. The two of them worked together and they died together.

Stephen Covaci's descent began on the roof of an office block five storeys high. He was a security guard who worked nights in the building. I was standing 3.4 metres from Matt Crosby at exactly 22.07 when it happened: a copper in uniform about to take the number of a car parked on double yellows. As a policeman, I'm expected to be precise about things like time and distance. The coroner wouldn't have accepted a vague assessment. He expected a meticulous account of what I observed and that's what he got. The only thing he didn't get was how it made me feel. The truth is, I never got over what I saw that day: two twisted, broken bodies, lying one on top of the other, like figures in a gruesome tableau by Hieronymus Bosch; a stream of blood coursing along the gutter; an exposed brain and a bashed-in face; the other man's face contorted in the pose of a hideous gargoyle. I'd been trained to react quickly to events, but I stood gaping like an idiot while I struggled to take in what had happened.

We're expected to face disturbing scenes with fortitude, but I was a quivering wreck that night. When they saw how badly I was taking it, they put me in a box labelled PTSD, offered me counselling and ordered me to take sick leave. But next night I turned up at work as usual. I wanted to be the one who found the truth.

It seems Stephen Covaci, middle-aged and unmarried, regularly took his breaks on the roof of the Broadgate office complex. Every night at 10pm, if the weather was fine, he opened up a fold-up table and a fold-up chair and ate a takeaway meal that he'd bought at the Romanian restaurant round the corner. Asked why he did it, he said he loved the night air (although the atmosphere was thick with pollution). As an amateur photographer he could sometimes be seen standing at the edge taking pictures of the street life below him. And then one day he toppled over the edge to his death.

Stephen was heavily in debt and had previously tried to take his own life. Faced with this troubling information, the coroner recorded a verdict of suicide: case closed. But for me there were still questions. Why didn't he leave a note? Was he really the type who'd kill himself over money worries? Why did he bother eating a plate of meatballs if he planned to do away with himself? Why did he take the trouble to throw the takeaway carton into a wheelie bin parked near the stairs? And most curious of all – why was he clutching a bulb of garlic in his closed fist when forensics examined his body? But these unanswered questions were brushed aside. It was convenient to move on. We had a heavy caseload to deal with.

All that happened six years ago. Matt Crosby, the innocent victim of someone else's death, was only 17 at the time and that was what really got to me. That was why I found it hard to leave the case alone. The image of a young man my son's age lying mutilated on the pavement was more than I could face. I became obsessed. I let the job slide, and I took early retirement. For weeks I sat at home thinking about the Covaci case and working on theory after theory. *Did he jump or was he pushed?* My wife Sally was understanding and even chipped in when I wanted a fresh eye on something. But eventually my obsession cooled; Stephen Covaci drifted into the background.

Until I got a call from Elaine Hawkins.

"You won't remember me," she said. "We used to go to school together. I want to talk to you about Steve Covaci. I have a confession to make. I want to get it off my chest before I die."

***

The place was a modest semi on the main road out of town. I parked on the grass verge and walked nervously up the garden path. I was unsure what I was going to discover after six years. There was a small wooden cross fixed to the front door, suggesting Elaine Hawkins was religious. The door was opened by a man of around 30 in a black T-shirt with the words *Continental Vinyl Store* emblazoned on the front in red. His blond hair was tied back in a ponytail. I detected a faint odour around him that reminded me of French cooking. "Hello," he said, "you must be PC Bennett."

"That's ancient history," I replied. "I'm plain *Mister* Bennett now but you can call me Mike."

He introduced himself as Jason Hawkins and showed me up the stairs. "Mum's expecting you," he said. "I don't know what she wants, but please don't wear her out. Half an hour, that's all."

Elaine Hawkins was sitting up in bed in a blue nightie, drinking from a mug with a picture of the Beatles on the front. The curtains were drawn and a TV was clamped to the wall. She was watching a game show but hit the remote when I came in. "It's rubbish anyway," she said. "I don't know why I bother with television."

I knew she had to be my age – late-fifties – but she looked ninety. Her face was grey and gaunt, her hands thin and bony. And yet she smiled like she was pleased to see me.

"Take a seat, Michael," she said. "I'm so glad you came, I bet you don't remember me."

I did remember her, but it was hard to equate this sick, weak woman with the red-headed teenager who used to sit at the back of 4B screaming out songs by Queen.

"How are you, Elaine?" I said. Stupid question.

"Well to be honest, I'm not too good but you can tell that, can't you." Her son was standing just outside the door. She called out to him. "Jason, would you make our guest a cup of tea. How do you take it?"

I asked for a black tea, no sugar, and Jason disappeared down the stairs.

I sat beside the bed feeling awkward. I wondered how long she had to live, and she seemed to read my mind. "It's progressing slowly," she said, "so I could have another nine months. I thought it was about time to...what is it they say? Put my affairs in order."

"To make peace with God?" I suggested, thinking of the cross on the front door.

"Well, I wouldn't put it quite like that. I don't really hold with all of that nonsense."

I got straight to the point. "So what about Stephen Covaci? Why am

I here exactly?"

She reached for a folder on the bedside table and began to sort through a bundle of faded news cuttings. She picked one out and handed it to me. "Well, I knew you were involved in the case because I saw your name in the paper all those years ago. I kept the cuttings. You were at the inquest, weren't you? You were quoted. I thought you were the best person to call. I've got to tell somebody."

I recognised the headline straightaway: *Suicide verdict on night owl whose death leap killed colleague.* I'd read the report dozens of times.

"Tell somebody what?"

She sighed deeply. "This is difficult. Just give me a few minutes to compose myself. I need to get my thoughts together."

We sat in silence, while she stared into her hands. Jason brought me my tea. "Can I get you anything, Mum?" He reached over to the bottom of the bed and straightened the crumpled duvet. "Stop fussing," she said, shaking her head impatiently. "Just leave us to it."

After he'd gone, Elaine looked up at me and seemed about to speak, but the floor on the landing creaked and she hesitated. Jason was standing outside the room, listening. I wasn't sure if that mattered, but she obviously thought it did. She asked me to close the door.

And then Elaine Hawkins told me her story.

***

"It was my husband," she whispered. "It was Jim who killed Steve Covaci. I'm certain of it. And it was all my fault."

Now as a policeman I learned to be suspicious of what people told me, so maybe she didn't get the reaction she was hoping for. "Is that right?" I said rather blandly. In truth, I wondered if her illness was in the mind and she was acting a fantasy.

"Jim died eight weeks ago, of a heart attack. Jason has looked after me ever since and he drives me mad with his fussiness. But without him I'd be lost. I wouldn't want to live. I get a bit sharp with him but he's my whole life really." She sighed. "Now that Jim's gone, I can finally get this off my chest."

"Why do you think your husband killed Stephen?" I could sense Jason was listening but Elaine seemed to forget he was just outside the door. Emotion took over and she raised her voice. "Because Steve and I were going to run away together. We'd been seeing each other for months. I loved him, or at least I thought I did. It depends on your understanding of love. Anyway, as I said, we were about to run away together." She smiled. "Run away. Funny turn of phrase, isn't it. We weren't going to run anywhere. We were going to get the train to Gatwick and take a night flight to to Bucharest. Steve was completely broke but I had some money put aside. He was planning to quit his job, and we were going to spend a few months with his sister in a place called Brasov while we decided what to do. It's somewhere in Transylvania." She slumped back, exhausted, and closed her eyes for a few moments.

When she opened them, she looked hard at me, perhaps sensing that I was sceptical. She would have been right. I didn't want her memories, I wanted evidence. We both fell silent. I wondered how I could check that she really knew Stephen Covaci and then I remembered the photos taken at the mortuary.

"Elaine," I said, "Stephen had a tattoo on his chest. Can you describe it to me?"

She stared into her hands again and, without looking up, she spoke slowly and deliberately. "It was a bat in flight. A pipistrelle, I think." She smiled and looked up at me. "That's right, isn't it?"

I nodded. "Yes, that's right, Elaine."

***

After she'd told her story, I was satisfied it was somewhere near the truth. She had a lot of detail that was never published: facts about Stephen Covaci's life. He had Romanian parents; he worked as a night porter before going into security work; he received a caution for assault in a disco; his middle name was Marius. She knew those things. They first met in a pub while she was out with friends and she stayed with him that same night. She was bored with her husband and drawn to Stephen by his dark good looks and overpowering magnetism. There was something sinister about him, she said, but that made the attraction more powerful.

At first she kept up the façade, but she was terrible at keeping secrets and didn't delete Stephen's texts from her phone. Her husband confronted her. She promised to end the affair but had no intention of doing so. On the day of Stephen's death her husband was jumpy. He wouldn't touch his dinner and left the house mysteriously around nine o'clock.

That's how she came to suspect that her husband killed Stephen Covaci. To the DPP it would have been dismissed as circumstantial but I thought she was probably on the right track. She asked me what I was going to do about the information and I said I didn't know. She looked serene when I left her. She had found her peace.

Jason stopped me at the bottom of the stairs and whispered that he wanted to talk to me in private. He tugged at his right ear lobe constantly while he spoke: an odd nervous habit. Again I noticed that bitter smell that made me think of Sally's coq au vin. Inside the lounge he invited me to make myself comfortable while he went to the kitchen to make tea. I mooched around the room looking for clues about his dad's life. There was a filing cabinet in the corner. While he clattered around in the kitchen, I opened it up. Marvel comics dating back to the mid-1970s had been neatly filed away in cellophane pockets. I rifled through them carefully. Each one was in pristine condition, with not a tear or a dirty mark anywhere. A CD rack stood against the wall, filled mostly with heavy metal albums: Iron Maiden, Black Sabbath, that kind of thing. There was a picture on the shelf of Jason posing outside the Continental Vinyl Store.

Another photo showed him with an older man standing next to a yellow VW. Jason looked to be about seventeen. I put the photo back just as Jason walked in the room with the teas. He placed the tray down on the table and darted frantically across the room towards me. I thought he was going to attack me but he just grabbed the photo and put it back in its correct place. "Me and my dad," he said, laughing nervously. "He used to call that car his big yellow taxi, used to nag me to learn to drive. It took me a while, but I did in the end." And he shrugged.

Once we were sitting down, he began to grill me nervously about his mother. What did she want? Was she in trouble? How were we connected? Were we talking about the old days? I told him that what we discussed was confidential; he would have to ask his mum. And then he began to open up. He told me how close he'd been to his dad and how devastated he'd been when he found him dead in the lounge. Now his role in life was to look after his mother and he knew that soon he would be losing her too. Her nagging drove him mad. *Don't do this, don't do that. Stop fussing.* I tried to reassure him; told him it was the illness making her behave like that. Yes, he said, he knew that and he'd miss her so much when she was gone.

Jason continued to tug at his right ear lobe. I don't think he realised he was doing it. He spoke about his father as if he was a hero, and maybe he was. He'd fought in the Falklands clearing landmines and saw two of his mates blown up. When he came back he was a changed man, so people said. He withdrew into his shell, lost his job and spent most of the day watching TV. He had three spells in a psychiatric unit. Jason said his mum couldn't cope with that and soon she started going to the pub every night. He and his dad became even closer then.

Jason seemed to run out of steam after a while so we sat silently drinking our tea. And then he said something completely out of the blue. "He's evil, you know."

"What? Who are we talking about? Your dad?"

"No, not my dad. I mean Stephen Covaci. I heard you mention his name up there. That's who you were talking about, wasn't it?"

I ignored the question and asked why he'd described Stephen as evil. He thought long and hard, and then he said, "You wouldn't understand. No one would. My mum changed when she met Stephen Covaci. He sapped her will. She invited him round when my dad had to go into hospital and I watched them together. He had total power over her. And then one day I realised where that power came from."

I asked him to elaborate but I didn't get an answer. He just shook his head and mumbled incoherent sounds. He gave me the impression he'd said too much and wanted to let it drop. I needed to talk more but after we finished our tea he said he had to get to work and ushered me hastily towards the door. I left feeling there was still a lot I needed to know about Stephen Covaci's death.

***

And back home I pondered what Jason had said. *He's evil, you know.*

Not he *was* evil. He used the present tense. Did I misconstrue what he said, or did Jason Hawkins believe Stephen had survived that five-storey drop from the Broadgate office building?

The following day I stood in the shadows across the road from the Continental Vinyl Store. In my old grey tweed coat and Ray-Bans, I felt like Cormoran Strike, like I was playing at being a private eye. I'd seen Jason Hawkins go into the store at ten past nine, and that was all I needed really – to know he wasn't home. But I was curious about him so I crossed the road to get a closer look. Album sleeves had been blue-tacked to the window so I was able to take a peek through the glass without being seen. Jason had on the same black T-shirt with the red motif, and I noticed he had a crucifix around his neck. I hadn't seen that before. Again, I noticed that nervous habit as he talked to customers: the persistent tugging of his right ear lobe. At his home I hadn't studied him carefully – there was no need to – but today, peering through the window, I spotted traits that suggested relentless unease: sudden, rapid eye movements, a fixed expression of apprehension as if he was waiting for a bomb to go off. A general restlessness suggesting he was constantly hyper-alert.

But I wondered if I was making too much of this. Perhaps he had nothing to add to the Stephen Covaci story.

I rang Elaine Hawkins' doorbell not really expecting a response, but the door opened and there she was – still buckled under the burden of disease, but with a smile across her face. She was pleased to see me.

"I have good days and bad days," she said as we drank tea in the lounge. "Today is a good day. It's probably the effect of the drugs, but what the hell!"

I'd made up a story to explain why I was there: I said I was fascinated by her account of her relationship with Stephen Covaci and wanted to know more about him. She was happy to talk. He'd told her about life in Romania under Ceaușescu before the 1989 revolution: the austerity, the poverty and the terror of the secret police. She remembered it all and gave me a half-hour lesson in Romanian social history. I took hardly any of it in. I was waiting for the right moment.

Surprisingly, it arrived in a way I didn't expect. She was in mid-sentence when suddenly she nodded off in the armchair.

Upstairs, there were three rooms off the landing – Elaine's bedroom, the bathroom and a tiny box room stacked to the gunnels with black plastic bags. I guessed they were full of Jim's clothes waiting to go to the charity shop. A metal ladder led to an attic room. That was the one I decided to check out. Reaching the top of the ladder, the first thing I saw was a crucifix attached to a wooden beam. There was a crucifix over the bed, too, and a crossbow attached to a nearby wall. Posters embellished the other three walls – most of them promoting heavy metal albums and old horror movies. On a dusty table sat three bulbs of garlic. Idly I picked one up. It felt smooth and somehow comforting in my hand. Without thinking I dropped it into my pocket. The room was sparsely furnished. There wasn't much to see, really, but a picture was beginning to form.

I heard Elaine calling my name, but before I went back down I picked up a book on Jason's bedside table, opened it, saw it was his journal and began photographing pages at random on my phone. I remembered to flush the toilet and slam the bathroom door loudly. She had no idea I'd been snooping in Stephen's room.

Elaine apologised for dozing off and we chatted for a while about the old days – life at Highfield Comprehensive and the after-school discos, that kind of thing. Surprisingly, she told me I was her first crush. That was, she admitted, one of the reasons she decided to reveal her secret to me and no one else. I like to feel we made a connection that Saturday afternoon. If she'd been fit and well, who knows what might have happened? At the front door, as I was leaving, I gave her a hug. I think she had tears in her eyes. I never saw Elaine Hawkins again.

***

But I did see Jason later that day. I was waiting outside the Continental Vinyl Store when he came out at five-thirty. When I told him I wanted to talk further he was remarkably compliant. We went to a back street pub, where I bought a couple of beers. The jukebox was turned up loud, playing old rock 'n' roll hits, so it was the perfect setting for a confidential chat. I asked him whether he had anything to tell me about the death of Stephen Covaci. I waited patiently while he considered the question.

"Can I trust you with the truth?" he said at last.

"That depends on what the truth is."

He thought for a few moments more. And then: "I'm taking a chance here, OK? When you hear what I've got to say I want you to promise you won't dismiss it out of hand. That you'll give it a fair hearing."

I said I would. And then he proceeded to confirm what I already knew. Those handwritten words in his journal had told the full disturbing picture.

He has to die but I have to trust in the ways of killing prescribed in those ancient stories that people dismiss as myths. He clings to the night, avoids the light, so that leaves me with one option. The wooden stake. I will prepare myself. A garland of garlic bulbs around my neck, another necklace bearing a crucifix, a bag containing a hammer and six wooden stakes. What will happen when I hammer in the first stake? Legend has it that his body will dissolve into dust. I have to trust that this will happen and that I will not be overpowered by his pure evil.

"You believe he was a vampire!" I said.

"*Is* a vampire. And yes, I knew it from the moment I saw him. And then there was all that stuff about Transylvania. I've always known vampires exist. Most people think of Christopher Lee in cheap horror films or Buffy the Vampire Slayer, but Dad used to tell me stories about vampires. He'd seen them too, you know, that's where I got my instincts from, it's in my genes, being able to spot one. After the way I saw the power he held over Mum, I knew Covaci had to die."

When Jason took the stairs to the roof of the Broadgate office building that night, Stephen Covaci was sitting on the edge taking photographs. He didn't turn around until the last minute and when he did, he was surprised to see his lover's son holding a hammer and a piece of wood. Covaci lost his balance, reached out with his hand and grabbed Jason's garland of garlic cloves. The garland snapped and Stephen Covaci fell to his death.

And Jason, knowing that death had not been delivered by the prescribed method, genuinely believed that the spirit of Stephen Covaci had survived.

He's evil, you know.

And because of this bizarre belief, Jason felt the need to protect himself with crucifixes and garlic. It was obvious really. It was the smell of garlic I detected whenever I was in his presence.

I sat, quietly listening to his confession. When he finished, Jason sat back in his chair and grasped the silver cross that hung on a chain around his neck. "So," he said, "will you go to the police? He's out there somewhere, you know. I failed dismally."

I shook my head. "He's dead Jason, I saw his body, you have to accept that." But he leaned forwards conspiratorially. "These creatures don't obey the same laws of nature that you and I are subject to. Covaci's spirit survived and one day he will come for me. I just hope I am prepared."

***

Three weeks ago I heard that Elaine Hawkins had died. I can picture Jason sitting at her bedside at the time, holding her hand, perhaps crying a little, listening to the feeble breaths intermittently easing their way out of her diseased body, wondering whether the breath he'd just heard was the last one.

Holding the truth from her was an easy decision to make. Knowing the reality of Stephen Covaci's death would have torn her apart. She would have lived her remaining months tormented by the possibility that at any day her only son, her carer, would be taken from her.

After she had gone, I had another decision to make: whether to hand over Jason's journal to the police. That was another easy decision to make, really. The evidence was overwhelming: maybe he was a poor damaged soul but he was, by his own admission, a killer. There was just one thing to do. It was only right that I should confront Jason and tell him what I was planning.

As I'd done before I parked on the grass verge outside the house and walked nervously up the garden path. The first thing I noticed was that the small wooden cross – which had been fixed to the front door – had been torn off and was lying in the middle of the flower bed, snapped in two. I knocked on the door and waited. There was no reply. I stepped on to the lawn and peered through a gap in the curtains. The house appeared to be empty.

So that afternoon I walked into the Continental Record Store and approached the manager, a chubby middle-aged man who introduced himself as Ron. I said I needed to speak to Jason. But he said Jason hadn't been in all week. He hadn't phoned or emailed.

As I was leaving Ron called out, "You're not the first person who's come looking for Jason. Some weird foreign bloke was asking after him one evening just as I was about to shut the shop."

I stopped in the doorway. "Really? So what did you tell him?"

"I told him I didn't know where he was. I'm not sure if he believed me because he just stood there staring at me. And then he said, 'When you see him, tell him an old friend of his mother needs to talk to him.' He said it kind of menacingly and it made me feel really strange, sort of light-headed. After he'd left I went outside to see where he was off to, but he'd gone, disappeared."

As I drove away from the Continental Record Store that afternoon I was aware that I'd broken out in a sweat. The sky clouded over quite suddenly and as I passed St. John's churchyard my hands started to shake. I knew it was illogical but I reached into my pocket and wrapped my fingers around the bulb of garlic that I'd picked up in Jason's room. I'd forgotten I had it. Eventually the shaking stopped and I began to breathe normally again.

    I realised it was time to put Steven Covaci behind me.

Aanjay's Heroic Deed
David Reading

A telephone call at four o'clock one Saturday morning reminded Aanjay that the day had arrived for the annual celebration of his birth. His Uncle Harish, a well-respected resident of Mumbai, appeared to have disregarded the time difference between their two cities so Aanjay was perplexed at being woken suddenly from an amusing dream about a hat-wearing fish. But when he realised who was calling his mood lifted.

Uncle Harish. It is so good to hear from you.

Happy birthday, Aanjay. May God shine upon you today as he does every day most probably.

Oh yes of course. It's my birthday! Thank-you for reminding me.

The conversation was brief. Uncle Harish provided news about Aanjay's friends at the Department of Drinking Water and Sanitation. They all pined for him, especially Deepak, who missed their weekly game of Twister. Uncle Harish said there was a parcel in the post for Aanjay.

Aanjay returned to his bed hoping to meet again the hat-wearing fish of his dreams but the sound of his neighbour's radio removed any chance he might have had of further sleep. The disc jockey seemed to be a devotee of the type of popular music known as 'heavy metal'.

Aanjay had a fondness for most styles of music but realised his ambition to return to sleep that morning would be unfulfilled. So he sat at the window of his little flat, watched the sun rise over Whitechapel and observed the starlings squabbling over scraps of food.

Just after seven o'clock Aanjay had a fine breakfast of Supersave Multigrain Hoops, which had been relinquished by the previous tenant. The tiny black specks he took to be weevils and he was encouraged by the fact that these would provide him with extra protein. He wondered whether they had been a purposeful addition by the manufacturers but could find no mention of them on the box. He enjoyed his birthday breakfast.

At nine-thirty the doorbell rang. Standing on the landing holding a small parcel was his neighbour, a stout fellow named Karl. Aanjay had enjoyed many interesting conversations with Karl in the past. Karl believed that all immigrants should be shipped back to their countries of origin and he believed Aanjay was one of those who did not belong on English soil. On several occasions he had voiced this point of view in no uncertain terms. Aanjay liked the cut and thrust of debate and would look forward to his lively conversations with Karl.

This morning, however, Karl appeared to be pressed for time and chose not to engage in small talk. The parcel he held in his hand was for Aanjay; it had been wrongly delivered. Although Karl had been tempted to keep it for himself he was worried, so he said, that the parcel might contain a bomb. Aanjay thought this was an unlikely prospect but understood that all manner of things were possible in life. He took the parcel and wished Karl an enjoyable weekend (not realising they were destined to meet again that very day in rather alarming circumstances).

AANJAY'S HEROIC DEED

Aanjay opened his parcel with enthusiasm. Although he had learned that having unrealistic expectations leads to much sorrow, he could not stop his mind from imagining what the parcel might contain. It was cube-shaped, suggesting it might be some kind of delightful decorative ornament. Aanjay felt that his little home needed brightening up. He had few possessions: just his clothes, his toothbrush, a bar of soap, an electric kettle, his copy of a James Bond novel and a picture of his mother which hung over the fireplace. As he tore away the brown paper wrapping, he saw it was not a delightful decorative ornament after all but a ceramic mug. An amusing inscription on the side of the mug read: KEEP CALM AND CARRY ON.

Aanjay was delighted with his gift and inspired by the message it conveyed. As he set about making tea, he noticed that inside the cube-shaped box there was also a greeting card. On the front of the greeting card there was a picture of a man playing golf and above that a simple communication: Happy 21st birthday. Uncle Harish had signed his name inside and added a brief message: *I am sending you this gift thanks to that most wondrous of inventions, the Internet.*

What a delightful start to the day! Aanjay thought to himself.

He left his flat that morning with a spring in his step, determined to tell all and sundry about his new mug and the humorous message it expressed. He promised Mrs Patel, the newsagent, that he would show it to her one day soon. *You will be tickled pink*, he said cheerily. Aanjay bought a packet of Rolos and the local newspaper and decided to eat his Rolos and read his newspaper sitting beside the pond opposite his flat. And that is exactly what he did.

Aanjay was dismayed to read that a woman had been sold an out-of-date pasty; and that the Mayor had been criticised for his choice of hat.

But before he could read much further he heard a terrible hullabaloo coming from the direction of his flat. Looking round he saw a small crowd of people, who were shouting and pointing towards an upstairs window. Pouring from the window was a cloud of smoke. Aanjay knew it was the home of his neighbour, Karl.

Abandoning his newspaper, and his Rolos, Aanjay jumped up from the bench and sprinted across the road towards this scene of apprehension. He heard a siren wailing in the distance. Reaching the building, he raced through the foyer and up the stairs, realising that waiting for the lift would waste too much time. He arrived at Karl's flat to see black smoke swirling out from underneath the door. There was a cry of distress from inside. His first instinct was to ring the doorbell, which he did, but after a few seconds it became plain that the poor fellow was in no position to answer the door. For a moment Aanjay shared the emotions he supposed Karl was feeling. A sensation of cold dread coursed through his body. But then he remembered the rousing message written on the side of his new mug. And immediately he felt energised.

A door further along the landing opened and a chap he knew as Mr Herring appeared. *What's up?* the fellow cried. *We have a problem to be solved,* Aanjay called back, *there is no doubt about that. The poor chap in here will fry to a crisp unless I can save him from such a fate. Mr Herring – keep calm and carry on!*

Aanjay leaned heavily on the door but it was clear his small frame would provide insufficient force to achieve his aim of breaking through. Another solution came to him in a flash. He entered his own flat, opened the window and eased his way along the narrow ledge towards Karl's window. He paused for a moment. A flock of pigeons whirled and swooped around him. He felt the air from their flapping wings brush his face. Aanjay loved all wildlife and marvelled at the iridescent colours displayed on their wings. But this was an unwanted distraction, so instantly he returned to the job in hand. Pushing against Karl's window had little effect at first, but he noticed to his satisfaction that the window was off the latch. He pushed harder, the window opened a little, and he squeezed through the narrow gap. The room was filled with smoke, the kitchen area was aflame, and Karl was lying in a heap on the floor.

Aanjay had got as far as taking hold of the fellow's shoulders, preparing to heave him to his feet, when a third figure entered this scene of potential calamity. Aanjay was relieved to notice that it was a representative of the local firefighting department. He – if it was a he – wore a helmet and a gas mask. Aanjay addressed the firefighter directly. *This chap seems to be in a bit of a quandary. We need to get him to safety. Can you help?* He was pleased that he had taken command of such a difficult situation.

The two of them dragged Karl through the dense smoke, out on to the landing and on to an awaiting stretcher, where a rather delightful woman wearing a green uniform was ready to administer medical assistance. *Take care of him*, Aanjay pleaded. *Underneath his gruff exterior there is a good heart.*

Karl opened his eyes briefly. He looked shocked to see Aanjay holding his hand and tried to pull away. The smoke had filled his throat and his lungs and his eyes were streaming. He tried to speak. He was mouthing something at Aanjay.

Anjay smiled, squeezed his hand and spoke gently to him. *You are welcome, my friend.*

Bait
Alexis Krite

By the 15th of October, Rita Komarov had been waiting a month. Sitting on the stone doorstep of the cottage, a red tartan rug wrapped around her shoulders, she celebrated her 34th birthday alone. The ocean lay in front of her and she could hear the waves rolling onto the beach, sucking up the pebbles and spitting them back against the rocks. In her hands she cupped hot tea diluted with a generous amount of Jameson whiskey. The moon hung low in the night sky and its reflection quivered gently on the water.

She knew Alek would come eventually, drawn by those little love messages she'd left for him, dozens of them stuck to the bedroom wall of their flat. She imagined his disbelief when he saw that she'd gone. And then his dismay when he fully understood what she had done. She allowed herself a little smile. She knew he would come, because his life depended on it.

It was Sarah, her sister, who'd told her about his affair. About Alek finding his *real true love,* as he put it. Unfortunately his real true love turned out to be Rita's best friend Janice.

At first, Rita believed it would be easy to win Alek back. And so she tried all the ways she could think of to diminish Janice in his eyes. To prove that she, Rita, was so much better than her. But if she was drunk and flirty, he feigned tiredness. When she was sober and witty, he appeared bored and flicked on the TV. Thinking she may have let herself go, she lost weight, put highlights in her hair and even got herself an A level in psychology. To her mind, she was quite the catch now. But for some bizarre reason, in the end he preferred to be with Janice.

And so she had left. Left the town where they had lived together for so long, left her friends, her family. Familiar surroundings. And made her way to the southern coast of Ireland. To the land of her forefathers. And it was here, now, that she waited.

As she sat there, in the chilly salt-tainted air, a cloud drifted across the face of the moon and for a few moments Rita sat in darkness. Pitch blackness. From the shadow of the woods behind her, a vixen screamed. Rita drew the rug tightly around her and told herself she had nothing to be afraid of. Sarah was the only person who knew about this place. But that would change. Eventually, under pressure from Alek, Sarah would cave in and tell him where to find her. And once he knew where she was, then there was no way he would miss her birthday. She was sure of that. When he arrived, Rita knew he would be angry with her at first, but then he would listen and see that she was right. She would agree to give him what he wanted, but there would be conditions. He would have to abandon Janice and take Rita back. She wanted a new car; she wanted them to move somewhere hot, away from everyone who knew them. A fresh start.

And she wanted a baby. In the end, he would, she was sure, realise that she, Rita, was actually his real true love.

The cold seeped out from the stone beneath her and from the Atlantic air around her. It was time to go indoors and light the log burner. She still hadn't got the hang of the wretched thing and the room filled with smoke almost immediately. It took all the kindling and a whole box of firelighters before the flames began, reluctantly at first, to dance.

Now she smelled of smoke so she picked up the bottle of Sicily and sprayed her hair, her wrists and then she opened her shirt and sprayed her breasts. It was late but he still might come tonight. And so she touched up the foundation on her face and gently brushed blusher across her cheek bones. Her Irish cheek bones. She looked at her reflection in the mirror and fluffed her hair up: not bad for thirty-four.

She filled a hot water bottle and tucked herself into bed, wrapped the duvet behind her back and watched the flickering flames through the bedroom door. She couldn't get used to sleeping alone. She missed Alek lying beside her and she missed Carla, their Doberman, sprawled out at the end of the bed. She'd been stupid to let him keep Carla, but the dog loved him more than her – and loved Janice as well. *Pair of bitches,* she thought as a stab of fury shot through her. Her heart began to race and for a moment she was consumed by thoughts of their betrayal.

She curled up and waited for Alek's car to pull up outside. After a while, the searing heat of anger slid into the chill nothingness of loss. She allowed herself to weep, just a little. The darkness pressed in, cocooning her in loneliness. She pulled her phone out of her pyjama pocket. She wanted to call him, but the screen was blank: there was no reception. The company had said nothing about the fickleness of the phone signal when she'd booked the cottage, or the absence of broadband. She covered her head with the duvet and put her fingers in her ears so that she wouldn't hear the silence.

***

The next day dawned bright and crisp with a cloudless sky. The sun washed away the dark thoughts of the night before and Rita's optimism returned. The village was five miles from the cottage and most days, mainly out of boredom, Rita drove there to look around and buy a few essentials. Today, she hesitated about leaving the cottage in case Alek turned up, but although he had missed her actual birthday, they could still celebrate with a bottle of wine and surprisingly, the village store had a decent selection.

The road from the cottage was pot-holed and fists of grass thrust up through cracks in the tarmac. As she negotiated a particularly sharp bend, a sheep wandered into Rita's path and she slammed on her brakes, narrowly missing it. She sat there for a second remembering the squirrel she had hit a week ago. That only required a hard tap with a stone to finish it off. A sheep would be far more difficult. She resolved to keep a shovel in her car in future.

The main village street consisted of the post office, pub, church and supermarket. There was a hardware shop and a shop for repairing electrical goods down a side street. Just where the village gave up and the farmland began again, there was a country store.

There didn't appear to be a police station.

Just as she parked the car, her phone lit up. This was obviously a local hotspot for Vodafone. She checked it for messages, hoping that finally there would be one from Alek. But as usual there were only promotions and a cheery text from the provider telling her she now had signal. Well, *that* was obvious. She threw the phone on the back seat in annoyance and got out of the car, slamming the door hard.

Sycamore seeds were scattered on the pavement and as she crunched through the tree litter, the leaves exuded the scent of autumn. She had always found it odd that fumes from the dying year excited her and stirred something almost thrilling in her. Most people probably felt that way about spring.

Rita headed for the Applegreen supermarket, which sold most of the items she needed. Her tastes had changed since she'd arrived in Ballyspit. She'd given up trying to buy fennel or chia seeds and was resigned to eating local produce, which for her vegetarian taste was mostly Hegarty's Cheddar, eggs and potatoes. She picked up a litre bottle of Jameson and a Villa Maria Sauvignon Blanc. Out of habit she stood for a moment by the dog food section staring at the tins of Chappie and bone-shaped biscuits.

As usual she tried to spark up a conversation with the checkout girl. Today it was Mary, the franchisee's daughter. Despite her homely appearance, it was clear that the portly Mary would rather be in Dublin or London and Rita thought she would have welcomed the sophisticated banter of a Surrey woman. But apparently not.

"Hi Mary, super day isn't it."

"Would you be wanting a bag? Five cents."

Rita pulled out her re-usable, biodegradable carrier from her handbag.

"No, it's fine thanks, got my BFL – my bag for life. You know, take an old bag shopping!" Rita laughed.

Mary looked at it and grunted.

"Forty-eight euros."

Rita handed over a fifty euro note and Mary dropped the change onto the belt.

"Keep the change. Buy yourself some chocolate." Mary looked up in surprise.

"Well goodbye then, have a nice day," Rita called as she let the door slam hard behind her.

She hoped Alek would appreciate the sacrifice she was making while she waited for him – stuck with these country bumpkins in the middle of nowhere.

Back at the car, Rita put the shopping on the passenger seat. She saw the door to the church was open. She hadn't been in a church since Sarah's wedding ten years ago. She and Alek had tied the knot in the local registry office and then only under pressure from her. He was drunk the night he agreed to marry her. When he sobered up the next day, she refused to let him back out. She laughed off his suggestions that she was trying to force him into marriage. When she revealed that she'd already told her father, he knew he was beaten. Jimmy McGuiness was one of the few people that Alek had to tread lightly with.

Outside the church she glanced around to make sure no one was looking; she was very much a lapsed Catholic and felt weirdly guilty entering the Church of the Suffering of Christ. She ran up the steps two at a time and tucked herself into a pew at the back. It was even colder in the church than outside. She shivered. She wasn't sure why she had gone in. Perhaps she was looking for reassurance that she had, in the end, chosen the right path.

But as she sat there, Jesus looked down at her, sagging from his cross. *You should be careful Rita,* he seemed to be saying. *You should listen to me.* But the paint had chipped off from one of his eyes and now he had a white spot in the corner. It gave him a cockeyed look. "I can't take you seriously, looking like that," Rita whispered.

The church smelled of damp and incense. She looked around but found nothing to comfort her and the Stations of the Cross just made her think about death. On the way out she dipped her finger in the holy water by the door. It had obviously been some time since the water had been blessed. A fly was floating in it, surrounded by a film of grease. She quickly made the sign of the cross and then wiped her hand on her jeans. There was a collection box next to the door and she stuffed a 50 euro note into it. Perhaps even Jesus could be bought.

It was good to get out into the air again. A breeze had started to chivvy up the fallen leaves but the sun was still warm. She couldn't face going back to the cottage just yet. She put her car keys in her pocket and walked back past the post office, the pub and the supermarket. She kept on walking until the village ran out, brought to a halt by a large prefab that housed Mulligans Country Store. She needed a new pair of wellies. The expensive pair she'd bought in Chelsea were already worn on one side, making her limp slightly.

Mulligans smelled of animal feed and leather. As she walked around, she saw farm tools that looked like implements of torture. There was an entire shelf with axes of various sizes and degrees of lethalness. She picked up a tomahawk style hatchet with an easy-to-grip handle and weighed it in her hand. She wanted to feel its sharpness, to run her thumb along it, but the blade was protected with a plastic sheath. It wasn't cheap but that really wasn't an issue at the moment. Mulligans had a few shotguns displayed in a glass cabinet, but she assumed it would probably be really complicated to buy one here. All that paperwork nonsense.

The only problem with a hatchet, she reflected, *was that you needed the element of surprise*. She sighed, remembering how she used to kiss Alek's head, how soft his hair was. A shotgun would be so much quicker. But she decided to buy the hatchet anyway. It was, after all, only a last resort. A final option should her plans come to nothing.

There were various items of ironmongery, household cleaning products, bags of compost and bird feed. In one section there was a ladies' fashion rail. Rita examined the nighties hanging there. She picked up a knee-length baby pink affair with lace around the neck and modesty buttons down the front, found a mirror and held the nightie against her.

As she was looking in the mirror, she saw a man standing behind her, watching her, a bag of chicken feed in his hand. She smiled at him. He shook his head slowly and smiled back. *He's right,* she thought, *I am not the brushed cotton sort*. She was a little disappointed when the man moved away and her instinct was to follow him. But instead, she went in search of the footwear section.

She found it at the back of the store and chose a pair of blue, very practical Wellingtons and two pairs of thick wool socks. They would come in useful for walking Carla.

As she ambled through the car park back towards the main road, a large German Shepherd ran up to her wagging its tail. It seemed friendly enough and Rita put down her bags so she could stroke it. The dog began to sniff her hands and clothes in a very business-like manner. She cupped its head in her hands and whispered menacingly, "I'll forgive you your bad manners because you have lovely brown eyes. *But don't mess with me.*" She gave its ear a hard squeeze and the dog yelped.

Rita watched as it trotted away, its tail between its legs, towards the same man who'd been standing behind her in the store. He was loading animal feed into the back of a police car, which seemed rather odd. The dog leapt into the car and watched Rita from the safety of the back seat, clearly shaken. The man stood up straight and looked at him, a puzzled expression on his face. He followed the direction of the dog's gaze and saw Rita standing there.

"He's lovely," she called out. "I was just getting my dog fix."

"He can a bit *too* friendly sometimes, not really something you want in a police dog!" And the man laughed. She smiled and turning quickly, made her way hurriedly out of the car park.

As she was driving back to the cottage, her phone pinged with another text. She reached round to get it from the back seat but she couldn't twist far enough and steer at the same time. *Probably just junk*, she thought, she'd check it later. But when she pulled up outside her gate, she saw the front garden was heaving with sheep. They were pulling at the roses that grew over the porch and tugging the chrysanthemums from the borders. She didn't really care about the garden but she didn't want to lose her deposit, so she spent the next twenty minutes herding the sheep out through the narrow gate. She completely forgot about the text.

Back inside the cottage, she was shocked when she saw herself in the mirror. Her hair was plastered to her face with sweat and her mascara had outlined the contours of her cheeks. *Oh my God!* she thought, *what if he turns up now?* She dashed into the bathroom, tore off her clothes and stood in the shower. There was just enough warm water in the tank to wash her hair and soap the sweat from her body before it ran cold.

***

It was late afternoon by the time she'd dressed, styled her hair and put on her make-up. The cottage was gloomy and the single-glazed windows had allowed the chill autumn air to enter. She sighed as she realised she had no kindling left. She took up the tartan rug and wrapped it around her. At least there was gas in the kitchen. She was standing by the hob, her hands over the flames, when a car crunched to a halt at the front of the cottage. For a moment she didn't move. She knew this could go well, or very, very badly. She had rehearsed this moment a hundred times but now her heart was pounding as if she'd just run a marathon. The waiting was over, her patience had paid off and her optimism had been justified. She walked slowly towards the front door. A dog was scratching on the wood. *He's brought Carla with him!*

She took a deep breath, pressed down the thumb-latch and pulled open the door. A dog rushed past her, almost knocking her over. But it wasn't Carla – it was the large German Shepherd she'd met earlier.

"Finn! Here boy!" Standing in the doorway was the man from the car park. "Sorry, he's a bit of a workaholic, has to investigate everything," he said. He grabbed the dog and pushed him outside.

On the doorstep were two Mulligans shopping bags. The man picked up the bags and held them out to her. "I think these are yours." She took the bags from him. "Goodness, I'd forgotten all about them." She smiled, expecting him to turn and leave. But he just stood there.

It seemed rude not to invite him in. But when she spoke her voice was flat with disappointment. She had been sure it would be Alek at the door, not this stranger. "Would you like a coffee or something?" she said.

"That would be grand, thanks." He had to stoop to get through the door.

"There's a cake in one of the bags, to welcome you to Ballyspit," he said. "By the way, that's a vicious looking hatchet you've got there, I hope you know how to handle it." He held out his hand. "Ruairi Byrne."

Rita took his hand. "Rita Komarov. How did you know where to find me?" For a moment she wondered if he'd stalked her.

"Small village, Rita. What are you doing out here anyway, in the middle of nowhere? Are you a writer or something? Jeez, it's cold in here."

"A writer? No, I thought I'd try to track down my relatives. I'm doing the family tree." She had rehearsed this explanation to ward off any inquisitive locals. There was actually a vague element of truth in it. She knew the McGuiness family was from somewhere in the wilds around here. Rita filled the kettle and put it on to boil. But suddenly she remembered the text. It was probably junk, but it might have been Alek.

"Coffee won't be a moment. I've got to get something from the car," she called as she headed out of the door.

Rita opened the car and picked up the phone. There was a text, but it wasn't from Alek – it was from Sarah. *Yo Rita! He made me tell him where you are, he'll be there today. And guess what? The cow is pregnant! Call me and STAY SAFE. Xxx*

For a moment she felt nauseous. A baby! But hold on, Alek was on his way to *her*. Janice had frightened him off. She'd got herself pregnant thinking she could hang on to him but the opposite had happened. Relieved, Rita slumped back against the car and smiled to herself.

The sound of wood being chopped broke into her thoughts and she remembered the policeman in the house. She felt a wave of anger.

What the hell was he doing? She raced round to the log store to see Ruari slicing wood with her new hatchet.

He looked up and smiled. "You didn't have any kindling, but you've got enough now for a few days." He carried a bundle of sticks into the house and she followed him through the door. In minutes he had got the wood burner going. *Not a bad thing*, Rita thought, *everything perfect for Alek*. The wood burner blazing, a home-made cake on the table. But Ruairi seemed in no hurry to leave.

Just then Finn began to growl. "Sounds like you've got another visitor," Ruairi said. A car was pulling up round the side of the cottage. Rita hurried outside, almost tripping on the doorstep.

And there, at last, was Alek.

He was getting out of a little Fiat with the name of a hire car company emblazoned on the side. His face was pale and drawn. There was a bruise on his cheek and he had a row of stitches above his eye.

"Alek!" she called out. She rushed up to him and threw her arms around him.

But Alek grabbed her by the neck and pushed her head down onto the bonnet of the car with one hand. In the other he held a pistol. "What have you done with it, you bitch? They're going to kill me, you stupid cow." He jerked her up by the hair, threw her to the ground and kicked her leg.

"What have you done with it?" he said again, calmer this time. "You've no idea who these people are. You've got me into serious shit, Rita."

Rita lay in shock, her face in the dirt. This wasn't how it was supposed to be. Above the pounding in her ears, she heard a loud click and looked up to see Ruari moving towards them, holding a shotgun pointed at Alek. "I think you'd better calm down, lad," he said.

Alek looked confused. He held out his arms in front of him and dropped the pistol. "Who the hell are you?" he said.

Ruairi glanced down at Rita, "I'll sort this out. You go inside." He reached out and helped her to her feet. She wiped the grit from her cheek and lifted her hand to touch Alek. He jerked away from her with a look of disgust and suddenly she realised it was over. She turned her back to him and limped slowly towards the cottage.

Alone in the kitchen she pulled on a pair of rubber gloves and tugged open the oven door. She pulled out a plastic carrier containing smaller bags full of white powder. Outside Finn was barking hysterically as Alek screamed at Ruari. The two men appeared to be at the front of the cottage now. Hugging the bag to her chest, Rita slipped out of the back door to the yard, and then round to the side. Alek's car was unlocked and she opened the boot and threw the bag in. Just as she clicked the boot closed, Finn appeared, and jumped frantically at the car whining loudly.

**

She was back in the house, standing by the kitchen table, when Ruairi came in. "Are you sure you're all right?" he asked. "I've got him handcuffed in the pickup. Who is he anyway?"

"My husband." Rita spoke softly. She waited for the inevitable questions but Ruairi simply put his arm around her and held her. "You're safe now, I'll take him into the station at Kinsale." He turned sharply. "What's that dog barking at?"

Ruairi walked out into the yard and pulled Finn away from the Fiat. The dog had scratched the paintwork on the boot, frantic to get in there. Ruairi opened the boot and looked inside.

He promised he'd be back within the hour.

***

As soon as Rita heard the pickup pull away, she went into the bedroom. The cash was hidden in a shoe box in the roof space above the bed and she checked to make sure the trapdoor was securely in place. At the last count there had been half a million.

She sat on the edge of the bed for a moment and dropped her head into her hands. Ruairi wouldn't be very long. When he got back, he was bound to ask some awkward questions about Alek. She needed to think. She lifted her face and looked around the room. On the bedroom dressing table there was a rosewood jewellery box that Alek had given her for their first Christmas together. She lifted the lid and sifted through the contents until she found what she wanted.

***

"Rita, what did he mean? He asked you *where is it?* Where's what?"

The two of them were sitting by the log burner, drinking whiskey. Rita's hands were shaking as she put her glass on the table. "I'll show you," she said. She stood up and went to the bedroom. When she came back, she held out her hand. On her wedding finger she wore a ring.

Ruairi whistled. "Are they diamonds? The size of them! It must be worth a fortune."

"Alek gave it to me when we got engaged. It belonged to his grandmother, I know it's really valuable, but I didn't care about that."

Gently she turned the ring on her finger until the diamonds caught the firelight. She sighed. "Alek left me for another woman and his brothers went crazy when I wouldn't give the ring back. He's terrified of them, that's why he attacked me. He wasn't always like that," she said quietly.

"Well, the ring is yours," Ruairi said, "and Alek won't be seeing the light of day for a good long time. Don't let his family frighten you either. We're pretty sure it was cocaine Alek had in the boot of his car, we'll be sending it off to the lab to check. Didn't you have *any* idea your husband was a dealer? You must have been suspicious."

"I'm so naïve. Alek used to talk about selling high end furniture to Arabs and rich Americans. I thought that's where the money came from. I knew he had contacts in Dublin but I just thought they were other antique dealers."

"Dealers, yes, but not in antiques." Ruairi downed the last drop of his whiskey. "Anyway, I'd better be getting back to the station before I get too comfortable here. I've left my number on the kitchen table, ring me any time you need anything, or if you're worried."

As he walked towards the door, he hesitated. "I'll have to come back tomorrow, Rita. We'll need to take a formal statement. You know how it is."

She nodded. "Of course. I'll be here."

When he left, she poured herself another whiskey. Things hadn't worked out exactly as she'd planned. She had lost Alek. She looked across to the log basket where the hatchet was embedded in a piece of wood. But, she thought, things could have been so much worse.

She stood on the bed and opened the loft hatch. She took down the shoe box and pulled a suitcase out from under the bed. She placed the box inside and tucked her clothes around it. If she got a move on she could make the ferry to Roscoff. The huge ring caught on her new cashmere pullover and she pulled it from her finger and threw it in the box with the rest of her costume jewellery.

    She could afford to buy the real thing now.

Angelina
Alexis Krite

The taverna perched precariously on the edge of the ancient road from Paramethia to the port of Igoumenitsa. On the mountainside below lay the rusting carcases of vehicles whose drivers had failed to negotiate the hairpin bends.

Cafe Kostas wasn't a place that invited tourists to stop. The gravelled yard was littered with rusting feta tins and a few scrawny chickens pecked in the dirt. Inside, a fug of yellow cigarette smoke hung suspended below the wood panelled ceiling.

Above the bar in the corner, the television was showing a football match with the sound switched off. Kostas, the owner of the taverna, was watching the game with his only customer, a truck driver from Agios Donatos. Kostas' mother, Angelina, sat by the kitchen door, bent into an S-shape like a shrunken figure carved from ebony.

The driver, Yannis Mavroyannis, had stopped at the taverna on his way home from the port. Although he only lived in the next village, he had used the weather as an excuse to be late. A storm had blown in and rain was sheeting down onto the road. Yannis flicked the end of his Karelia Light at the ashtray. It overshot and landed on the ground. He grunted, reached out with his boot and rubbed the cigarette stub into the composite marble floor. From the depths of her black headscarf the old woman in the corner hissed disapprovingly.

Yannis shrugged and unhooked his arm from the back of his chair. He slid his hand up under his T-shirt and dreamily scratched the folds of hair-carpeted belly. Extracting his hand, he examined his fingernails. Lightly embedded in the black grime were a couple of hairs. He raised his hand to his mouth and pulled the hairs free with yellowed teeth and then spat them out on to the floor. He looked over at the old woman but her head had tipped forward. Her hands were clasped together on the crook of her walking stick. She appeared to be asleep. Or dead, Yannis thought. *Ah well, that's life.* He poured himself another glass of retsina from a copper-coloured carafe and then, with some effort, lifted his right cheek slightly and passed wind.

A huge Scania refrigeration truck pulled into the yard and moments later the driver opened the door and slid to the ground. He stood for a second, stretched and hitched up his trousers. Then, head down against the rain, he barrelled towards the door. Spotting Yannis through the window, he raised an arm in greeting.

Yannis pulled up a chair and called out to the inn keeper. "Eh Kosta! Another glass." The driver of the Scania pushed the metal framed door open and the wind whipped it back with a clash. The windows continued to shiver long after the door had closed. He sat down next to Yannis and held out his hand. "How are you, Yanni?"

Yannis grasped his hand and shook it, then tipped his head from side to side and replied, "So, so. And you, Aki? And the kids?"

Akis shifted his huge behind uncomfortably on the chair. His buttocks spread over each side, engulfing the rush seating and the wooden frame. "Yeah, fine thanks," he answered. With the greetings over, he swept his hair back across his bald patch. "Bloody weather!

They've closed the new motorway because of some accident. If I miss that ferry, I'll be sleeping in Igoumenitsa tonight."

Both drivers looked out at the rain beating against the glass. To undertake the old mountain road now would be lunacy.

Kostas appeared with a small tray. He rested it on a neighbouring table, picked up the full ashtray, spread a new paper cloth over the metal table and set down the glass, a meze of feta cheese and olives and a clean ashtray. "When the hell you gonna get some decent chairs in here, Kosta?" Akis grumbled.

He tipped his head at the woman sitting in the corner. "I see the old crone's still breathing then." Angelina began to cough and hacked a lump of sputum into a tin on the floor next to her. "Ah disgusting," Akis muttered under his breath, "someone should put her out of her misery." Angelina lifted her middle finger and waved it at him. "Senile too," Akis sneered.

"Maybe. But she's not deaf." Kostas sloped back to the kitchen, pausing to watch Panathinaikos score a goal against Olympiacos.

Akis eyed the new Karelia Light that Yannis had drawn from his pack and raised his eyebrows. "You smoking *those* bloody things now, Yanni? Is it that wife of yours?" he asked in disgust.

"Yeah, she's working on my health. *Cut down the fags Yanni, cut down the booze Yanni, cut down the coffee Yanni*. Only one thing she doesn't ask me to cut down on and I did that years ago, voluntarily." Yannis sniggered at his friend.

Akis sighed. "These women. They trap you with their cooking, feed you up until you're so fat no other woman would be interested in you, wait a few years until you got more hair on your backside than your head and then they start trying to make you cut down on everything."

Yannis nodded. "That's right, once they think they got you, you're done for. Eleni's put me on a diet." He called out, "Hey Kosta, chicken and fried potatoes over here and another carafe!"

Akis looked at him in disbelief. "A *diet*?"

"Yeah. She's frightened I'm gonna have a heart attack. Worried about where the money would come from then. Three daughters and not one son to keep her in her old age, she says, as if it's *my* fault."

Yannis lit his cigarette. "I caught her sniffing round the truck the other day, seeing if I had any baklavas hidden there!"

Akis smiled sympathetically. "And did you?"

Yannis slapped his belly and laughed. "She was too late!"

"Our women, you know, they say they're cleaning the cab but we know what they're *really* looking for."

Yannis raised his eyebrows. "Baklavas?"

Akis roared with laughter. "Something far sweeter than that, my friend!"

Yannis looked confused.

"Listen man, these foreign women, they'll do anything for a lift. And you've got to *be prepared*." He winked at the other man.

Yannis felt a pang of envy. The European jobs had always brought their share of perks but lately all he'd had were the sheep runs to the local abattoir. Not much chance of picking up a foreign woman on those.

Akis rested his arms on the table and leaned forward conspiratorially.

"Anyway, there's this woman I know, she lives in Igoumenitsa." He glanced at Angelina dozing in the corner and spoke in a whisper. "She's no spring chicken, but she's very *broadminded*, if you know what I mean." Yannis didn't know what he meant.

Akis sat back and closed his eyes for a second. He pictured Salomi and tried not to think of her moustache. "She's a big girl, very adventurous. But you know, heart of gold. I take her over on the ferry. Sometimes Brindisi, sometimes Ancona." He paused and dragged heavily on his cigarette, tipped his head and blew the smoke in perfect rings, up towards the ceiling.

"Anyway, she has this *thing*," Akis added with a lascivious grin. "Very erotic!"

"What sort of *thing*?" Yannis said, trying to show some interest.

Akis leaned forward. "A thing about food."

Yannis couldn't see what was so erotic about that. *He* had a thing about food, especially now he was on a diet, but it didn't make him feel randy. A full stomach usually had quite the opposite effect in fact.

He turned back to Akis. "So what is it, oysters? Does it get her going when she eats them?" He'd never really believed oysters were an aphrodisiac; they usually gave him heartburn.

Akis shook his head slowly. "She doesn't *eat* the food. She likes you to rub it all over her!"

That seemed like a terrible waste to Yannis, whose growling stomach was starting to sound like Liza, his father's ferocious sheep dog.

"What kind of food?" he enquired.

"Well, first it was fruit, in a light syrup, she likes to watch her weight you know." And he laughed. "Then last week, it was tinned sardines."

Yannis opened his eyes in astonishment.

Akis acknowledged his surprise. "Yeah, well can't say I was too keen on that one."

"Anyway, I picked her up a couple of days ago and when we got off the ferry at Brindisi, she opened a bag with about twenty bottles of tomato ketchup in it. I said, *no doll, let's save that for next time.* I was running late you see."

With his mind still on food, Yannis asked, "So what did you do with all the ketchup?"

"Hid it under the bunk in the cab. Then this morning, Maria does her usual inspection. *Stinks of fish in here,* she says. So I told her, *yeah, had a bit of trouble with the refrigeration unit, lost a few kilos of pilchards.*"

"Ah yes," Akis continued, forgetting now to lower his voice. "They're so easy, these women. Tell them you love them and you can get away with murder!" A loud snort from the corner drew his attention. Angelina was peering at him, her eyes like misted obsidian.

"Anyway," said Akis, dropping his voice again, "so Maria went off back to the house. I got in the truck and opened the locker under the bunk to get out another packet of fags. Then I thought, that's funny. Something not right here. Something's *missing.* And do you know?" Akis winked at Yannis. "All the ketchup had gone! I reckon Maria reads the same magazines as Salomi!"

A gust of wind hurled the rain against the windows. Akis threw his hands up in frustration. "Now it looks like I won't even make the crossing today."

"Still, you've got the woman in Igoumenitsa." Yannis tried to keep the bitterness out of his voice. Some people had all the luck.

Kostas arrived with a plate of chicken and fried potatoes, swimming in grease. He set it down on the table along with a bowl of cooked beetroot leaves doused in oil.

In the corner, Angelina suddenly banged her stick on the floor and Kostas rolled his eyes at the two drivers. Shaking his head, he went to help his mother out of her chair. He placed his hand gently under her elbow and with his help and by leaning heavily on her stick she managed to get to her feet, swaying slightly.

She lifted her head and her black headscarf slid back, revealing an almost bald skull. The handle of her cane, Yannis noticed, was carved in the shape of a snake. She turned to Akis and grinned at him. He nodded: "Kyria Angelina." He acknowledged her as politely as he could, but it was difficult. He felt revulsion at her gaping toothless mouth and the few sparse hairs on her head. He shuddered, thinking of Salomi and Maria. *Please God*, he thought, *that I die before they get like that.*

He turned back to Yannis, who was getting up from the table, his meal untouched. "You off?"

"Yeah, be my guest." And Yannis pushed his plate across the table. He had an urge to get home. He was thinking of his wife Eleni and wondering if he should pick up some tinned peaches from the minimarket on the way.

"Rain's lifting," he said, turning back and looking out of the window. He threw twenty euros on the table, nodded to Kostas and Akis, and headed out to his truck. A line of blue sky slashed through the grey clouds above the mountains and steam was starting to rise from the pot-holed tarmac of the old road.

Back in the taverna, Angelina, now upright, staggered for a moment and then hobbled with unexpected speed, through the bead curtain hanging in the kitchen doorway. It swung gently from side to side for a moment, and then she was gone.

Akis wiped the grease from his chin and reached for the ketchup bottle but all that was left in it was a congealed rim, like dried blood, around the lid. "Hey Kosta! Bring me some sauce!" he shouted.

A few minutes later Kostas came back and shook his head. "No more sauce, mate."

Akis banged his hand on the table. "I can't eat chips without ketchup. What sort of a place are you running here?"

Kostas raised his shoulders in a gesture of helplessness. "I picked up a carton yesterday from the cash and carry. Maybe my mother's put it somewhere." He tapped the side of his head. "Mama," he called, "where's the ketchup?" But Angelina didn't reply. Kostas shrugged again. "Sleeping." And he walked away from the table.

Akis stared down at the naked fried potatoes. *Really, what's the point of chips without sauce?* he thought. Then, thinking of Maria and his surprise supper, he grinned. By the time he had finished and had smoked three more cigarettes the rain had stopped completely. He made his way over to the truck and heaved himself up into the cab. He switched on the ignition and waited for a few seconds until the *wait to start light* had gone out and then he turned over the engine. He pulled out on to the road in the direction of the port.

The road fell away in front of him, shimmering with its coating of rain. He eased the truck around the bends. The ferry would be leaving in an hour. He changed gear and accelerated as he came out of each bend. He spotted a coach, dangling on the edge of a precipice, ten metres below. *Amateur,* he thought.

A few minutes later he felt that the engine was losing power. It began to stutter. He cursed loudly, "Blasted cheap Russian fuel!" He changed gear again, pressing the brake as he came to the next corner. Without warning, the lights on the dashboard died. He pressed the brake harder and wrenched the stubby gear stick into second. Still the truck kept going, silent now except for the hiss of tyres on the wet road. Akis shifted forward and clutched the steering wheel, trying to turn it as the truck sped towards the sparse vegetation that hemmed the very edge of the tarmacked curve ahead of him.

He heard nothing for the first twenty metres as the blue Scania tumbled gracefully through the fine silver mist that cloaked the roughly-hewn cliff face. As it hit the tarmac on the road below, Akis exploded through the windscreen. He was deafened by a hideous scream. *Was that him?* he wondered *or the metal skin of his truck being ripped from its chassis?*

The driverless truck somersaulted spectacularly and then sprang down onto the next loop in the road far below. In all, it bounced and flipped five times, each landing taking it closer to the port. It finally came to rest off-piste in the rocky riverbed that formed the base of the gorge. The water rushed through the open cab windows and flowed down the valley until it reached the Ionian Sea.

***

Kostas carried the lunchtime bucket of scraps into the yard and tipped them in a heap under the scanty shade of a cypress tree. The chickens clustered around him and as he pushed them away with his foot, he noticed a box sticking out from behind the tree trunk. A bright red tomato beamed at him from the carton. He bent down to pick up the box and there, beside it, were ten empty ketchup bottles. He pushed them with his boot, shaking his head. Perhaps it was time Mama went to live with his sister. He'd had his share of dealing with her dementia; it was Katerina's turn now. He began to collect the bottles and place them back in the box. Just then, something black caught his eye. He reached down and plucked it from the mud. He wiped it on his jeans and examined it: it was a fuel cap.

He turned it over, and stamped in capital letters across the middle, was one word: *Scania*.

The Life and Death of Harvey Patton
Jane Churcher

When the agent told us the house backed on to a graveyard it didn't stop me wanting to see it. I'm not the sort of person who scares easily. The agent said it was built in the '80s and as we turned into the driveway I thought he meant the 1880s, but when we drew closer I realised it was built to look that way. I imagine the phrase would be mock-Victorian.

As soon as he'd opened the front door, and as we stood in the hallway looking up those winding stairs, contemplating all that space, I said, "We've got to have it." But Matt said, "Hold on, Cathy, we haven't seen the graveyard yet," so the first thing we did was take a walk up those long, winding stairs to the back bedroom and we looked out of the window.

There are graveyards and there are graveyards. Some are bleak and scary like they've been dreamed up by Edgar Allen Poe; others are clean and white, well cared for, adorned with flowers. The one we could see through the bedroom window – *our* bedroom window – was one of those latter ones. The people in those graves had living relatives who spent their Sunday afternoons watering the flowers and clearing away the dead leaves and petals. There was nothing scary here. We took a look at the rest of the house and when I said, "Shall we take it?" Matt squeezed my hand. "It's perfect," he said.

We looked across at the agent. He should have been dancing a jig at that point but he was staring at his shoes. "Look," he said, "it's going to take several weeks for this to go through so I'm going to mention something. You're bound to find out pretty soon anyway. Three other buyers found out about this and pulled out at the last minute, wasting everyone's time. So I'm going to say it now to save us a lot of bother."

He paused and laughed nervously. "You may have heard of a man called Harvey Patton. Patton was a notorious thief and a conman. He was not a nice man. He was rumoured to have been one of the *Brink's-Mat* Robbers, although the police could never prove that. OK, so Patton is buried out there in the graveyard, and people say they see things." He took a deep breath. "To put it bluntly, they say they see Harvey Patton wandering around out there. This is crazy, I know, but I want to get this problem out the way so I know we can proceed with confidence."

I looked at Matt and Matt looked at me. Matt laughed.

I hesitated. "So you're saying there's a ghost hanging around the place?"

The agent continued staring at his shoes.

"So why on earth would you think that's a problem?" Matt said. "This place really is perfect for us. What do you think, Cathy?"

The agent sneaked an awkward glance at me.

I paused for dramatic effect. And then I said, "You're right. It's perfect. Where do we sign?"

Three months later it was as if we'd always lived there. Matt had done the wiring, I'd painted the walls and we'd got a team in to do the rest: lay the carpets, carry out a few repairs to the woodwork and do a bit of plumbing.

And then I saw Harvey Patton looking at me through the open kitchen window. I'd seen Harvey's photo in an old newspaper at the local library so I knew I was looking at him now. It wasn't the dead of night, when these things are supposed to happen. It was about two in the afternoon while Matt was at work.

In the movies, the delicate leading lady grabs hold of her cheeks and screams when scary things happen. It's traditional. But I didn't do that. I looked Harvey Patton in the eye and I shouted, "So what's your story, Harvey?"

I can't understand why a ghost would look startled – surely they're the ones who are meant to do the startling – but Harvey's expression was a picture of astonishment.

"You can see me?" he said.

"Of course I can see you. It seems a lot of people can see you. You're notorious."

Neither of us spoke for a while. What do you say to a ghost and what does a ghost say to a living person unless it's Whoooooo? Harvey didn't say that. He was lost for words.

Finally I thought I'd better break the ice, so I said, "You'd better come in."

Harvey looked to the left and then to the right. "Where's the door?" he said.

"Aren't you supposed to walk through walls?" I asked.

"I don't know," he said. "I'm new to this."

"But you died years ago. Five years, wasn't it? You've had plenty of time to learn."

"But I've never got this far before," he said. "Normally I just gawp at people. A lot of people can sense me and they freak out. It passes the time but I don't know what else to do. It's not easy being dead."

"Well you'd better start learning the ropes," I said. "If you put your mind to it, I'm sure you can be creative."

Harvey stepped back, adopted the position of a runner at the starting blocks, and sprinted forward.

"That's it, I knew you'd do it," I said. He was standing in the centre of the kitchen.

"Wow," he hollered, "that felt weird. I wanna go again."

The ghost of Harvey Patton was wearing a dark grey suit, white shirt and purple tie. His black brogues were spotless. You'd have thought that hanging around in a graveyard for years would have scuffed them a bit.

"So what's your name?" he said. He was giving me the look of a man who hadn't felt a woman's touch for years, and of course he hadn't. It wasn't a sleazy look. In fact he was an old-fashioned romantic. He should have been carrying a bunch of roses.

"It's Cathy," I said. "Nice to meet you. I know exactly who you are. You're that notorious thief."

We chatted for the best part of the afternoon. Harvey was a very perplexed ghost. He didn't have a clue why he hadn't gone to where all the other dead people go. In the early days he had a chance to find out when he got a visit from a man in a blue suit who said he was a kind of overseer. He was a bald bloke, talked with a Liverpool accent. Harvey asked a lot of questions about why he was still here in the land of the living but the man – the overseer – brushed them aside impatiently. All he would say was "Don't ask me, it's the Law of the Universe."

After a couple of hours, I asked Harvey to stick around and meet Matt. But suddenly the atmosphere changed. "I'm sorry," he said, "but I have to go." And without another word he left the same way as he arrived – by taking a run at the kitchen wall. It seemed his rapid exit was triggered by something he saw through the window, something out there in the graveyard. I took a look but all I could see was a little girl kneeling at one of the graves.

***

Explaining to your husband that you've had a conversation with a dead gangster is easier than you'd think. I didn't tell Matt straightaway. I left it until halfway through the evening, when he'd drunk half a bottle of red wine and we were curled up together on the sofa. "Matt," I said, "would you describe me as well-balanced?"

He made a joke about marrying me because he liked crazy women so I asked him again but in a different way. "If I were to tell you something utterly insane, would you still have trust in me?"

"Totally," he said. "I mean that. We said for better or worse, remember?"

"You really won't think I'm going crazy?"

"Come on, out with it. You're starting to worry me," he said. And so I told him about my new best friend Harvey, who'd walked through the side of the house and had a serious conversation with me. Matt listened. And then to my amazement Matt said, "This is such a relief!"

His head flopped back and he breathed deeply. "Such sweet relief! I wanted to tell you but thought I was cracking up."

"Tell me what? You've seen him too?"

"I've been agonising about this all day. I tried to tell you about it when I got in but I had a crisis of confidence. I saw him myself through the bathroom window as I was getting ready for work. He didn't see me. I don't even know if ghosts see people."

"They do."

"He was standing on the footpath next to that statue of Jesus with its head knocked off. A couple of joggers were running past him. They didn't seem to take any notice. I guess not everybody can see him. I knew it was him because of that old photo we saw at the library. Same face, same build, same hair, same everything. Even the same suit."

"Come on," I said. I jumped up off the sofa, grabbed his hand and pulled him towards the door. "Get your shoes on. We're going out."

It was just after nine when we got out there in the graveyard. It was dark. Harvey was standing looking at one of the graves, which turned out to be his own. After all that time you'd wonder what he found to be of interest in the same slab of grey stone.

"Mr Patton," I said. "I want you to meet my husband Matt."

"Call me Harvey," he said.

***

We sat together, the three of us, in front of Harvey's grave. The inscription read: 'In loving memory of Harvey Patton. Sorely missed by his wife Jane.'

"So what happened to Jane?" I said.

He pointed to the headstone next to his. The inscription read: 'Here lies Jane Catherine Patton, much beloved by all who knew her. A life too short.' She had died two years after her husband.

"I'm so sorry, Harvey," I said. "Do you have any idea what happened?"

"I think it was some kind of a road accident," he said. "They turned up one day with the coffin and the headstone. There was a whole bunch of them dressed up in black. Uncles and aunts and cousins, the whole pack. I stayed away, on the other side of the cemetery. Don't ask me why. I guess I couldn't face them. Most of them were boring as hell when I was alive so why should I have anything to do with them when I was dead. But I did hear my Aunt Deb saying something about a lorry driver and a court case. So I guess that was it."

"So what was it that upset you today?" I said.

"You noticed? OK, I'll tell you. There's this little girl who turns up at my grave a couple of times a week. I've no idea who she is. It started about a month ago. She looks about nine years old, pretty young thing with curly red hair. She's not family – I'm pretty sure of that. So who is she?"

"So why don't you follow her and find out?" Matt said.

He looked at Matt like he was dumb. "You don't think I'd like to? The problem is that I'm confined to this sorry patch of soil. However much I try, I can't get away. I get through the gate and get about 200 yards down the road and then it's like there's an invisible force field stopping me going any further. It's like something out of that movie – what's it called? – Forbidden Planet. I'm stuck here."

"But why here?" I asked. "I thought ghosts were meant to hang around at the place where they died."

Harvey laughed. "That's the big joke," he said. "This *is* where I died. I was in here paying respects to my old man. He's buried over the other side. Plot 42. I was kneeling at his grave blubbing when I had a heart attack. Anyway that's what I assume it was. I was all hot and sweaty and felt like someone was kneeling on my chest. I lay there in agony for half an hour and then croaked. The trouble was, my soul – or whatever you want to call it – didn't go anywhere."

"Harvey," I said. "This girl who turns up at your grave. When do you think she'll arrive?"

***

The little red-headed girl always seemed to turn up just after four. Harvey knew the time because you can see the church clock from the graveyard. He assumed she may have come straight from school because she wore a navy blue school uniform with a badge on the pocket. It was never a weekend. It was usually a Friday.

So for the next few days, at four o'clock exactly, I sat on the patio waiting and watching. It was on the Wednesday afternoon that she turned up. She carried a leather satchel and, as Harvey said, she was wearing a school uniform. It was the uniform of the Catholic school down the road.

Harvey had promised to stay out of the way. I approached her quietly and discreetly. She was kneeling in front of Harvey's headstone, her hands clasped together in prayer.

"Sorry to disturb you," I said. "Was he your father?"

She looked up at me, surprised. "No, I didn't know him."

"You didn't know him? So he's not a member of your family?" I knew they weren't related. I was just fishing.

She stood up and turned to go.

"I'm sorry," I said, "I didn't mean to disturb you."

"It's OK," she said. "I was going anyway." She looked me in the eyes, a worried expression on her face. "He was a thief, you know. He stole from people. He stole from my mum. He took my gran's jewellery. Now my mum hasn't got any money and we're going to be thrown out of our house. I thought that if I came down here he might somehow tell me where the jewellery is. It was never found. It's worth thousands of pounds."

I was confused. "But how can he tell you where the jewellery is when he's dead?"

"It sounds silly, but I thought that if I prayed hard enough God would make him tell me where it is. But it hasn't worked."

"Well not yet," I said. And then I thought hard. "Come back here on Friday at the same time and I'll see if I can be of any help."

After she'd gone I told Harvey about the conversation. "So the jewellery, Harvey. Where is it?"

"Get a spade," he said, "and follow me to Plot 42."

***

And so Harvey Patton was able to do his last good deed. The little girl's name was Fay. It turned out her mother had met Harvey in a pub and had been beguiled by his charm. She took him home and they spent the night together. Next day Harvey had gone. And so had the jewellery. He'd buried it at his father's grave.

I made Fay promise never to reveal who'd given her the jewellery. She kept her promise.

The last conversation we had with Harvey gave us a clue that his time here was near the end. Funnily enough he was starting to fade away at that point, like he was made of gas. He said he'd had another visit from that overseer with the Liverpool accent. He'd been told to expect good news.

"I've just got one piece of advice to leave behind," Harvey told us. "This is my gift to you. Ready for this?"

"OK," we said together.

"If you think you might be about to die, put on a pair of comfortable shoes. These brogues are killing me."

The Lesson for Today
David Reading

Mrs Pyminster stepped up to the lectern and peered out at the congregation as the final verse of Jesus My Redeemer drifted lethargically around the church. When the last line had died away she coughed lightly to clear her throat. The Rector said *please be seated* and the congregation took their places.

In a voice modelled on the Queen's Christmas Speech, Mrs Pyminster informed the congregation of the passage she was about to read.

Today's lesson is taken from Isaiah. In which there is a message of redemption in a world weary from sin.

The Rector, sitting a few feet to her left, nodded gently as a way of indicating to his flock that he knew the passage well and it pleased him greatly.

Now it came to pass in the fourteenth year of King Hezekia...

Mrs Pyminster hadn't rehearsed the passage but she'd been a reader at St Hyacinth's for 15 years and could take anything the Old Testament threw at her. She didn't need to check out the difficult words because, for her, there weren't any. Her rich, southern English tones carried the authority of Margaret Thatcher. And if she did slip up and mispronounce the occasional Biblical name, she would stop suddenly and stare at the congregation daring her listeners to make something of it.

Then came forth unto him Eliakim, Hilkiah's son...

The Rector had put on his serious face, signalling that this was a significant passage that required full attention. For him, the message proclaimed by the prophet Isaiah was just as true today as it was when it was written.

But something wasn't quite right. The Rector couldn't put his finger on it but it was as if a sixth sense had kicked in and his unconscious was trying to tell him something.

And Rabshakeh said unto the assembled throng, Say ye now to Hezekiah, thus sayeth the great king...

Mrs Pyminster ploughed on. Every Sunday she fulfilled one of her chief missions in life. She saw herself as more than a reader of words: she was vessel of God, delivering His message to the faithful; a message that, she hoped, might fall upon fertile ground and bear fruit a hundredfold.

What was it exactly that wasn't quite right? The Rector made a conscious effort to hold on to his serious face and not allow it to lapse into the anxious one. He tried to grasp the sense of the words he was hearing from Mrs Pyminster in order to work out what was wrong but his anxiety was clouding his concentration and all he could hear was a collection of sounds. Sounds like *Hilkiah* and *Asaph* and *Shebna the scribe.*

And that was it! Shebna the scribe wasn't meant to be here, not in today's reading. Mrs Pyminster had opened the Bible at the wrong place.

But what was the problem with that? Who would care? If the reading from Isaiah was different to the one that had been printed in the service sheet, so what?

He allowed his shoulders to relax, breathed deeply, closed his eyes and smiled gently at the thought of his own irrational anxiety.

But something still nagged at him. Mrs Pyminster ploughed on.

How then wilt thou turn away the face of one captain of the least of my master's servants and put thy trust on Egypt for chariots and for horsemen?

The Rector concentrated hard on that sentence from Isaiah, struggling to maintain his serious face. That voice from the unconscious was still trying to get through to him, to tell him what was amiss.

And then he got it. It came to him as a flash of awareness. Mrs Pyminster was heading down the road towards catastrophe. The reading that had inadvertently found its way on to the Sunday schedule was not just any passage. It was *that* passage: The one that had brought the house down when he was a 13-year-old schoolboy at St Bidolph's. The passage that Derek Flagtail had read out during a wet lunch-hour in the biology lab, sending 4B into fits of giggles.

The Rector struggled to recall the exact words Isaiah wrote: the words that were about to be read aloud by Mrs Dorothy Pyminster MBE, chairwoman of the Townswomen's Guild, secretary of the flower arranging group, past president of the WI.

Derek Flagtail had read out the passage so many times that every boy in 4B knew it by heart.

But Rabshakeh said, Hath my master sent me to thy master and to thee to speak these words? Hath he not sent me to the men that sit upon the wall, that they may eat their own dung and drink their own piss with you?

That was what his unconscious had been trying to signal. Mrs Pyminster was expecting to convey a message of spiritual inspiration but instead she was about to speak words that should never be heard emerging from the lips of a 59-year-old country wife from Hampshire. As he came face to face with this awful predicament, the Rector experienced the kind of body-shock you would feel if you suddenly realised you were about to drive your car over a cliff. He glanced sideways at Mrs Pyminster, who was still in full, glorious flow.

Denial seemed to be an option. Was there really a problem? He looked across at the congregation to survey the faces: the face of Mrs Polkinghorne, sitting in the front pew with her ten year old daughter Charlotte; the face of Miss Whitebait and her fiancé Captain Rillington-Dogge; the faces of the Longcock family, just back from Kenya where they had been shooting warthogs.

But of course there was a problem! Anything would be better than this. It would be better for the church to burn down, or for old Major Pumphrey at the back to die of a heart attack, or for someone to interrupt the reading to prove beyond doubt the non-existence of God. All of that would be better than the social calamity that was to follow.

By now there was a trickle of sweat running down his back. His scalp itched. His face was on fire. His right eyelid was twitching. His serious face had slipped into a look that suggested psychosis. He thought back to his divinity training. Had there been preparation for a moment like this? His mind was blank on that score.

Then said Eliakim and Shebna and Joah unto Rabshakeh, Speak I pray thee unto thy servants in the Syrian language....

Mrs Pyminster was still riding that runaway train to disaster, unaware that the lowest point of her entire life was moments away: death by embarrassment.

Fantastically absurd solutions flickered through the Rector's imagination: he could set off the fire alarm but that would mean scuttling off into the vestry to hit the red button; or he could shout and point towards an imaginary intruder at the back of the church.

In the end he did nothing.

And so the moment arrived: Mrs Pyminster drove her four-by-four into that metaphorical blazing oil tanker. In the world of his imagination, the Rector was her fellow traveller, attempting to jump free from the passenger seat at the last moment but unable to undo his seat belt and dying with her in the inferno.

For the Rector, what happened next seemed like a miracle from God. Without stumbling or hesitating, without tripping over those taboo sounds, Mrs Pyminster read aloud the words written in Isaiah Chapter 36 verse 12.

And the world carried on as if nothing had happened.

If she was aware of what she was reading, Mrs Pyminster didn't show it. And as for the rest of the congregation, they simply didn't notice. Their minds were on their holidays, or their fuchsias, or their dinner plans, or tonight's TV, or on shooting warthogs.

After the service, over coffee, Audrey Polkinghorne said, "Very nice reading, Mrs Pyminster."

Thicker Than Water
Alexis Krite

"I wouldn't do it if I were you," Kevin said nervously, wiping away the rim of froth from his lip.

Cara smiled at her cousin, puzzled at his concern. "It's fine Kev. I really don't mind. I could do with the extra cash."

She drew out a Marlborough and placed it between her lips. As she scrabbled in her bag for a lighter, Kevin's business partner, Sean, leaned across the table and flicked his Zippo. She brought her face close to his, accepted the light and pulled hard on her cigarette, blushing slightly. Sean and Kevin were over from Ireland on one of their regular business trips and as usual. Kevin had asked Cara to join them for a drink at the Anchor, a run-down pub near the seafront. But it was Sean, really, that she was so pleased to see.

Sean clicked the lighter shut, extinguishing the flame. "It's none of your business Kev. She *wants* to do the extra shift!" He jabbed Kevin sharply with his elbow. "Hear that? None of your business son."

"Ah come on now boys, don't fall out over *me*!" Cara laughed and held out the packet of Marlborough Lights to her cousin. "Here you go, Kev, I won't tell Mammy!"

Kevin shook his head. "No, you're all right."

"He's got a weak chest, haven't you Kevvy?" Sean wrapped his arm around Kevin's shoulder. As he tried to shift away, Sean held him fast.

"So tell me Cara, what's this job you've got that's so important?"

"All I know is they're having a conference at the Belle View, big shots from Aldershot, army types apparently. Now it seems some last-minute VIPs are coming too so they want me to do a late stint in the hotel bar."

"The Belle View, eh?" Sean said. "That's very interesting." He turned to Kev and raised his eyebrows.

Kevin scowled at him and pushed Sean's arm away. "Do you really have to do it Cara?" he pleaded.

"What do you mean?" Cara said. "Do I have to go to work to earn the money to pay for me digs? You bet I do."

"But are you sure it's a good idea? You know what squaddies are like, they'll be all over you like a rash." Kev's hand went to his neck and he started to fiddle with the Saint Christopher that his Da had left him.

The cousins were close. And even though Cara was five years older than him, Kevin had always looked out for her. But now he was making her feel uncomfortable, being over-protective. She rested her hand on his arm.

"You worry too much, Kev. I can take care of meself. I'm keen to do a bit of overtime and anyway it might turn out to be an interesting night." She saw Sean give Kevin a nudge with his elbow and wondered what he meant by it. She changed the subject. "So Sean, when are you boys heading home? I wish I could be coming with you but, you know… too many commitments."

It was always Sean who arranged the schedule. He didn't trust Kevin to do the important stuff. He said they would be driving up to Liverpool the following afternoon and getting the night ferry. "It's been a good trip – very good for business," he said. "We've just got a few odds and ends to tie up before we go." And he squeezed Cara's leg and smiled at her. She made a half-hearted attempt to remove his hand.

Sean ordered Kevin to get in another round and he moved off obediently to the bar. He glanced briefly at Cara over his shoulder while he waited to get served. She realized something was bothering him, but she had no idea what. That was the thing about him; sometimes he would just clam up. *Probably something to do with a girl*, she thought.

When he returned with the drinks, Cara looked at her watch. "Jesus, I'll have to knock this back in a hurry. Three more minutes and I'm going to have to love you and leave you."

Suddenly Kevin started up again. "Are you sure about this, Cara? Yer mammy wouldn't be too pleased at you canoodling with the British Army. Give it a miss and stay and have a few drinks with us."

"Let it go, Kev. My mind's made up. Like I said, I need the money."

"If you're short of cash, girl, I can help you out."

Suddenly Sean slammed his glass down, slopping beer onto the table. "Look Kevin! It's none of your business!" And he pointed his finger menacingly in Kev's face. "Hear that son? None of your bloody business."

This was the side of Sean that sometimes scared Cara. She shifted uncomfortably on her chair and then drained her Martini, stubbed out her cigarette and got up to leave.

Suddenly Kevin leapt up. "Don't you have a friend who can do it,

Cara? I thought yer mam was going to cook up a special breakfast for us tomorrow, being our last day here and all." He snatched Cara's coat from her chair and held it tight to his chest.

She frowned at him, puzzled at his concern. "What are you so worried about? I'll be finished by six, I'll still make the fry-up. Come on now Kev, give us me coat."

"I'll walk you to the hotel then," Kevin said.

"For fuck's sake let the lady go!" Sean roared. "She's a big girl now. Leave her be."

"I'll be fine, Kev," Cara said quietly. "Don't worry. It'll only take me 20 minutes. Here, give us a hug." And she put her arms around him and pecked him on the cheek. "Spikey! You'd better have a shave before you kiss me Mam" – she wrinkled her nose – "and a quick scrub under the armpits wouldn't hurt either!" She turned to Sean. "Bye, Sean. Don't let him drink too much."

She walked towards the exit and turned back to give them a smile. Then the door swung closed behind her.

Sean pulled out a cigarette and lit it. He didn't say anything for a few minutes. He took a long pull, drawing the smoke down deep into his lungs. Finally he said, "What the hell were you thinking, son? You don't seem to know when to keep your mouth shut. Now go and get me a whisky. And make it a double."

"I need a piss. Give me a minute." Kevin walked around the side of the bar and out of the back door towards the Gents.

***

It was unusually warm for October. The wind whipped up the salted spray from the beach and blew it into Cara's face as she walked along the seafront. She stood for a moment watching the inky water boiling and slapping up against the piles of the pier. The noise of the wind and the sucking and spewing of the waves filled her ears and deafened her to all other sounds. There were few people out at this time of night and those that were, had their heads bowed against the angry breath of the English Channel.

She walked on and for a second the wind dropped, before summoning its strength for the next round of battering. She shivered and turned to look over her shoulder. The darkness spilled out behind her, the streetlamps ineffective against the strength of the night. Had she heard something in that brief silence? She began to regret refusing Kevin's offer to accompany her.

She couldn't work out why he'd been so sulky when she told them about the job. She'd hoped Sean might walk her to the hotel but he'd shown no enthusiasm. She was disappointed, but it had been the same the last time he and Kevin had made the trip to England: Sean, angry and curt, bossing her cousin around like a baby brother and Kevin subdued. She didn't know why they were partners. It wasn't as though her cousin was a great businessman. As far as she could see, he was just the driver. But Mam was always pleased to see them, well Kevin at least. Cara had a feeling her mother had reservations about Sean, despite the way he tried to charm her.

She turned off Western Parade with its tired hotels and swinging *no vacancy* signs, into the lane that led to Queens Avenue. She wouldn't normally take this shortcut, but her shift started in fifteen minutes. She should have left the pub earlier. The narrow alleyway was sheltered from the wind and now the only sound was the clack of her heels on the cobbles. She was almost at the end when she caught an echo. Fear pressed into her back. She remembered something she had heard on the telly: *never look like a victim*. If she ran, if she *could* run on these bloody heels, if she bolted now, she would pull the predator with her. Ahead of her she could see the odd headlight on Queens Avenue. Just keep walking. Clack clack clack. Nearly there. Her body buzzed with electricity, sending shooting pains into her hands, into her stomach. Her hearing became painfully acute. She heard the rustle of clothing, the stiff creasing of an anorak. She braced herself to run, her muscles taut, her fists clenched.

***

He held her head down with his foot as he taped her mouth and expertly drew the black hood over her face. She was struggling, but it took little effort to lift her over his shoulder and lay her on the floor of the waiting van. She kicked out with her leg and caught him on the shin with the heel of her shoe. He opened his mouth to swear but closed it before the thought had become a curse. He took both her hands in one of his, using the other to bind the gaffer tape around them. Just before he slid the van door closed, he tucked a blanket around her. Her sounds were animal-like, the howls caught in her throat, choked by the tape across her mouth. Soon she gave up and lay still, snatching breaths through her nose, sick with the stench of petrol and the motion of the van.

The van pushed through the night. Every once in a while, the flash from a headlight penetrated the black cloth that covered Cara's eyes. Her head rolled from side to side. Her body slithered on the bare metal floor. She was swept helplessly into the side, pressed into sharp metal objects that probed the blanket and dug into her skin.

Eventually the surface changed and instead of the tyres humming on the tarmac surface of the road, they began to grind against stone and rock. She slid forward as the van descended. The driver pressed the brakes each time they seem to speed up and very slowly the van rocked downwards until it came to a halt.

For a moment there was silence. Cara braced herself, the fight returning. She would bloody well run this time. She heard the van door slide open and felt his hands on her ankles. As he pulled her forwards, she bent her knees and then shot her legs out in front of her. Her heels made contact with something soft and she heard him gasp. He released his hold and her legs dropped over the side of the van. She tried to sit upright, but before she could raise her body, he gripped her arms and pulled her up. For a second, he held her close to him. She could smell the beer on his breath and the stench of his sweat.

With his hands under her arms, he guided her, stumbling, across the jagged surface. Far in the distance she thought she heard the lowing of a cow. And then further away still, the sigh of waves licking the shoreline. On the warm wind she smelt the bitter scent of fox.

He pushed her down and she sat, her back against rough bark. She felt the cold blade of a knife slice efficiently up between her wrists, cutting the tape that bound her. Free for a second, she snatched at the air and her hand brushed the rough stubble on his face. Then he held her arms and drew them behind her back, binding her to the trunk with soft cord. His breathing was rapid, short breaths that sang of fear; of time being siphoned away. She felt his hand slip up, trembling, under the hood and she called out in pain as he eased the tape from her mouth.

"Let me go! I won't tell anyone, let me go!" But still he said nothing.

She heard the crunch of his feet moving off into the distance. The van choked into life and soon she was alone.

Next to the tree, a battered medallion glinted dully in the moonlight.

***

"Did you hear about the bombing, Mary? Sure wasn't it shocking?" Maeve had phoned her sister as soon as she had seen the news. "Doesn't Cara work in some hotel over there?"

"She does, but it was her day off yesterday, thank God. She'll be round later. She and the lads are coming by for a farewell fry-up. Though I must say I thought they'd all be here by now. Cara's mother looked out of the window, helicopters were circling round and a pall of black smoke hung over the rooftops down by the seafront.

"Well, get Kevin to give me a call before he leaves for the boat."

"I will so, Maeve. Love to Jim and the girls." Mary sat down and pressed the remote control. It was all over the BBC. Five dead, many injured.

Terrible.

And then she began to hum: *And we're all off to Dublin in the green, in the green, where the helmets glisten in the sun, where the bayonets flash and the rifles crash, to the rattle of a Thompson gun.*

Aanjay in a Troublesome Spot
David Reading

An advertisement pinned to the notice board of the local grocery store declared that there was a vacant post at the Ritz Cinema just a mile from Aanjay's little flat. From the telephone box outside the shop, Aanjay called the number written on the card and found himself talking to a rather serious fellow named Mr Salmon. Mr Salmon said he was the manager of the establishment, a role that he felt to be one worthy of respect in the community. A visit to the cinema, Mr Salmon believed, was an important part of social interaction in a world where people were becoming more and more remote from each other.

Over the telephone Mr Salmon stipulated that the successful candidate would be enthusiastic and hard-working. Aanjay felt he met both of those requirements. He had succeeded so far in life due to his gusto for living and learning. In the past, fellow students had been amazed at his vigour. While many of them were engaged in their night-time revelries, he would stay up until the early hours of the morning, reading books, checking facts and writing notes.

Mr Salmon proceeded to describe the role Aanjay was expected to perform. After the presentation of each film he would be required to patrol the auditorium picking up plastic cups, popcorn cartons, confectionery wrappers and any other debris discarded by members of the public. Next he would be required to sweep the floor of dust and dirt. Finally he would mask unwanted smells by means of a pleasant coconut and lime air freshener. *People come to the cinema expecting a high level of hygiene,* Mr Salmon said earnestly. *Therefore your role in the successful operation of our business is crucial.*

A week later Aanjay entered the Ritz Cinema as an employee, having landed the rather grand post of senior maintenance manager (a title that drew a gasp of admiration from Uncle Harish during a telephone call from Mumbai). The role would last for the entire summer, after which Aanjay would return to his studies. Mr Salmon's assistant, a young lady named Harriet, provided Aanjay with a broom, a plastic sack and a badge on which his name and his position were written. Unfortunately his name had been misspelled, for which Harriet apologised sincerely. Aanjay felt this to be inconsequential, believing that a person's name was nothing more than a row of letters. One's identity, he told her, was something more complex than that: something fashioned by one's genetics and experiences. Harriet was wide-eyed with admiration at Aanjay's understanding of such matters.

On his first day Aanjay was surprised to see how much litter had been cast aside by members of the public. He was certain that one plastic sack was not enough, an opinion that he conveyed to Mr Salmon. As a result he was given a second sack: a promotion of sorts. At the end of each film presentation both sacks were filled to bursting with plastic, cardboard and paper.

On his second day, Aanjay discovered a bomb taped underneath one of the seats in the back row of the cinema. Members of the public had already begun filling the front seats in readiness for the afternoon showing of a cartoon about a talking horse. Aanjay noted that the film had received flattering reviews, and soon the cinema was likely to be filled to the very brim. This concerned him. He wondered whether it might be possible to borrow a pair of scissors from Mr Salmon and cut the wires, but this was not a plan that was ideal. He had once seen a documentary on the television about a bomb disposal chap named Trevor, and Trevor had made it clear that the disposal of a bomb was not a trouble-free enterprise; simply cutting the wires at random was fraught with potential hazards. Exploding the bomb inadvertently would not be a satisfactory outcome.

Mr Salmon was shocked and alarmed when he heard news of the bomb. Aanjay could see panic in the poor fellow's eyes and urged him to remain outwardly composed. A calm demeanour is essential, he said. *We must keep a clear head.* Aanjay instructed Harriet to telephone the police, which she did, but he was concerned that the bomb might explode before they arrived. Therefore he decided to act. *Mr Salmon,* he said, adopting his most solemn voice, *please ensure that the building is evacuated. This must be done with the minimum of fuss, as you will readily accept. You must leave too. Find a place of safety and allow me to deal with this rather prickly situation.*

Alone with the bomb, Aanjay wondered what his Uncle Harish would advise. No doubt he would recommend Aanjay's swift departure from the scene of the problem, but this was a poor option. There would be a grave risk to anyone who had tarried behind and remained in the foyer. He lay on the floor next to the bomb and carefully studied the wires, attractively coloured blue, green, yellow and red. He tried without success to remember Trevor's approach.

Aanjay looked around him and noticed, with satisfaction, that Mr Salmon had successfully cleared members of the public from the auditorium. It was then that he heard a voice cry out.

Mummy!

On the far side of the cinema he could see a little girl. He realised Mr Salmon, in his panic, had overlooked her. Aanjay got up and walked across the auditorium, to where the little girl was sitting. She cried out again.

Mummy!

Aanjay now faced a taxing dilemma: whether to return to deal with the bomb, or to tend to the little girl's requirements.

What is your name, my precious? he asked.

It's Jasmine, she replied.

Jasmine, where is your Mummy?

She's not very well. She's gone to the toilet.

Aanjay tried to take hold of Jasmine's hand, but she pulled away and clung tightly to the arms of her seat.

We have to leave, he said in an impressively commanding manner. *Let's find your mummy together.*

She said I must wait here, Jasmine countered.

Aanjay had heard people use the expression *between a rock and a hard place* and he thought this turn of phrase described his present predicament admirably. He had no further time to mull over the aptness of the metaphor or the seriousness of the situation because at that moment the bomb went off.

Aanjay found himself propelled forwards on to the little girl. There was a dreadful roar as the walls and the ceiling disintegrated, covering him and his new friend with debris. As the sound died away and the ceiling stopped falling, he could see Jasmine's face pressed up against his own. Her eyes were wide open with shock, which Aanjay thought to be understandable. He tried to move but the weight of the debris held him down. His first thought was that it would be his job, as senior maintenance manager, to clear up this mess.

His second thought was that he might die. This seemed a likely prospect, but Aanjay had lived a rich, fulfilling life and death was not an overwhelming concern. In a conversation about reincarnation, Uncle Harish had once remarked that he, Harish, had been a shoemaker living in Madras in a previous life. Aanjay thought this to be unlikely. He believed that we were all here to enjoy this present life as far as possible, and help others to enjoy theirs, with the knowledge that one day we will all pass into what amounts to little more than a deep sleep. If anything, this was a prospect that was quite satisfying: he liked sleeping.

He remembered another interesting discussion with Uncle Harish, which took place during the funeral of their good friend Ishaan. Uncle Harish said that a person on the point of death might see the events of their life parading before their eyes, as if watching a film. Uncle Harish believed that if Ishaan had experienced this phenomenon himself, he would have been reminded of his many good works as a clerk in the Ministry of Heavy Industries and Public Enterprises. Aanjay thought back over his own short life. What had been the most memorable event? There had been many. But one he cherished was listening to his mother as she spoke on her deathbed in the Bhagwati Hospital . *Aanjay,* she said, *remember the meaning of your name and draw strength from it. You are The One Who Can Never Be Defeated. Live up to that name.*

Aanjay's thoughts returned at once to the little girl named Jasmine.

He sincerely hoped that whatever his own fate, she would be protected from harm, having been shielded by his body.

He was mulling over these thoughts when he felt the weight on his back lighten. He heard people speaking. Someone pulled him gently from the rubble. He found he could stand up without help. He looked up at what was once the roof of the Ritz Cinema and saw the blue sky. It was then he realised he had been holding Jasmine's hand tightly in his. She tugged at his hand and with the other pointed past the rescue workers to a woman in a red coat. *That's my mummy,* she whispered. As she was carried away, Aanjay called after her: *Always honour your mother, Jasmine. Remember – she is the one who named you.*

The House Sitters
Alexis Krite

Rupert walked quickly back through the orchard, away from the sound of splashing and the desperate, muffled calls echoing up from the bottom of the well. Last night's rain flicked off the toes of his sandals, and his feet skidded on the wet leaves. In his hurry he slipped and fell awkwardly onto a pile of rotting apples. A haze of inebriated wasps rose haphazardly up into the trees. He covered his ears with his hands and lay there, his heart thudding, until he thought the cries had stopped. Three, four, perhaps five minutes went by and when he moved his hands away, all he could hear was the abusive complaints of the wasps. Relief swept through him and he felt almost giddy with euphoria. By tomorrow afternoon, no-one would be any the wiser.

***

Rupert and Pauline had arrived at Elmwood House four days earlier. As per the instructions, the keys were located under a plant pot next to the old stable. The front door was solid oak and seemed reluctant to let them in. Rupert found he had to shove it brutally with his shoulder at the same time as turning the key before it relented. He rubbed his arm and called to Pauline in the driveway. "You'd better carry the cases in. I can see this is going to stir up my rheumatism." Pauline nodded, heaved the cases out of the boot and carried them up the stone steps to the house.

The door opened into a wide entrance hall and they stood for a moment, looking around them. Persian rugs lay on the dark, polished floorboards and sunlight drifted through the mullioned windows and rested on walnut, mahogany and oak furniture. Pauline dropped the cases just inside the door. "Blimey Rupert, we're going to have to be very careful. Wipe your feet. Better still, take your shoes off."

Rupert did as he was told and then ran his hand around the frame of an oil painting which was hanging on the carved panelling in the hall. It depicted a couple of dogs ripping apart a stag. He whistled in astonishment. "Henry certainly isn't short of a bob or two."

"Time he gave you a pay rise then. Still, it's very generous of them to let us stay here."

"They're not letting us stay here Pauline, we've got a job to do."

"We're only babysitting a little cat. It's just like a holiday really."

"So where is this cat, then?" Rupert said, and pulled a packet of cat treats out of his pocket. "What's the betting it's some poncey Siamese? Puss, puss, puss, come on." He rattled the cat treats.

"It's got a name, Rupert." Pauline ducked her head under a Pembroke table and then peered behind the grandfather clock, calling as she did so. "Horatio, Horatio!"

There was a thud from upstairs, followed by a long, painful cry. Another call heralded the arrival of an enormous grey cat. It sat down on one of the rugs and glared disdainfully at its minders. It wailed again. Rupert dropped a cat treat on the floor and Horatio pounced, trapping it with a huge paw. He looked up at Rupert, his eyes narrowed, his ears flattened against his head and he hissed threateningly.

"Aggressive little thing, isn't he," Rupert said.

"I expect he just wants a bit of love." Pauline bent down to stroke its soft fur. "Who's a lovely fluffy boy then?"

Horatio struck with extraordinary speed and raked a claw through her forearm. She screamed and looked at Rupert in a state of mild shock.

"So that's the way it's going to be!" she snapped, nursing her sore arm.

They saw little of their charge for the next couple of days but diligently cleaned the cat litter tray, left food and water and washed his bowls each night. They would see him occasionally, glaring at them from the top of the bookcase in the lounge or hunched under a cupboard. They learned to give a wide berth to every piece of furniture that provided shelter for him. He had taken to shooting out a scythe-like claw each time they passed him. After a day of bleeding ankles, they chose to wear thick socks over their jeans.

There was a terrace butting up to the back of the house, with a pergola covered in jasmine. The flowers were brown now but still exuded a faint sweet smell. It was here they ate their meals, looking out across the wooded valley where a line of pylons marched, bringing electricity to the hamlets and villages of this half-forgotten corner of Devon.

But on the third day it rained and so they were forced to eat inside.

Pauline called up the stairs, anxiously looking around to check that Horatio wasn't lying in wait for her. "Do you want dinner in the dining room, Rupert?"

"As long as we can shut that bloody cat out!" He hoped the Bennetts hadn't bugged the house before they left for the Caribbean.

Later they would wish they'd eaten in the kitchen.

Rupert blamed Pauline for what happened. He'd wanted to indulge her. She seemed to relish a taste for the high life and insisted first of all that they sat at either end of the Georgian mahogany table like a country squire and his wife. But it became a nuisance each time one of them had to pass the salt or ketchup, so halfway through his fish fingers, Rupert picked up his plate and sat next to Pauline. His place mat had an image of an old master's painting of pheasants and rabbits being plucked and skinned by a large, rosy-faced woman. He moved his plate to cover the worst of the carnage.

He was careful to place his wine glass on the little round coaster Pauline had set before him.

After dinner Pauline offered to wash up so Rupert could adjourn to the lounge to search on the NHS website for suspicious moles. Nothing, as yet, seemed to match the irregular shape he'd found on his thigh. But then the NHS hadn't been too clear about the stabbing pains in his abdomen or the lump that had grown between the toes of his left foot. He decided to try an American website. They seemed to offer a more varied range of symptoms and diagnoses.

Suddenly Pauline called out in alarm. "Rupert! Can you come here a minute?" She was back in the dining room, wiping the table frantically with a cloth.

"Look at this! Look at this mark, Rupert! Just look!"

She pointed to a heart-shaped stain next to Rupert's place mat.

He studied it closely, spat on his finger and rubbed it. The spot remained, staring up at them, more mouth-shaped than heart-shaped now. Pauline gave it a rub with the cloth; it made no difference.

"Oh my God, Rupert, this table must be worth *thousands*. What have you done?"

"It wasn't me. I used the mat. I used the coaster. I didn't spill anything."

"Well, it certainly wasn't me. I was nowhere near it. It *must* have been you!"

"OK, OK, don't panic. I'll look on the Internet, there must be a simple way to remove it."

Rupert fetched his laptop and began tapping away.

"Right, it says here, to remove wine stains mix toothpaste and bicarb of soda, rub the mixture in, leave it and polish with a cloth."

Pauline rummaged through the kitchen cupboards. Rupert ran upstairs and grabbed the toothpaste from the bathroom. They prepared the mix, rubbed it in to the mark and smoothed it off with a cloth.

The stain had broadened now, its edges creeping out across the deep red sheen of the wood.

"Oh God, it's got bigger. What else, what else?" Pauline's voice was rising in panic.

Pinterest suggested car wax. Rupert found the key for the garage, unlocked the up-and-over door and found the wax stored in a box labelled *car cleaning materials*.

The mark didn't disappear but at least now it was quite shiny.

Pauline was anxiously searching the Internet. She looked up from the screen. "This site says mix a little mayonnaise with paint thinner and gently rub with wire wool".

They looked at each other in alarm. Paint thinner?

Pauline brushed her hair back from her face, took a deep breath and rested her hands on the table. "Let's just wipe it down with a damp cloth and leave it till morning. Maybe it will vanish overnight once it's had time to absorb the toothpaste and the bicarb and the car wax…" Her voice trailed off.

They went to bed. Soon Pauline was snuffling and sighing as she always did. But Rupert lay awake. He listened to the rain slapping against the window and the creaking of the rafters. He couldn't stop thinking about *the mark*. He began to sweat. A fox barked and in the trees behind the house two owls started up a conversation. Rupert stared into the darkness.

His boss had trusted them.

His boss's wife had trusted them.

They would both be livid. It wouldn't be easy finding another job at his age.

Tomorrow he would try paint thinners.

Morning came at last. Rupert dressed and went down into the dining room. Pauline followed, hardly noticing that Horatio had attached himself to her dressing gown and was being dragged like a polishing mop across the floor.

She peered over Rupert's shoulder. "Still there?"

He nodded. "Bigger."

And it was true. The mark had spread now, resembling a map of Ireland.

They tried the thinners. They added more mayonnaise. They gave it a light dusting with fine wire wool. The mark grew in front of their eyes.

That night Rupert lay awake again. There must be *something* that would shift it! In his mind, he concocted potions and unguents to disguise the mark. Finally he drifted off briefly but woke with a sudden pain in his jaw and pressure on his chest. He moaned. This was it then, finally, a heart attack. But he didn't have the strength to get up and turn on the Internet or reach his phone to call 999. He nudged Pauline. "I'm dying".

She threw an arm out and immediately the pain and the weight were gone. "It's just Horatio lying on you. Go back to sleep."

Sleep! Ha! Rupert wiped his face and felt the dampness of his own blood where the cat had scored him while he had been asleep. The beast was sitting on Pauline now, purring noisily. Horatio's eyes reflected the sickly light from the moon as he stared into Rupert's face.

The next day they were back in the dining room first thing. Rupert bent over the table, this time applying a topcoat of vinegar and brown shoe polish. The mark had grown again and now it was a fair representation of Winston Churchill.

Suddenly there was a loud tap on the windowpane. An old man in a flat cap was peering through.

"What the hell you doing in there?" he called out. He pushed his head through the half open window: "I see you! Buggering about with that table. That's Mrs Bennett's pride and joy, been in the family for years. It's worth a bloody fortune. What you doing to it?"

Rupert jumped. "Nothing," he said. In a panic he covered the mark with his hand, feeling like a small boy who had been caught out. The man pushed his cap back and Rupert realised it was Reg, the old retainer who supplied the house with wood, looked after the chickens and generally fixed things that needed fixing.

Reg disappeared from the window and next minute there was a rattling at the back door as he let himself in. He appeared at the entrance to the dining room and took off his boots. "Let me have a look at that," he growled. Reluctantly, Rupert lifted his hand.

Reg stood over the mahogany table, shaking his head and muttering. "Bloody hell! You're really in for it! They'll be mad as hell!" And he stabbed a gnarled finger at the shape that now seemed even more conspicuous. "I warned them not to trust anyone in here, I told them to put the cat in a bloody cattery but they wouldn't listen. They didn't want him to be disturbed they said. Disturbed! They'll be disturbed when they hear about this. What the hell did you do to it?"

Rupert stood up straight and attempted to sound confident. "Look, we're sorting it out. There's absolutely no need for the Bennetts to be bothered with it."

Reg narrowed his eyes, shook his head and looked slyly at Rupert. "They'll be bothered, all right. 'Cos I'll make *sure* they know about it."

Having said his piece, he shuffled towards the door.

Pauline seemed unperturbed. She was thumbing through a copy of the Yellow Pages. "Rupert, look, I've found the name of a furniture restorer based in the town. Let's give them a ring."

But Rupert's confident manner had abandoned him. He held little hope now that anyone would be able to return the table to its former glory.

Pauline dialled the number and someone answered almost

immediately. She made an appointment for the following morning and believing all was now well, went back to the kitchen to prepare lunch. Through the window Rupert watched as Reg, the only witness to this debacle, shambled off down the gravel path towards the orchard.

Suddenly Rupert rushed to the door, pulled on his sandals and raced after him. He wasn't sure yet what he was going to do, but there had to be *something*. Panting, he caught up with Reg as he was throwing down corn for the chickens in the orchard.

He decided to appeal to the man's better nature. "Look Reg, it'll be fine. We've got a furniture restorer coming tomorrow, so there really is no need to worry the Bennetts with this."

Reg didn't even look up. "You people always seem to think you can get your own way," he sneered. "I saw what I saw and that's that."

Rupert wasn't sure what Reg meant by *you people*. He tried another tack. "Well, how much then?"

The old man straightened up and faced Rupert. "You what?"

"How much not to tell them? I mean they won't know. It will all be sorted by the time they come home. Probably."

"How much? You ruddy townies are all the same, think you can fix everything with a bit of cash." He tipped the last of the corn on the ground and shook the bowl. "But you can't, see? Because you can't buy *loyalty*." Rupert wasn't entirely sure he agreed with this and was considering arguing the point, but Reg rambled on: "I been working here 60 years, that's three generations of Bennetts." He wiped his nose with the back of his hand. "They trust me see, because I'm *loyal*." He moved off, still muttering about loyalty and then turned and called over his shoulder. "I warned them. You can't trust strangers, I said, and

I was right." Rupert saw the self-satisfied look on the old man's face and his panic turned to anger.

"Can't trust strangers," he repeated. "Anyway, I got work to do."

Rupert tagged along after him, furiously kicking apples as he went and disturbing a couple of sheep who were dozing under the trees.

In the middle of the orchard was a small enclosure. Propped up beside it was an old bath. The green scummy water that lay in the bottom was obviously intended for the sheep. Reg tutted at the bath and then climbed over the rickety wooden fence. On the other side was a circular concrete surface with a metal lid in the middle. Grunting with the effort, Reg lifted the lid, which was the cover to an old well. He saw that Rupert was standing there watching him and spoke gruffly to him. "Hand us that bucket."

Rupert looked around and saw a galvanised bucket with a piece of rope tied to the handle. The other end was attached to the fence. He passed the bucket to Reg, who took it without even saying *thank you*. Reg dropped the bucket down through the open wellhead and began to draw up water. Suddenly Rupert's foot slipped and caught on the now taut rope. He moved his foot to the right with a sharp jerk, as if to free it. Then somehow, quite by accident, Rupert told himself later, the rope came loose from the fence. The bucket shot back down the well and Reg, still gripping the rope tightly, lost his footing and disappeared with it.

***

Now that the splashing had stopped, Rupert stood up. He batted away the disgruntled wasps and walked casually back towards the house. The sun came out from behind the clouds, bathing him in light. For the first time in days, he felt calm. He would sleep tonight.

A white van had pulled up on the gravel drive. It sported the sign: *Antique Restoration Ltd.*

Strange, he was sure the chap Pauline had phoned was arriving *tomorrow* morning. Oh well, the important thing was that he was here.

Pauline was standing next to the van talking to a tall man in overalls. She threw her hands up when she saw her husband approaching and shouted. "Rupert! Would you believe it? This is the furniture restorer, but not the one we phoned. The Bennetts had already booked this gentleman before they left!" She was almost hysterical with relief.

The man laughed. "Yes, apparently one of the grandchildren spilled nail varnish remover on the table when she was painting her granny's nails." He picked up a small toolbox from the back of his van and almost as an afterthought, turned to Rupert and called out.

"By the way, how's old Reg these days? Haven't seen him in a while."

Rupert looked down at Horatio, who was sitting at Pauline's feet. The cat stared up at him, unblinking. Rupert locked eyes with the smug grey cat, and answered in a remarkably steady voice that surprised even him.

"How's Reg? Well, I believe."

Superstition
David Reading

Children often accept things their parents tell them without question. And this was one of those things. Suzanne had been told as a child that bad luck always comes in threes. Her mother had said it, and Suzanne had never questioned it. It had become almost a scientific fact.

On this particular day, she slipped while coming downstairs in her socks and landed painfully on her tailbone. Later that morning she backed the car into a statue she'd bought at the local garden centre: the image of the Greek goddess Artemis. It had stood in the front garden for years without incident, and now it was missing an arm.

And then came occurrence number three. Throughout the afternoon she'd been waiting for something to happen. And here it was. Arriving home from her yoga class she found her husband on the landing crouching over a dead bird.

"My God, what happened?" Suzanne asked.

"She's got a broken neck. She must have found her way into the bathroom," Craig said quietly.

"How do you know that?"

"It's obvious. You must have forgotten to close the window when you went to yoga. She probably flapped around the bathroom for a while, found her way on to the landing and flew smack bang into the wall."

Suzanne was standing rigid at the top of the stairs. "Why do you keep saying *she*? How can you tell a crow's sex?"

"It's not a crow, it's a raven. The female raven is a bit smaller than the male. That's how I know it's a she. If you'd bothered to educate yourself you'd know about these things."

He looked up at Suzanne and saw she'd turned away from him. Her head was bent forward, pressed against the landing wall. "Oi, what's the matter with you?" he said. "It's only a bird."

"You know what the matter is," she bleated.

"What?" Craig stood up, holding the dead bird roughly in his hands. "What are you going on about?"

"You know what I'm going on about."

Craig thought about this. And then it came to him. "It's that bloody woman in the Waitrose car park, isn't it."

Suzanne's silence told him he was spot on. "For God's sake, wise up. You don't really take that seriously, do you?"

"She predicted it," Suzanne said. "No, not *predicted*. She made it happen."

"Made what happen? Come on, don't have one of your crazy turns. How the hell could anyone have made this happen?"

"She said there would be a sign, remember? A black bird."

Suzanne didn't have a coherent explanation but she knew there were people who had what her mother called *The Gift*. And they could use that gift for good or evil.

Craig took the dead bird outside and buried it in the garden next to the compost heap. He was worried a fox might dig it up and leave its carcass in the middle of the lawn. Then all this superstitious nonsense would start all over again. He found a rock and placed it on top of the newly-prepared bird grave.

Suzanne stood watching him through the window on the landing. And in her mind she replayed the incident that had happened ten days before.

She and Craig were heading towards the exit at Waitrose. Craig was pushing a trolley loaded up with bags full of shopping. It was the day before his 30th birthday and Suzanne was planning a special birthday dinner. But Craig was not in a good mood. There had been a row with a woman who'd parked her trolley across the aisle, and then he'd lost his temper again when the checkout girl rang up a pack of smoked salmon twice.

As they left through the exit, Suzanne saw a woman in the car park with a purple shawl wrapped over her shoulders. On her left arm she held a basket and in her right hand a sprig of heather. There were looks of mild discomfort on the faces of the other shoppers. They glanced up at the sky, down at their feet, towards the other side of the car park, anywhere but into the eyes of the woman who was hoping to persuade them to part with their cash. The clever ones veered away before they came anywhere near her sphere of activity.

But the old woman was standing next to Craig's BMW. They couldn't avoid her.

Instinctively she seemed to know Suzanne was the vulnerable one. She pushed her offering under Suzanne's nose.

"Lucky heather, dearie? This will bring you years of good luck."

Suzanne was indeed the vulnerable one and mechanically she reached into her pocket. But Craig got in first. Before she could pull out her purse, Craig, already in a bad mood, began to yell abuse at the old woman. Later Suzanne couldn't remember exactly what it was he was shouting, but it was the force of his anger that shocked her rather than the words he spoke.

His rage subsided as quickly as it had erupted and as they got into the car, Suzanne thought the episode was over and opened the window to take deep breaths. But suddenly the old woman reappeared, banging the flat of her hand ferociously on the car roof. And leaning through the open passenger window, she spoke the words that ten days later would come back to haunt Suzanne.

Listen hard to what I'm telling you. Be sure that you will regret this day. I declare that misfortune and calamity will fall upon you. The sign shall be a black bird. When you see that sign you will know that one of you will surely die.

Craig opened the driver's door as if to get out but then thought better of it. Shouting more abuse, he reversed out of the parking space and pulled away.

Suzanne was silent for the rest of the journey home.

***

When Craig came inside after burying the dead bird, Suzanne tried to explain why she felt the way she did, but in the end she realised it was pointless. Craig was the pragmatic one in their relationship, a hardcore humanist who didn't have an ounce of belief in him. He got into one of his moods. They hardly spoke to each other for the rest of the day.

Next morning Suzanne lay on the bed staring at the patterns on the ceiling. She fought against the image of the old woman in the Waitrose car park. She wanted to believe the woman was a mad old bat and the raven turning up like that was just a coincidence. She heard the front door slam as Craig left for work, still so irritated with her that he didn't even say goodbye.

She took deep breaths and pictured quiet pastoral scenes in order to exorcise the images playing around in her head. When she'd come off her medication, the doctor had given her mental and physical exercises to perform whenever she felt a panic attack coming on. He'd told her to imagine she was sitting on a riverbank on a peaceful sunny day, surrounded by flowers. Nothing could upset her. He'd told her to breathe deeply from the pit of her stomach, allowing her imagination to focus on beautiful things: flowers, birds, trees, the ripples in the river, and so forth.

Lying on the bed with her eyes closed, Suzanne breathed in, breathed out, saw a bright golden light, saw cuddly bunnies, bluebirds and a tiny fawn like Bambi. She began to relax. But then her imagination took her to another place. There were black birds, thousands of them, mobbing her relentlessly, swooping down and pecking at her eyes. This was no longer Disney, it was Hitchcock.

Suzanne got off the bed and threw on some clothes. She left the house, got into her car and headed off into town. She knew what she had to do. She had to find that old woman and put all this to rest. Unless she did that, she would never sleep again.

***

The road was wet that morning after a night's rain. She drove in a frenzy, doing 40 in a 30 limit as she came along the main road into town. She had to brake hard when the lights at a pelican crossing turned red. She sped off again, skidded on the wet surface, hit the kerb, turned the wrong way down a one-way street, did a three-point turn to get back on to the main road.

She pulled into the Waitrose car park, found a parking space, turned off the ignition and took deep breaths. *Am I going crazy?* she thought. *Is this just going to make things worse?* She got out of the car and looked around for the old woman. And there she was, lurking at the store entrance, her basket over her arm.

As Suzanne approached, the woman turned and smiled. It wasn't a pleasing, welcoming smile. To Suzanne it was a malevolent grin. She hesitated, alarmed by the menace she sensed. The woman stepped forward, thrusting a sprig of heather out in front of her.

"Lucky heather, dearie?"

Clenching her fists, she struggled to remember the script she'd put together in her head. But the only words that came from her lips were: "I'm sorry."

"Come on, dearie, this will bring you years of good luck."

To Suzanne, those words seemed like a taunt.

"I really am sorry," Suzanne said, a little louder. "We didn't mean to upset you." She ignored the sprig of heather that had been pushed under her nose.

"What do you want?" the woman demanded.

Suzanne hesitated.

"Well, what do you want?" she repeated impatiently.

"I want you to remove the curse."

For a second, the woman looked blank. "The curse?"

"The curse you put on us. You said one of us will die."

The old woman raised her eyebrows. "Ah yes. *That* curse."

"It's nonsense, isn't it. You were just trying to frighten us."

"Frighten you?"

Suzanne wasn't sure whether the woman was completely on the ball with this. She ploughed on. "It was a few weeks ago, here in the car park. My husband upset you. You said one of us would die."

The old woman narrowed her eyes and stared at Suzanne. Then she sprang into life. "Yes," she said, "yes it's true. One of you *will* die." Suzanne was aware someone else had joined them but she ignored the newcomer and pleaded again. "Look, can you stop all this? Please."

The old woman stared at the ground. She was silent for what seemed like the best part of a minute. Her friend didn't interfere.

"Please," Suzanne said.

The old woman looked up sharply. "It is already written," she replied. "I cannot change what is already written. I say again. *One of you will die*. It has to be."

Suzanne turned around, walked back to the car and got in. There was nothing more to be said. It was true then. *One of us is going to die*, she said aloud, slumped over the wheel. *So which one of us will it be?* She knew she couldn't live day in, day out, with the excruciating anxiety, waiting for fate to answer that question for her.

She said it aloud again, to herself. *Which one of us will it be?* The answer came to her. Suzanne knew that at 5pm exactly, Craig would be getting off the train. And at 5.15 he would be taking his usual shortcut through the copse at the back of the house. She reached under the driver's seat for the tyre lever that she kept there for protection. She cradled it in her hands for a few moments. Then she started the engine and set off.

Outside the store, the old woman's friend watched as Suzanne drove away. "Who was that, Ethel?"

Ethel shook her head as she stared at the departing BMW.

"I've absolutely no idea," she said blankly.

Father's Day
Alexis Krite

When the end finally came, it came suddenly. Mick was in the yard when he saw the black Range Rover gliding ominously up the track towards the farmhouse. Three of them got out and he knew what they were there for. They looked sympathetic as they told him the news but he still felt angry. They had come with an order: stop milk production immediately or face the consequences.

Mick didn't argue. He was prepared for this moment, catastrophic though it was. Everyone had warned him: his neighbours, the Agency, the vet. People were amazed he'd got away with it for so long.

And now the big bony Holstein cows had gone. Sent to market to line the pockets of other, more efficient dairy farmers. Mick leaned on the gate of the yard. Farming was all he had ever known. He gazed at the stack of silage bales and breathed in the sweet smell of fermenting grass, tightly packed in black plastic. Unused, the bales would moulder and eventually slip down onto the cracked concrete. He could look for a buyer, but he knew the effort of phoning around and negotiating a sale wasn't worth it. Let them rot.

Just then, a breeze sighed through the empty milking parlour. It set the loose rusting sheets of corrugated iron keening as they lifted and fell with the wind. Funny, he'd never noticed the sound before.

But now it filled the silence. All his life he'd lived with the background of lowing cows, a bull bellowing, calves calling for their mothers and the pump humming as Dad started on the milking. Thinking about it, it was after his Dad's death that the rot began to set in. Jenny couldn't deal with his depression and left him and their boy Rob. But the lad wasn't interested in farming, and now all he did was the bare minimum and spent his time boozing with his mates and goodness knows what else. Mick knew he should be bitter but he just didn't seem to have the energy, even for that.

He shifted uncomfortably in the June heat, sweat trickled down his back and his blue and white checked shirt clung damply to his belly. Where the buttons were missing, or where the barbed wire had snatched at the fabric, tiny breaths of air poked and flickered against his skin, bringing some relief from the heat.

The cat brushed his leg and reaching down to stroke her he saw a red elastic band, dropped by the postman. He picked it up, scraped his straggling white hair into a ponytail and looped it into the band. He rubbed his neck, enjoying the coolness of the air on his skin, then stretching his back he pushed himself upright against the top bar of the gate.

Narrowing his eyes against the sun, Mick looked up towards the hill. He could make out a clump of sheep lying under the oak on his neighbour's land. He cursed. They would have pushed their way through the fence and spilled onto the lush grass next door. He turned and whistled for Rosie, who lay panting in the shade of the old Ford Escort that was parked up next to the track. Moss lined its door seals and the windows were green with filmy layers of mould. One by one the wheels had been removed to replace those on some trailer or other.

When he'd bought the car for Rob's seventeenth birthday, Bahama Blue and shiny and only 40,000 on the clock, he'd imagined the boy's excitement. But Rob had taken one look and said, "I ain't learning to drive, Dad, no way." And that had been that. Gradually it began to rust and settle into the earth. Now Rosie used it for shade and the chickens laid their eggs on the back seat. The house seemed to be composting down too. The window frames were soft to the touch; you could push your finger right through the wood. There was mould in the kitchen and the bedrooms and the carpets were covered in filth. Outside, ivy had colonised the stone walls.

He'd have to shift those sheep. He gave Rosie a nudge with his foot and reluctantly she stood up. For a moment, her legs trembled. She shook her matted black and white coat and then after a few stiff steps she seemed to remember where she was. She looked up at her master, barked and slowly wagged her tail. Mick flipped her ear affectionately. "Come on then, girl, let's get them buggers." Rosie followed him as he shambled along the track: limping, humped over and worn out by the wet, the wind, and the price of milk.

***

When they got back to the farmhouse, Rob's quad bike was parked carelessly in the yard with two wheels up on an old railway sleeper and the boy was sitting in the kitchen eating beans from the can. A motorcycle magazine was open on the table in front of him. Mick kicked off his boots and went to the fridge. "Where've you been all morning?" he barked. "You moved those pigs of yours yet?"

Rob looked up from his magazine and shrugged. "I've been busy."

"Doing what? No don't tell me – you've been wasting your time with those so-called mates of yours."

The boy swore under his breath. Mick ignored him and pulled opened the fridge door. It was empty except for a carton of milk and six bottles of cider. He took out a bottle and held it up. The liquid inside swam with clots of apple sediment. He hadn't been desperate enough before to drink it, but now with the milk cheque gone…

He turned to his son.

"So come on, what are you doing about the pigs? They been in that wood for weeks now."

The pigs were Rob's latest enterprise. He'd bought fifteen piglets and set them free in Fosters Copse. It had seemed a good way of getting more money from the government; the grant was given for maintaining woodland. Fifteen pigs should clear the brash without him having to lift a finger. But there had been complaints that the pigs were extending their territory. The police had been to the farm twice now and told them to fence off the copse.

"I can't deal with that today," Rob snapped. "I've got the lads comin' round."

Mick gave a sigh of exasperation. "What are you doing hanging around with that lot. All stoned out of your heads half the time. Call yourself a farmer?"

Rob stood up and threw the empty can into the rubbish bin. "No, I don't. Not after watching you make a right mess of it." And he strode towards the door.

"Go on then, bugger off out of here!" Mick hurled the full bottle of cider at the boy. It missed and smashed against the wall. The yellow liquid ran across the flagstones, snaking through the piles of dirt and broken glass before disappearing down a crevice under the Rayburn.

Rob turned, a sneer on his face. "Oh, by the way, Dad. Happy Father's Day!" And he disappeared out of the door.

Mick sat down at the table and stared at the debris: unopened bills, cracked plates with congealed food stuck to them, a carburettor wrapped in a filthy cloth. That was where he'd found the note from Jenny. Right there on the kitchen table. Almost five years ago. A note on the table after 18 years of marriage. Didn't even have the courage to tell him to his face.

Mick opened the drawer in the kitchen table and took out a screwdriver. He got up and moved slowly through the doorway into the hallway, wincing from the pain in his knee. Since his fall in the barn, he'd slept downstairs in what had been the parlour in his mother's day. He opened the wardrobe door and sank stiffly to the floor, using the foot of the bed to steady himself. He listened for a moment. All was quiet except for Rosie's snoring in the kitchen.

In the corner of the wardrobe was a pile of clothes. He moved them to one side and swept away the dust from two screw holes. He'd fitted the wardrobe himself and had left one floorboard that was easy to take up. Turning the screwdriver, he liberated the screws, prised up the board and heaved out a heavy tin box.

Inside lay his Dad's war medals and his Mum's wedding ring. He picked up a small soft bag and weighed it in his hand. It contained his childhood collection of foreign coins. *Fat lot of use now*, he thought, *all bloody euros.*

Next to the bag was a roll of ten pound notes: the only money he had left in the world. He counted it out: just fifty pounds. It was the last of the good times money – from the days when he could hide away the price of a prime milker or a batch of spring lambs. He stuffed it in his shirt pocket, closed the box and carefully placed it under the floorboard before heaping the clothes back on top.

He changed out of his muck-covered jeans into his slacks. They had a few stains on them but the washing machine was broken and he couldn't be bothered going to the laundry. It was still hot outside and so he changed his work shirt for a yellow t-shirt with *'Florida!'* emblazoned on it in red. The souvenir of someone's trip of a lifetime. These days he bought all his clothes from charity shops. Not that he bought much at all.

In the kitchen he looked in the mirror that hung above the sink. He should tidy up his beard really. It had separated now into two long white tails. But what was the point? He'd get round to it sometime.

He left the dog in the cool of the kitchen and got behind the wheel of his pickup. He usually went to the local supermarket just a few miles away but today he fancied going a bit further and he didn't want to bump into any of his well-meaning but nosy neighbours. The county town was a good twenty-five miles away.

***

Mick parked up in the supermarket car park among the four by fours. It didn't look like any of them had ever seen mud, let alone been stuck in a tractor rut. *Money to burn*, he thought.

He filled the trolley with tins of beans, canned soup and instant mashed potato. He avoided the freezer cabinets. At home the ice box was impossible to penetrate. It had become a cave of ice and old fish fingers. On the way to the chiller cabinet, he passed along the seasonal aisle. It was buzzing with children and their mothers. He looked at the Father's Day cards and remembered the ones Rob had brought home from school. It couldn't have helped, Jenny leaving like that, but maybe he should have done a better job with the boy. He fancied a couple of bottles of beer but instead, he thought he'd treat Rob and so he threw in an apple pie and a pot of cream.

At the checkout he unloaded the trolley and waited while the girl wiped streaks of milk from the belt with cleaning fluid. He was standing there, his bags open as he got ready to pack, when he noticed a debit card still in the payment terminal. He pulled it out and lifted his hand to give it to the girl.

Then without thinking, he slipped the card into his pocket.

***

He loaded the shopping into the pickup and checked his watch. It was twenty past three. He felt for the debit card in his pocket and before taking it out, placed his thumb over the raised letters of the account holder's name. He didn't want to know whose card it was; that would make it stealing, and he wasn't a thief. In the top left corner was a symbol with four curved lines. He didn't use a card himself, he preferred cash, but he had watched people using these things. They seemed to tap the card on the payment machine and bingo! Shopping paid for.

He'd never stolen anything before and he couldn't really understand why he didn't just go back to the shop and hand in the card. But he closed the pickup door and turned the key in the lock. He wasn't ready to go back to the farm. He fancied a wander around the town, to feel clean tarmac under his boots for a change, instead of the usual mud and muck.

The place was busy. Everywhere he looked he saw young Chinese people, foreign students no doubt. The girls were dressed in tiny skirts and skimpy tops and the boys in knee-length shorts and expensive looking t-shirts. They ambled along in groups, chattering and slurping drinks through straws. The boys seemed to be carrying all the shopping: paper carrier bags with flashy names on the side. Then there were mothers pushing prams, some tripping along in heels with their phone held to an ear, others in trainers, aggressively shoving pushchairs in front of them, their white bellies hanging out over the top of too tight jeans. *So many people.*

He looked through the shop windows at the queues of customers waiting to pay for purchases and wondered at the amount of money changing hands. Of course it wasn't really *money* it was all plastic and credit and overdrafts. You wouldn't catch anyone at Molton livestock market taking plastic. It was cash or nothing. He felt the card in his pocket and scratched his nail over the numbers. Probably by now it had been reported missing and stopped. Probably.

He saw a sign in the window of a men's outfitters: Father's Day Sale. *Why not?* he thought. In the shop, his eye was caught by a row of dazzling summer shirts. He stood by the rail and slid the hangers along one by one. He stopped at a particularly bright shirt with a Hawaiian design: green palm trees with an orange volcano rising up in the background and two red parrots thrown in for good measure. He unhooked the hanger and held the shirt up against him. As he was standing there an assistant came up. "Want to try it on?" he asked. Without thinking, Mick nodded and followed the lad to a changing room.

The shirt hung airily over his belly and felt cool against his skin. He pulled the elastic band from his hair and let it fall onto his shoulders. He smoothed his beard into one long tail. The curtain moved and the assistant put his head into the cubicle. "Nice fit, sir."

"Think so?" Mick turned and peered into the mirror again. The boy seemed to have a point. And hard as he looked, he couldn't see the farmer in his reflection at all.

"And some trousers perhaps?" the assistant suggested, looking down at the stained beige slacks. Mick thought of the last few pounds in his pocket.

"No, just this, ta."

At the checkout, the till rang up £15.99. He started to reach for his wallet and then realised the groceries had pretty much cleaned him out. He might even have to miss out on an evening pint at the pub. He looked at the payment terminal.

"Contactless?" the girl at the counter asked. "Just tap the card please."

He drew out the card and holding his breath, gingerly touched it on the machine. A loud peep and the receipt began to print.

"Do you need a bag sir?" she asked. He nodded and just like that she slipped the shirt into the bag and handed him the receipt.

As he was walking away Mick heard the girl talking to the next customer. "Oh sorry, there's a £30 limit on contactless. I'll need you to put your PIN in."

Thirty pounds? Back in the sultry late afternoon heat he opened the bag and the tropical shirt stared right back at him.

Emboldened by this first success, he quickened his step and headed for the department store on the corner. The men's section was upstairs and as he held on to the rubber handrail on the escalator his hand began to sweat. Ahead of him he could see a red *sale* sign above a row of jeans and other assorted trousers. He glanced at his watch; he'd had the card for fifteen minutes. He snatched a pair of chinos from the end of the rack: 44-inch waist, regular length. They would do. He hurried up to the counter and as the assistant rang up the price he banged the card on the machine.

"You were a bit quick there sir, I'll have to start again."

His heart started to beat faster and he could feel his face was flushed. But the assistant didn't even look at him as he rang up the price again. "Twenty-four ninety-nine please." This time Mick laid the card carefully on the terminal, again a beep and the receipt was printed.

"Do you need a bag? Five pence."

"No you're all right, thanks." And Mick stuffed the trousers into his carrier bag on top of the Hawaiian shirt.

In the square outside the shop, he dropped heavily onto a bench. His body crumpled forwards and between his legs he could see his spoils sitting in the open carrier bag. He folded over the top of the bag and lifting it up tucked it under his arm. His armpit felt wet and he could smell the rank vinegar stink of his sweat.

As he made his way back to the pickup, he looked up at the town clock. It was only four o'clock. What the hell. He turned and strode into the large chain chemist next to the express supermarket. He picked up a basket and filled it with spray deodorant, shaving balm and shower gel. In his head he totalled up thirteen pounds. While he was waiting in the queue he threw in a bag of disposable razors.

Tap, beep, and the receipt was stuffed into his pocket.

He straightened up and walked confidently out of the chemist and into the little supermarket next door. He left with a bottle of wine, an avocado, a jar of olives and a packet of brie.

***

Rob walked in to his father's bedroom, swaying slightly. "Bloody hell, Dad! Smells like a brothel on a Friday night in here!"

Mick was sitting in his underpants pulling on his socks. "And you'd know what that smells like would you?"

"Are you off out then? What about me dinner?"

"It's skittles night, remember? You'll find some food in the fridge. But don't you touch that avocado. It's mine, see?"

"Yeah, but Dad, aren't we gonna watch Deal or No Deal?" He sounded like a small child again and for a moment Mick softened. "Sorry boy, I can't, playing Willerton tonight, big match. Get some of your mates to come round." And then added quietly, "if they're not too wasted."

Rob slumped sulkily out of the bedroom and pulled a pouch of tobacco out of his pocket.

"And don't you smoke that indoors," Mick called after him.

He was glad to see the boy take his cigarette off up the lane. He wanted to slip into the pickup without any stupid comments about his new shirt and trousers. He felt the card in his pocket dig into his thigh and wondered if anyone had reported it missing yet. In the driving mirror he could see Rob behind him. The boy was leaning up against the hay barn, flicking his ash onto the ground. *Bloody idiot*. Mick started to open the door to get out and give him a rollicking but then he thought of the comments he'd get in his new outfit and pulled the door closed again.

***

The pub was packed with the skittle teams and their supporters. Mick nodded and waved as he made his way through the crowd to the bar. "Pint of the usual please, Sandra," he called out. The landlady raised her eyebrows as she took in his new shirt. "Sure you don't want a dark rum instead, Mick?"

He felt a nudge in his ribs. "Aye up, Mick! Better get me sunglasses on!" Pete Lee, the Willerton captain, was standing there with his mate, Des Brown. In his hand he was holding a glass tankard with World's Best Dad engraved on it.

"Yeah well, you can push off, Pete. You won't be so cocky when we demolish you lot tonight. Nice glass by the way, that from your boy?"

Pete smiled and nodded. "Yeah, he's a good lad, real hard worker."

"Lucky man," Mick muttered under his breath, as he tapped the card on the machine that Sandra held out to him.

"Unfair competition I call it – trying to blind us like that," Des said with a laugh. "Hey Sandra, give us a tequila sunrise, old Mick's put me in the mood for something exotic!"

Pete moved in close and spoke more quietly. "Joking aside, Mick, sorry to hear about your problems. You'll miss that old milk cheque. How's Rob taken it?"

"Lazy sod's well pleased. He don't have to get up before dinner time now."

"Still, it can't be easy."

The three of them stood for a moment silently staring at the optics. You were always one sheep away from disaster in this game.

"Hello, Mick."

Mick turned to see a familiar face. She'd put on a bit of weight, her hair was yellow now, the natural blond long gone and of course she was a bit older. But he had no problem recognising her.

"Jackie Wilson! Well I'm blowed, haven't seen you in a long old while."

The two of them had been at school together and while Mick stayed on the farm, she'd moved to London, secretarial college or something. He'd always felt it had been a mistake to let her slip out of his life. But what would he have done in London? Farming was always going to be his destiny.

She smiled and gave him a hug. "It's Jackie Tucker now, remember?"

How could he forget? They'd all been invited to the wedding. He remembered the man she married. A bit stuck up, the locals thought.

Jackie turned serious. "Harry died, you know, heart attack."

"Yeah, I'd heard. I'm sorry. How are the kids?" Mick remembered she'd had two, or was it three girls?

"Well, they miss their Dad of course, but they've both got kids of their own now." She brushed her hair back from her face and smiled coquettishly. "I'm a glamorous granny!"

Jackie stepped back and took a long look at him. "Well Mick, you seem well. You got a bit of, I don't know, a bit of zest about you. Reminds me of the old days." She'd heard about Jenny leaving, about the depression he wouldn't admit to. It was nice to see him looking happy.

"Had a good day that's all," Mick said. He finished his pint and felt the card in his pocket. Worth one last try.

"Come on then, Sandra," he called across the bar. "Let's have a round over here for Jackie and the lads. On me. What you having, Jackie?"

"You sure, Mick? I heard things weren't too good."

He wiped the beer from his beard and looked at her closely. It was still there, he thought, the kindness in her eyes.

"Not so bad I can't treat me old girlfriend. Come on, what is it?"

Jackie asked for a white wine. The till rang up £25.90 and Mick tapped the debit card on the machine.

He raised his glass to his teammates. "Here's to a whitewash!" he said.

They moved off to the skittle alley and flipped a coin for the first team to play. Willerton won the toss and Des called out, "OK boys, phones off, you know the rules."

***

Half an hour later the door of the skittle alley burst open and the landlady rushed in. "Mick! They've been trying to call you!" She sounded frantic.

Mick was leaning forward, about to bowl. He stood up straight, the ball still in his hand. "What's going on?"

"There's a fire up at your place. Get up there fast."

Jackie grabbed her keys from her bag. "Come on Mick, I'll take you," she called out.

***

The hedges hadn't been cut on the Strawbridge Farm and they could smell the smoke long before they could see the black column spiralling up into the night sky. It blocked out the stars and spewed flakes of ash into the air. Mick wound down the passenger window and as he breathed in, the acrid stench of burning plastic caught in his throat.

Jackie pulled up behind the fire engine and Mick leapt out before the car had stopped. He ran towards the inferno but the heat held him back and he could feel the pricking of burning ash on his scalp. The barn was ablaze and wet blackened bales of hay were slithering to the ground where the firefighters had soaked them in an attempt to slow the flames. The house was hidden by a heavy pall of smoke but the occasional flare shot out through the broken windows and illuminated the wreckage.

Mick stood helplessly in the yard, shielding his face from the intense heat with his hand. He felt someone taking hold of his arm and looking round he saw it was a young firefighter. "Are you the owner, Sir?" Mick ignored the question. "I'm looking for my boy – lad in his twenties. I think he's inside."

"There's no one there," the firefighter said. "There's just a dog." Another firefighter was holding Rosie in his arms. She lifted her head when she saw Mick and her tail moved weakly. The fireman brought her over to Mick and he stroked the collie's singed back.

The quad bike was still in the yard, its tyres flat and smoking. Mick could feel his chest tighten and his eyes were stinging with tears and smoke. "Where is he then? My lad? He's gotta be here." He tried to get closer to the burning buildings, but the heat drove him back.

"There's no-one in there, Sir, I'm telling you. He must have driven off somewhere."

"He don't drive!" The feeling of panic was taking control. *Stupid, stupid man!* he thought. *Why didn't I tell him to put that bloody cigarette out?*

Then he had a thought. "The caravan. He's got to be in there." He turned to the fireman. "It's in the barn behind the house."

The flames hadn't reached the barn yet but the smoke had. Through the fog they could just make out the long green shape of the caravan inside. Mick tore off his shirt and wrapped it round his head, trying to breathe through the fine cotton.

The door to the caravan was closed and as Mick went to wrench it open he felt the skin of his hand stick to the handle with the heat. Someone came up behind him and pulled him back. "Come on, Sir, leave it to the professionals!" Mick lashed out wildly but the man was younger and stronger and heaved Mick away from the smoke and leaned him up against the fence. He dropped to the ground, weeping and calling his son's name. As he sat there, he realised Jackie was crouching down next to him. She put her arm around him. "Come on, Mick," she said gently, "if he's in there they'll get him."

Suddenly she began to shake him. "Oh my God, Mick! They've got him." Mick looked up to see his son's limp body being carried in the arms of the young firefighter. Behind them another boy was slumped between two men, his feet dragging as they ran with him away from the barn. A great cracking sound shot up into the air and flames licked along the ancient oak beams as the roof fell in, engulfing the caravan and sending sprays of shattered tiles like shrapnel over the heads of the onlookers.

***

Next day the weather broke and a veil of fine summer rain was cleansing the air of the stench of burnt plastic and scorched roofing sheets. Pools of black mud lay like spilled ink on the track and sagging oak beams tipped from the stone corners of the house. The roof was open and gaping like a huge mouth drinking in the rain. Des pulled up his collar. "Well, boy, it's a bit of a mess."

"You could say that!"

Mick had spent the night at the hospital. It was touch and go for a while but just after six Mick received the news that Rob and his mate were still in intensive care but over the worst. They allowed him to spend a few minutes with his son and for the first time in years Rob cried. "I'm sorry, Dad," he said. Mick put his hand on Rob's and spoke gently to him. "I told you smoking was bad for you, didn't I?" And they both managed to smile.

"You'll be home soon, boy."

The minute he'd said it, he saw the look in Rob's eyes. There was no home. Not anymore.

***

And now, as he stood in the charred ruins of the farmhouse, Mick wondered what *his* Dad would have said. When Dad had run the farm, the yard was spick and span, *a place for everything*, he used to say, *and everything in its place*. The cows were milked bang on five every morning and at five on the dot in the afternoon. All weathers. He'd left the farm in Mick's hands and assumed he would look after it in the same way. Mick felt a wave of shame. He hadn't been much of a son and now, he realised, not much of a father either. A plaintive sound at his feet made him glance down and there was the cat. He picked her up and ran his cheek along her fur.

Des stared at the blackened remains. "You got your paperwork in order, Mick?" He thought he knew what the answer would be.

To his surprise Mick replied, "Insurance you mean? Yeah, couldn't get that last loan from the bank without it."

"Well then, you can crack on and get this place up and running again or throw it away on a trip to the Caribbean. What are going to do?"

Mick thought about his Dad, thought about Rob.

"You reckon I could put a new parlour in, maybe one of them pre-fab barns? "

"Yeah, why not? Get your milk licence back." Des stood with his hands on his hips. "Bit of potential here, I'd say."

Just then Mick's mobile rang. He put the cat down and slid his hand into his pocket to get the phone. His fingers touched the debit card and the receipts of the day before. He let the phone ring.

"You believe in karma, mate?" he asked Des.

His friend looked blank. "I wouldn't know about that. Come on, let's go and get a pint. You and Rob can stay at my place 'til you get back on your feet."

The phone rang again and this time he answered it. "Mick, it's Jackie, you all right, love?"

He smiled. "Not so bad, Jackie. Could be worse." He pictured Rob in the hospital. "A lot worse."

"Well, come round to Linda's, I'll be there for a few more days. I'll cook us a meal tonight. Six o' clock."

He slipped the phone back into his pocket and pulled out the debit card. He stared at it for a moment. Then with a scowl he threw it into the slurry tank. The card sat on the scummy surface, slowly turned on its side and slid gracefully down into the mire.

One who cheats death.
Eight Letters, Ending in *R*
Alexis Krite

"I'm telling you, Sal, it will be amazing." Elaine closed her eyes, picturing the scene. "There you'll be, floating on your back in the Ionian Sea. Absolute bliss."

"Why floating?" I asked. "What's wrong with breaststroke?"

She shook her head, frustrated at my inability to visualise.

"Because the warm water will hold your body and the waves will gently rock you backwards and forwards. It will change your life." She made it sound like a baptism. "You'll lie there, with the sun on your face and all you'll hear is the creaking of the cicadas."

Judith came to life at that moment. "Cicadas! Three down. Seven letters beginning with C. *Insect with exceptionally loud song!*"

"Bloody hell Jude, you ruined the moment! Just for a minute I was back in Kefalonia." Elaine reached across and put her hand over mine. "Seriously Sal, you'll love it. It really *is* the best feeling ever," she whispered. "I only wish I could come with you."

Perhaps she wouldn't have said that if she'd known what was going to happen in Lefkada in two months' time.

It was the second semester and we were enjoying our usual lunchtime get-together in the mean staff area at the University's Centre for English. The daily crossword session had become a craze. Whoever finished teaching first would rush down to Reception, grab the Independent, dash back upstairs and slap the paper on the table.

Judith was in her usual upbeat mood. "Right. One across. Eight letters: *person in great distress*. Third letter is F." She looked expectantly at the circle of faces around the table.

Elaine leaned over, her arms folded beneath her. "Sufferer?" Judith, more often than not the scribe, wrote the letters in the blank boxes.

"OK. What's three across then?" I asked, peering over her shoulder.

"*Rush of water, transport,*" Judith replied.

Marion stopped raking through her pasta and prodded her fork towards the page. "Jet?"

Judith began writing it into the grid. "Yep, brilliant, so taking one across and three across, that makes *sufferer jet*." It had taken me months to realise that the two words at the top of the crossword were somehow connected, but Judith had sussed it out long ago.

***

I have always loved crosswords and this lunchtime ritual had become the highlight of my working day. There were usually five or six of us calling out clues and suggestions, in between mouthfuls of Pret sandwiches and over-priced salads. It was a brief respite from the thankless delivery of knowledge to rich foreign students in an effort to make them even richer.

The department had become a repository for returning teachers, desperate now to work in the UK. The elasticity of their youth had taken them to China, Japan, Spain and even Rwanda in one case, but as the shadow of middle age crept up over their tanned legs towards their sun-dried faces, the words *pension, security* and *mortgage* had replaced *adventure, escape* and *discovery*.

As far as crosswords were concerned, we all seemed to have our specialisms. I was the one they turned to for clues that had a religious element (my convent education qualified me for that). Mark, lanky and bespectacled, was the science expert. Elaine was the literature queen and Marion the historian. New members included Paul, the legal expert, and Angelo, who, despite struggling with the English language, was our economics ace.

At home, while I was cooking, I would sit at the table and work on one of the Guardian online crosswords. I made sure there was always a crossword book in my car, in my bag and even in the bathroom.

***

It was because of my obsession with crosswords that our lunchtime topic of conversation had turned to Greece. Three weeks before the start of semester two, I found myself sitting in the dentist's waiting room without a puzzle. On the table in front of me was a pile of magazines. I hate magazines. Whenever the hairdresser offers me one, I attempt to express my intellectual superiority by smiling politely and refusing. I then open my bag and lift out some weighty novel. But now, as I was waiting for a filling, I didn't have a novel *or* a puzzle. I picked up a magazine, noting it was the most recent addition (less likely to have been coated with weeks of germs) and flicked through it. And there was a crossword. No-one had attempted it.

I was alone in the waiting room. The receptionist was busy on her computer, presumably booking a weekend break and trying to look as if she were dealing with the accounts. She showed no interest when I took out a pen and began filling in the grid. I was quite scornful at the ease of the puzzle; this was nothing compared to what the Independent or the Guardian would require in terms of general and specialist knowledge. '*To tumble; a season.*' Well, *Fall* of course. I had almost finished when the nurse called me upstairs and, without thinking I slipped the magazine into my bag.

That evening I fished the magazine out and was about to put it in the recycling when I decided to finish the puzzle. While my potato was baking away in the oven, I quickly filled in the words and was preparing to bin it along with the empty wine bottles and cardboard food containers when I noticed something. The magazine was offering a prize for the first correctly completed crossword to be received. I glimpsed through the list of prizes, only half interested. I had never won anything in my life. The first prize was a week for two in Lefkarda, one of the Greek islands. The second was a £100 voucher for Lidl and for the ten runners-up, there were free meals at Pizza Express. *Oh what the hell*, I thought, and cut out the completed puzzle and entry form. I popped them in an envelope and stuck a second-class stamp on it. On my way to work the next day I stopped by a post box, mailed the form and then forgot about it.

To my astonishment I won.

***

"Who are you going to take with you then? Oscar?" Judith closed the paper with a satisfied slap, another puzzle completed in record time. She had a point: it *was* only me and my cat. It always had been. Not the same cat of course. They tend to expire after about 15 years, but there was no-one else. I hadn't spoken to my sister since she despatched both our parents to a care home. And there was no partner. I had never quite understood the dynamics of a relationship and despite my adroitness at crosswords I couldn't seem to read the clues in a real-life puzzle. I was always surprised when the latest man left.

A holiday for two. I looked around the tables. Marion had two young children. Elaine was great but she had an aversion to flying after a crash landing in Tanzania. Angelo was caught up in an ardent liaison with the geography teacher. And the thought of asking either Paul or Mark gave me the creeps. In the corner were a couple of retired male teachers who were only working, it seemed, because they couldn't bear their own company at home, or that of their wives. So that only left one person.

I smiled at Judith. "I suppose it will have to be you." She leapt up from the table, waving her arms. "Yeah! Take me to the land of Retsina and Ouzo!" Anyone else would have hugged me, but we looked at each other for a second and both unconsciously decided against any physical contact. I could see this would be a classic, booze-fuelled week for one of us. Jude would be off hunting among the herds of Greek men inhabiting the tourist bars and restaurants and I would be sitting by the pool. Doing crosswords. A glass of wine in front of me.

***

The hotel provided us with a pleasant two-bedroom apartment. My balcony looked out over the beach. As soon as we arrived, I stepped onto the warm marble tiles in my bare feet and leaned on the railings. The evening sun was low in the sky and seemed to be balancing on the water. *I should have taught in Greece rather than Poland*, I thought. I was standing there, breathing in the warm evening air, when I felt a slight tremble in the floor. The windows seemed to shiver for a moment and then stop. Judith called out to me: "Did the earth move for you too?" She thought it was funny. I wasn't so sure.

Elaine was right about the Ionian Sea. She was also right about the sun and the cicadas. The air was heavy with the scent of orange blossom and pine. The locals were friendly and very taken with the colour of my eyes, although while one waiter informed me blue eyes were considered lucky, another drew back a little, crossed himself and, I swear, spat into the sand.

I got up early in the mornings and wandered down to the little bakery. The smell of freshly baked bread and bougatsa will stay with me forever. Without waiting for Judith to get up, I would buy a slice of the cinnamon topped pastry and eat it as I walked along the beach, the warm sand pressing up between my toes. I discovered spanakopita on our first day on the island: *a Greek pie made with filo pastry, dill, feta and leeks. Eleven letters.*

Judith was very blasé about the whole experience. She had spent quite a few holidays in Greece and even a teaching stint in Athens for a while. Apparently that had ended badly. She looked shifty while she was telling me and I thought it best to leave the subject at the point where she said, "Of course everyone else knew the school owner was a sex maniac, but no-one thought to tell *me*."

On the fourth day I made a decision. I would rent out my house in England and move to Greece. It seemed there were at least six English schools on every street and they were all crying out for native speakers, or *naked* speakers as Judith called us.

We were due to leave for home on Saturday evening and in the morning I got up earlier than usual. Judith's door was open and her bed was empty. I'd heard her return around midnight with Nikos or whoever it was. The cement walls and floors carried every sound and I'd clamped on my headphones and tried to sleep, as Joni Mitchell serenaded me. Shortly afterwards the door slammed and I assumed they'd gone off to continue their bar crawl. Judith was obviously making the most of her last night here.

I wandered along to the bakery. The owner was pleased to see me and nodded towards the tray of bougatsa. I smiled and pointed to the steaming squares of spanakopita. "Ena, parakalo." After all, if I was going to live here, I should start to learn the language. She, however, was having none of it. "One piece of spanakopita, one bougatsa, anything else?"

I took a bottle of water from the fridge, paid and left with a "Yassou!" to which she replied, "Goodbye, see you tomorrow."

I strolled along the beach for a while and then settled down at the poolside, empty at this time of day. A disturbed night and the warm sun made me sleepy and I moved my sunbed into the shade of the overhanging balconies for fear of getting burnt. I soon dozed off, the half-eaten bougatsa on the table next to me.

The bottle of water, mercifully, was still tucked into my pocket.

"Quick! Train's coming! Hurry up or we'll miss it!" Mum was shaking me as the train thundered through the station. Or was it *under* the station? The platform was swaying and the train was spitting out fire and lumps of dust. I reached out to grab my mother's hand but I couldn't move. I couldn't find my hand. I tried to shout but my mouth was stuffed with something dry, something gritty, something that shouldn't be there. And still the platform rocked and still the train rumbled and thundered underneath me.

And then there was silence. Just for a moment. But soon the earth came back to life, it roused itself and creaked and groaned as it shook off the dust and rusted ribs of steel that had bound particle to particle. I tried to open my eyes but they were locked closed. I should stand up, brush my hair, and wash my face. I drifted back to sleep. Mum was there again. "You see? We missed the train! It's all your fault! There won't be another one for days."

My left hand was heavy, too heavy to move. But I managed to bring my right hand up to my mouth and hook out what I could with my forefinger. I tried to spit but I had no saliva. Something was pressing into my right thigh. It was the water bottle. I edged my fingers towards it and then wrapped them around the lid of the bottle. I gripped it and slowly, very slowly, drew it out and pressed it against my side. From there I brought it up to my mouth and caught the lid with my teeth. I turned the cap and almost choked as the water flooded into my mouth. But at least I could spit now. I poured a little on to my eyelashes and called out as the liquid dust stung my eyes.

There was a crack, a tiny opening, and through it I could see a pinprick of daylight. I shouted but no-one seemed to hear me. I drifted off again and the next time I managed to open my eyes there was blackness all around. I think I wet myself. For a while my legs felt warm and damp. It could have been blood though. I finished the last of the water and called out again and again.

There were times of light in the pinprick hole and there were times when all was dark. Sometimes I thought I heard movement, and once, I thought I heard voices. Crossword clues danced before my eyes: *catastrophic result of moving plates, not on a table. Ten letters.*

"Go away, Oscar!" He was sniffing in my ear. Sniff sniff sniff. I could feel his hot breath on my face. Someone lifted the duvet off and then a wet nose pushed itself into my mouth. I spat. "Disgusting cat!" The pinprick had become a sun now, in the darkness. I screwed my eyes up against the blinding light. There were voices all around me, arms reaching down and pulling me. A dog whining and scrabbling at me. A pain seared up through my leg and scorched into my groin. I screamed. More voices, loud, reassuring, gentle. And then a rush of air, tasting of blossom and moonlight, sea salt and pine, filled my space and shocked me into taking a deep breath. I gulped and filled my lungs.

As I allowed myself to be lifted from the rubble, I thought back to Elaine's words. She had been wrong. It wasn't my first dip in the Ionian Sea that would change my life.

It was being a *survivor*.

Carbon Copy
David Reading

Monday

Glenys picked up the envelope from the breakfast table and read the sender's name typed on the back. "Open it," I said. My hands gripped the edge of the table.

"It's from Wilson and Brown," she said.

"I know it is. Open it."

She tore at the envelope and let the letter fall out in front of her. "What does it say, Glenys?"

She glanced at it for a few seconds then threw it back across the table. "I'm sorry, it's not what you want to hear."

I steeled myself and picked up the letter. The word *regret* leaped off the page as if placed there on the end of a spring. The word had a desolate finality about it.

Three weeks earlier I had sent Wilson and Brown a copy of my novel, An Unbreakable Bond. They specialised in works set in the War years and my story was perfect for them. If Wilson and Brown weren't interested, no one would be. I threw the letter down and fell into a sulk.

Glenys leaned across the table, picked it up again. "They're very positive," she said. "Listen to this. *We honestly believe that you have a genuine talent but your work is not something that fits our portfolio at this present time.* That sounds like you came close to getting a deal."

"It's a standard letter. They never say what they really think, these people. They know how to let you down gently."

This was my third rejection in six weeks. I took one last look at the letter and stared hard, as if through telekinesis I could change the wording. But I was stuck with it. I placed it in a cardboard folder with the other rejections, tossed the folder casually across the table and prepared to get on with the rest of my life.

"Don't give up, Bob, please. Look at J.K. Rowling. She was shown the door dozens of times. Maybe the book just needs refreshing a bit."

Later that morning I went back to my latest draft, the one I'd sent to Wilson and Brown. I read through the first chapter wondering how I could improve it. But there was no way I could improve it. It was perfect.

Tuesday

Glenys picked up Wilson and Brown's second letter from the breakfast table and stared at their name typed on the back of the envelope. It felt like déjà vu. "Open it," I said. My hands gripped the edge of the table. "Give it to me straight. Have they changed their minds?"

As Glenys stared at the letter, I saw her face contort like she was in shock or pain. She didn't say a word. She just threw it across the table towards me.

I picked it up and began to read.

Further to our communication dated yesterday, March 13th, it began.

When I read those words I thought they had reconsidered, I really did. But then I saw that other word.

Plagiarism.

"What the fuck!"

Glenys was looking shocked, wearing the kind of expression I'd expect to see if she'd been shot in the back.

"This is madness," I said. "What the hell are they talking about?"

She stared menacingly across the breakfast table at me. "Tell me it isn't true, Bob. Tell me you didn't steal someone else's work."

"Of course I didn't steal someone else's work. If they're similar it's because two people had the same good idea."

"Not just similar," she said. "Read the third paragraph."

I read the relevant words aloud. I couldn't believe what they were saying. *Identical in almost every detail.*

Next thing I knew I was shouting, as if it was Glenys herself who'd written the letter. "That's impossible! I spent eighteen months dragging that thing out of the depths of my psyche. You saw me in there. Typing furiously, cursing, crying with anguish. Did I fake all of that?"

"I'm sorry, but this is just too incredible." She shook her head vigorously, clearly trying to make sense of what was happening. "Maybe someone hacked into your computer. Maybe he's the one who's the plagiarist."

"But why would anyone want to steal the work of a complete unknown? What would they get out of it?"

The letter from Wilson and Brown claimed that a member of

their marketing team had seen a print-out of my manuscript in a pile and decided to skim through it. When she read the opening pages something rang a bell. She did a spot of investigating online. And that was when talk of plagiarism began.

I read the final part of their letter. *This matter has been passed on to our legal team....possible action....plagiarism can be punished with a prison sentence.*

"And listen to this," I said. "Even the title's the same. An Unbreakable Bond."

"Bob, there's only one thing you can do. Give them a call. Get this sorted out for once and for all. Do it now."

And so I gave them a call. I got through to a receptionist named Sue, told her who I was and asked to speak to Anna Clemence, the name at the bottom of the letter. Sue, as cheerful as a lark, asked me to hold on. When she came back on the line she was a lot less cheerful. Ms Clemence would not speak to me. The matter was in the hands of lawyers. Wilson and Brown would write to me again as soon as their stance was clarified.

Sue hung up before I had a chance to plead my case. All I could do was wait for that third letter.

But no, there was more I could do. I went into my study, Googled An Unbreakable Bond, and this was what I discovered on Wikipedia.

An Unbreakable Bond is the debut novel by British writer Adam T. Chance. Published in 2009, it tells the story of two young brothers who, in 1940, are put on a train and transported to the Cotswolds as evacuees. The novel follows their respective adventures after they are separated by the actions of a heartless police constable.

Glenys came into the study to find me screaming at the computer. "What the hell is happening, Glenys? That's *my* story. Adam T. Chance stole *my* story."

By now she was unbearably calm, as she usually is in a crisis. "OK, answer this," she said. "When was his book published?"

"It says here 2009."

"And so?"

I answered slowly and carefully, like a child reciting a piece of prose from memory. "And so Adam T. Chance wrote An Unbreakable Bond eleven years before I typed my final paragraph. Eleven years!"

Wednesday

And so that third letter arrived and here it was sitting on the breakfast table, waiting to deliver a piece of news I knew I wouldn't want to hear. "Open it, Glenys," I said. My hands gripped the edge of the table. "Give it to me straight. What are they going to do about it?"

She tore at the envelope and let the letter fall out in front of her. "Read it, Glenys."

She read it quickly and threw it back at me. "Read it yourself, Bob. This looks bad and I really hope for your sake we can get it sorted out."

The letter had two scary words at the top: WITHOUT PREJUDICE. It consisted of three short paragraphs with Anna Clemence's signature at the bottom. Her name was becoming synonymous with menace. I'd never met Anna Clemence, but my mind had created an image for me to hate: early forties, black hair, thin red lips, fake smile. She had a husband shorter than her, who she dominated. She lunched at posh restaurants, shopped at Waitrose and drank Pavia Pinot Grigio with every meal. The three short paragraphs in her letter told me Wilson and Brown were taking no direct action. Anna Clemence didn't explain why, but reading between the lines it was clear that this was none of their business. Not directly. They had rejected my manuscript and so we had no professional relationship. But the final sentence told me this was all going to get worse.

We have been advised to contact the author of An Unbreakable Bond in order to draw his attention to the discrepancy.

Casually Glenys started to butter a piece of toast. "So they're leaving it to the author. That should get it sorted one way or the other, shouldn't it? What I mean is, you can expect a letter from Adam T. Chance any day. And then you'll be able to make all this go away."

Her relaxed attitude was beginning to annoy me. I stared across the table at her. "You believe them, don't you. You think I stole his work. You think I'm that unscrupulous. How long have we been married?"

She didn't answer. I have to admit that if it had been the other way round I wouldn't have known what to believe. I had no appetite for breakfast so I got up from the table and went into the study. There were a dozen copies of An Unbreakable Bond on Amazon. I ordered a copy and clicked next day delivery.

Thursday

I waited in all morning for the book to arrive but had to go out just before midday to buy wine. When I got back, a note had been pushed through the door containing a scrawled message from the delivery people saying a parcel had been left in the wheelie bin round the side of the house. I fished through the baked bean cans and cereal boxes and found a jiffy bag. It was stained with something that may have been ketchup. Back inside the house I poured myself a glass of wine and tore open the package.

It was a second-hand hardback copy with a coffee ring on the cover. It looked half decent but the artwork was amateurish, almost as if it had been self-published on the cheap. On the cover there was an image of two young boys in school caps getting on a steam train. They reminded me of characters in The Famous Five. I flicked to the end. Like mine, it was short compared with some of the stuff on the market: 272 pages. The title and author's name on the front were printed in an old-style typeface that was intended to suggest the War years. I looked at the inside cover for a picture of the author, but there was none. On the back I found a list of one-line reviews. *A tour de force*, said Publishers Weekly. *A very good read*, declared The London Review of Books rather lamely. There was nothing from the major papers, suggesting it wasn't worthy of their attention.

I placed the book on the table in front of me, next to a print-out of my manuscript. I poured out another glass of wine.

Glenys arrived at that moment. "So it came then. Have you started it?"

"I'm just about to."

"So what's stopping you?"

"Nothing's stopping me. I'm just getting psyched up."

"Look, just read it for God's sake. Let's get this whole thing over with."

So I opened An Unbreakable Bond at chapter one and began to read.

DAVID READING

I stopped reading at about half nine and Glenys opened a bottle of gin. I was in shock. She asked me about the book but I shook my head, saying I'd tell her about it once I'd finished. We drank, we argued, I became depressed. When we argue I sound like a whining child. She says it stems from me being abandoned as a two-year-old. Being brought up by a series of different foster parents gave me deep feelings of insecurity. That's her opinion, anyway, and who am I to argue?

Friday

I got up at six and read the rest of the book through the haze of a hangover. I turned over both sets of pages at the same time: comparing my words with those of Adam T. Chance. When the mail came through the door the noise of it hitting the doormat startled me. I expected to see a letter from Chance's lawyers, but it was just the usual junk mail. Glenys came down just before one o'clock and found me in the study looking depressed.

"My head feels like it's been kicked by a horse," she groaned. "So have you finished it?"

"Almost. I've just started on the last chapter."

"And?"

"Well, they're wrong. The two books are not identical. There are small differences in the language. He also uses a lot of semi-colons. I always avoid them. And there's a bit where he describes the sweet counter at the local corner shop. That's something I thought about but in the end I left it out. Too much unnecessary detail. But yes, the two works are almost identical."

I looked up at her in desperation. "So what do you make of that?"

She was standing in the doorway. There was an obvious distance between us. I looked carefully into her eyes. I saw scepticism in that look. She didn't believe me.

Glenys saw me staring, came closer and stroked my hair. "It's OK, I really do believe you. There has to be an explanation so let's find out what it is. A scam, maybe?"

"How could it be a scam? Copyright 2009 – remember? It's been around for years."

"I know, I know. I'm just grasping at straws."

I continued reading. And by the time I'd finished I knew what I wanted to do.

Saturday

We dropped into a posh-looking hotel in the main street at Chipping Campden and asked if they had any vacant rooms. There was a room free called The King's Suite, which was pricey but we took it. The girl on the desk asked what I did for a living and I said I was an author, which was a bit premature when you come to think of it. Obviously she'd been trained to take an interest in the guests and had a snippet of information of her own to offer: Graham Greene lived in the town in the 1930s. "Graham Greene? You know him? Brighton Rock?" I told her I didn't know him personally and she laughed at that. Under different circumstances I would have been thrilled to see the house where Graham Greene lived, but just hearing his name only served to make me feel more insignificant than I already felt.

The King's Suite was on the top floor, up a flight of dodgy wooden stairs without a banister. The door opened with a real key rather than a key card and once inside the first thing you saw were pictures of hunting scenes. A plaque on the wall said George the Third had stayed in this room on his journey to Stratford-upon-Avon. This seemed a flimsy reason to charge £215 for one night's stay, but it was the only room that was vacant.

"I'm terrified," I said as we started to unpack. "This could all go badly wrong."

"Clear it from your mind, Bob. For now, at least. This is a lovely town. Let's enjoy ourselves and worry about this tomorrow."

I took a copy of my manuscript from the case and threw it on to the bed. There was a point when I'd thought of burning it and deleting the file from the computer, but Glenys had suddenly come alive and reached for her phone. And before I'd had a chance to find out what she was doing, she was speaking to someone. "Kevin, it's Glenys Hawkins here. I need your help." It was that conversation that led us to this little town on a wet Saturday evening.

Sunday

We got out of the car and lingered for a while in the rain. We were outside a thatched cottage a mile from the town. It was a modest place, not at all showy. Adam T. Chance, it seemed, had not made a fortune from his writing but it was probably the kind of place you'd expect to find authors and artists who'd done moderately well.

"I'm not sure I can do this, Glenys."

"Yes you can. You just ring the doorbell and when the door opens you speak."

"What do I say?"

"You'll think of something."

"Is this really a good idea?"

A path of crazy paving led up to the front door. On either side of the door there was a large flower pot, each containing a shrub covered in white flowers. They were just like the ones I'd bought Glenys for Valentine's Day and she'd placed them outside our own front door. Spooky, I thought.

The house was called Hillside. Glenys had got the address from an old colleague who worked in IT at the Met. It seems you can find anyone if you have the right contacts. We walked up the path together and I rang the doorbell, clutching my manuscript in a large padded envelope. I couldn't hear a ring so I knocked on the door.

I didn't know what to expect, but what followed was certainly not on my list of possibilities.

Glenys said *bloody hell!* The guy standing there took a step back. His jaw dropped and that may sound like a cliché, but I swear it's what happened. His jaw actually dropped.

He was wearing a blue denim shirt like one I had at home. He had on a pair of black corduroy jeans. Exactly like a pair I had at home. But that's only a small part of it.

He recovered quickly and held open the door as a welcome. "*I know who you are,*" he said. "Come in. I'm Geoff. You must be Robert."

"But we're looking for Adam," Glenys said.

"That's my pen name, the name they gave me at the publishers. They said my real name made me sound too ordinary. They wanted me to have a name that sold books. Ridiculous, I know, but you go along with these things. My wife refuses to call me Adam and I don't blame her. Glenys is out at the moment. Hopefully you'll meet her later."

He led us into the living room and invited us to sit down. I fumbled with the package uneasily. He looked at it and smiled.

"I assume that's what the fuss is all about," he said.

We sat on the sofa and I looked around. There were copies of impressionist paintings on the walls. Exactly like ones we had on our walls at home. I glanced at the books in his bookcase: Len Deighton novels, John Le Carre, Alistair MacLean, alongside the more high-brow works of Shelley and Wordsworth. Just like our collection at home.

My eye was drawn to a photograph standing on the mantelpiece. It showed two baby boys sitting on a beach towel.

He got up, picked up the photo and stared at it. "Someone called me yesterday from Wilson and Brown. When they told me about your book I knew instantly who you were. I'd known for years that you existed but I could never seem to pluck up the courage to track you down."

He turned and stared intently into my eyes. "Didn't you ever get an overwhelming feeling: a feeling that part of you *was missing, or broken?*"

I thought back to those times when I'd been in the study writing and had been spooked by an eerie feeling that someone was with me, looking over my shoulder, standing right behind me. I'd just put it down to my over-active writer's imagination.

He placed the photograph of the two babies carefully back on the shelf and we sat down. He was looking at me, almost with a sense of wonder. I'd seen that look before, when Glenys had given birth and was holding our daughter in her arms for the first time.

"You know Bob..." And his voice had a tremble in it that made me feel quite uncomfortable. "I've read that twins have a psychic connection. But I had no idea how strong that connection could be." He reached across and touched my knee, as if reassuring himself that I was real. To my embarrassment, I saw he had tears in his eyes.

"I suppose that's why we called our book An Unbreakable Bond."

Jago Stark's Christmas Gift
Alexis Krite

Jago woke up with a start to see a face peering at him through the entrance to his makeshift shelter. The sun was catching the woman's blond hair and forming a halo around her face. For a moment he wondered if he'd died in the night. Then he noticed the sagging jaw line and crow's feet around her eyes. The woman dropped a plastic bag at the entrance. "Here you are love, there's some toothpaste, wet-wipes and a chicken sandwich." Then she shot back onto the path. Jago waited until she'd gone, crawled outside and tossed the carrier, with its contents, onto the grass verge next to all the other bags people had left. "Bloody do-gooder," he muttered to himself.

Back inside his shelter, Jago wormed down into his sleeping bag and pulled up the blankets. The wind had dropped and he realised he needed to get up soon and sort out the tarpaulin roof. One end of the lean-to was flapping where it had come loose from the fence; the other, weighed down by rocks, seemed fairly secure. He needed a piddle too. He'd give it another hour or so in case any more unwanted visitors called by. While he was burrowed in his sleeping bag, it was easy to avoid conversation. If he wasn't actually sleeping, he could pretend. He did most of his maintenance work in the dark, same as his ablutions and answering calls of nature.

He had arrived in this small country town in early November, almost two months before. His chosen pitch was up against a fence which enclosed a field and a bit of woodland. Although he'd set up camp on the footpath, he'd made sure there was enough room for pedestrians to pass by without having to bother him.

On the other side of the road there was a smart new housing estate and not far away a decent supermarket. Jago had been doing this a long time, at least thirty years now, and he had a good eye for a pitch. He'd been worried his new neighbours might take objection to him. He couldn't have been more wrong.

Jago heard a car pull up and a door slam.

"Evening Jago, I see you've had more visitors. We're going to have to get the council to clear all these bags. They're causing a bit of a health hazard." Jago peered out of his sleeping bag to see the local PC squatting at the opening to the shelter. This was one of the few visitors he was happy to see.

The PC opened a packet of cigarettes and handed one to Jago, who sat up to take it. The policeman leaned in and lit it for him. He tucked the rest of the packet just inside the entrance, then pulled out three bottles of cider from a bag and opened one for himself and one for Jago.

"Thanks, mate, you not on duty then?"

"No, I'm in my van, not the squad car." The two men were silent for a while, sipping their cider. "Quiet here isn't it," the officer said, thinking of his wife and their three teenage kids at home. With any luck, they'd be in bed by the time he got back.

"You warm enough?"

Jago nodded. "Yeah, had an ambulance stop yesterday, they dropped off a couple of nice blankets."

"You know, I can always put up the tent that the bloke across the road offered you."

"No, you're all right, thanks. This will do me fine."

"You had your dinner?"

"Yeah, shepherd's pie today. Number 43 brought it over an hour ago."

"Any good?"

"Not bad. Mind you, the liver and bacon from number 62 takes some beating. Oh, and number 44 give me some apple pie and custard."

"You OK for water? I can pick you some up before I go home if you want."

"No, the bloke from 59 got me a pack of six. Thanks anyway."

The policeman stood up, stretched his legs and groaned. "I'm getting a bit too old for this. Maybe I should consider early retirement." He looked up at the black clouds drifting in from the east. "They say it's going to snow overnight. My money's on a white Christmas. Are you sure you'll be OK?"

"I'll be fine." Jago was used to harsh weather. And with the blankets he'd been given he reckoned he'd do all right.

"I'll be off then, Jago," the PC said. "I'll call in on my way to the station tomorrow."

"Would you do us a favour before you go? Tell that old crone to push off, will you?"

A woman was hovering on the path, holding a large Sainsbury's bag. *What is it this time?* Jago thought to himself. *Why can't they leave me alone?*

The PC explained that the homeless gentleman had more than enough warm clothes and she scuttled away, relieved that she hadn't had to engage with the wild-looking vagabond whose head was poking out of his shelter, like a moth emerging from a cocoon.

After the PC had gone, Jago lay in his sleeping bag and began to reminisce. Christmas, eh? When he was younger, he used to enjoy Christmas Day at one of the homeless shelters. Those jolly volunteers doing their good deed for the year, a bit of banter with the other fellows and a slap-up meal. But for the last few years he'd given it a miss. One day was much the same as the next, but everyone had to keep reminding him about Christmas Day. He was in his sixties now and they said your long-term memory was better as you got older. He thought a lot, these days, about the past. Christmas Day on the Cornish farm had been a chaotic affair. Mum all red in the face and steamed up in the kitchen and then Grandad sitting in his chair shouting orders at the kids. There had been six of them then. Running around the place like demons, ripping up the wrapping paper from their presents and dashing into the kitchen to steal a mince pie, hot from the oven and getting a whack from Mum's wooden spoon.

And then Dad would get back from the pub.

That would be it really. The rest of the day would be spent trying to dodge the back of his hand and then creeping quietly upstairs so as not to draw attention to themselves. They'd huddle together, three to a bed, turning over their Christmas presents and sometimes swapping them. Whispered conversations in the dark until they heard Dad snoring and knew it was safe to come down for a secret feast of leftovers.

"Morning, Jago, do you know what day it is today?" Number 43 was stooping by the shelter entrance, looking inside. Jago opened his eyes and peered out from under his woolly hat. "Judgement Day?" he asked gruffly. Number 43 laughed. "It's Christmas Eve and I want to invite you to Christmas dinner tomorrow."

Jago closed his eyes. She was taking a chance. For all she knew he might not have any trousers on, or he might even be wearing a dress with stockings and suspenders. No one had actually seen him standing up, out of his sleeping bag, other than the creatures of the night.

"No thanks."

"Oh come on, Jago, I'll do the works: turkey, Christmas pudding." She stood up straight and towered above him.

"I've got a little gift for you too," she added.

Another pair of bloody gloves I suppose, Jago said under his breath.

He pulled his hat down over his eyes and pretended to sleep. But number 43 was persistent.

"Please Jago." He could hear the pleading in her voice. "Let me do this for you. I see you every day from my bedroom window when I get out of my lovely warm bed. It doesn't seem right that you should be out here. It just doesn't seem fair."

Jago thought for a moment. There was no way he was going into her house for dinner, but he hadn't had a bit of turkey for a long time. And he'd always been partial to sage and onion stuffing.

"Turkey, you say. What are you putting in it?"

"Sage and onion."

"Veg?"

"Roast potatoes, carrots and sprouts, although," she added hastily, "I can leave the sprouts if you don't fancy them."

Jago relented. "All right then, but you bring it over here." And then realising he ought to be a bit more gracious, he added, "Thanks very much."

"Oh lovely, thanks Jago." In a way she was relieved he hadn't agreed to come to the house. It was fine talking to him in the fresh air, but she wasn't sure she really wanted to socialise with him in an enclosed space, especially with the central heating turned up full.

A couple of hours later number 62 called out to Jago. "Cooee! Anybody there?"

Jago slid further down into his sleeping bag. *What was this? A bloody séance?*

"I know you're in there." Number 62 could see his bulky outline but he might of course be dead. She called out firmly. "Jago, Jago."

She wasn't going to go away, that was obvious, so Jago popped his head out.

"Ah there you are. Do you know what day it is tomorrow?" she asked.

He rolled his eyes. "Groundhog Day?"

"What?" Number 62 didn't know what he was talking about. "No silly, it's Christmas Day and I want to invite you to have Christmas dinner with me." Number 62 had struggled with her conscience over this. Jago could be surly and it was risky too. For all she knew he might be violent. But her Christian obligation had taken over and once she had made her decision, she was actually looking forward to it.

"No thanks."

Number 62 felt deflated. She ran a hand through her short-cropped grey hair, a distraught look on her face. It had taken a great deal of courage and much weighing up of risk versus reward. "Please Jago, I'm on my own you know." And then horrified that he might take this the wrong way, she added, "I've bought a whole turkey and Poppy and I will never manage to eat it all."

Jago didn't think she'd have much problem finishing a whole goose, let alone a turkey, judging by the size of her. And he remembered the precious Poppy. Every time number 62 brought him a hot meal her King Charles spaniel came snuffling into his tent, trying to lick his face. "What you doing for pudding?" he asked.

"Chocolate Yule log and double cream."

"Brandy butter?" That was the only alcohol number 62 was likely to have at Christmas.

"Yes, I can make some brandy butter."

"Yeah, OK then. But you bring it over here. Thanks very much."

Number 62 was slightly disappointed that Jago didn't accept her invitation to come to the house, but it saved her the embarrassment of setting up the dining table in the garage. She waddled back across the road, full of Christmas cheer. She might even have a sherry when she got home.

A familiar voice hissed his name. "Jago?"

"No peace for the wicked," he muttered under his breath.

"Jago, can I have a word? Do you know…"

"Yes, it's Christmas Eve and I'm waiting for the three kings!"

He knew by the smell of patchouli oil that it was Number 44. She was a bit of a hippie. He could only imagine what she'd be cooking for Christmas dinner. She was quiet for so long that he opened one eye to see her crestfallen face. Perhaps he'd been a bit sharp. After all, she made a cracking apple pie. He should make a bit of an effort. "Morning missus, you all right?"

"Well Jago…" She spoke in a half-whisper and Jago had to sit up to hear what she was saying. "I don't normally do Christmas, I prefer to celebrate the Winter Solstice you know." Jago didn't know. "But this year I thought I would make an exception, for you."

"No need to change your plans for me, girl." What was it with all these women? It's not as if he was the Saviour.

"I walk past every night and see you at one with nature. No walls, no possessions. I envy you, Jago, if only I had the courage to do the same."

Jago kept his comments to himself.

"So I'd like to ask you to join me and Dragomir for a meal tomorrow, in our house, to celebrate the re-birth of the year and the coming into the world of Jesus Christ." She breathed the words out in a rush and seemed exhausted at the end.

She was covering all options, then, which seemed a safe bet.

Jago took a moment to consider. "I don't like to be contained, see? I'm like the fox, I need to be able to sniff the air, to scent danger, to run if I have to." He couldn't remember the last time he'd run anywhere, but he thought this line would save him from having to refuse outright.

No 44 nodded. "Oh, yes, I understand completely. I should have thought of that, I'm sorry." She seemed genuinely upset. He thought again of her apple pie.

"Tell you what, why don't you bring the dinner over to me. I can eat it here and then I can share any leftovers with my fellow creatures." He hoped the residents hadn't noticed how the rat population had flourished since he moved in.

"Of course! That's a wonderful solution. I'll see you tomorrow."

"Oh by the way, what's on the menu?" He had a horrible feeling he knew already.

No 44 called back as she skipped off down the road. "Nut roast, quinoa and carrots with juniper and tahini."

As he lay in his shelter that night, the sky seemed to be whispering to him. He peeked out of the entrance and saw it had started to snow. The flakes were falling gently around him and soon the detritus that had been left by the passers-by had been transformed. Mysterious mounds hiding their secrets of scarves, socks and cheese sandwiches, now lined the pavement. A rat was sitting on its haunches by one of the mounds, with a crust in its paws. Jago watched as it dropped the bread for a moment and wiped a snowflake from its nose.

He lay back and pulled the covers up around him. *Christmas Eve eh?* He and his brothers used to club together to buy Mum a present. She always made out she was delighted with it. One year they gave her some cheap perfume from Boots and she cried and tried to gather them all in her arms. His older brother Bill laughed and told her not to be so soft, but Jago found himself crying too.

He slept late the next day and was woken by the sound of raised voices.

"Look, I asked him first, it's all here wrapped in tinfoil." That would be number 43.

"You must have misheard him, he obviously didn't want yours, or he'd never have agreed to mine." Number 62 sounded pretty angry.

"Ladies, let's not argue, this is a time for peace and goodwill." Number 44 was trying to calm things down. "And actually, I think he is going for a vegan Christmas dinner this year. He is an animal lover you know."

Number 43 snorted.

"I think I've got the solution. Come across the road for a moment." The man from 59 had taken control.

The ladies stopped arguing and once again Jago was left to himself. He dozed off for a while. The snow muffled any noises from outside; even the cars sneaked by silently. But then his stomach started growling. So much for a Christmas dinner! He'd have to rake through some of the bags outside see if the rats had left anything.

He gave it half an hour and then put his head out of the shelter.

"Merry Christmas, Jago!" And there they all were: numbers 43, 44, 62 and 59 plus quite a few others he'd seen as they walked their dogs.

The PC was crouching down outside. "Merry Christmas, mate, warm yourself up with this." And he handed Jago a bottle of whisky. Jago looked around. The snow was thick on the ground but someone had put up a gazebo. There were tables and chairs and a firepit under the gazebo. A pile of parcels wrapped in Christmas paper were heaped outside his entrance. Someone had hung paper chains on his shelter. The smell of turkey wafted through the cold air and even the aroma of sprouts whetted his appetite.

"Tuck in, son." The man from 59 held a plate out to Jago, piled high with turkey slices, roast potatoes and what looked like a very small portion of nut roast. "Ray Beckworth, from number 59." Jago nodded.

The woman behind him piped up. "Sally Turnbull, from number 43." And she handed him a gravy boat.

"Mary Corrigan, your neighbour from number 62. Christmas blessings, Jago." Her dog started to lick Jago's face. He felt like giving it a good kick but to his surprise found he was actually enjoying the sensation. Mary passed him a red paper crown.

"Morgana Windspirit and my partner Dragomir from number 44." The man bent down and nodded, his dreadlocks swinging into Jago's face. Morgana was holding a piece of mistletoe in her hand and Jago ducked back in quickly to the safety of his shelter.

"We'll let you get stuck in then, Jago." And the policeman, who introduced himself as Geoff, herded everyone into the gazebo where Jago watched them eating and drinking and laughing together.

After a couple of hours, people began to drift away. Number 62 (he couldn't think of her as Mary) came over to him.

"Thank you Jago," she said. "Can you believe it? I've never spoken to my neighbours before and do you know? They are lovely. I don't think I'll ever be lonely again." Morgana came up behind and put her arm around Mary. "You've given us a great gift, Jago," she said. He looked puzzled and shook his head. "You have shown us that we can all be generous of spirit."

"And I never realized how much more enjoyable it is to give rather than to receive. So thanks for that Jago." That was Sally from number 43. He thought she sounded as if she'd had rather too much Christmas cheer.

He looked at the three women, standing in a row, bundled in their winter coats, scarves and hats, smiling down at him.

Never mind the three wise men, he thought. *This was equality gone mad.*

Acknowledgements

The authors would like to express their gratitude to the following friends and relatives who gave the authors their help and support: Carolyn Bevan, Catherine Bowden, Pauline Brookes, Erik Brown, Angie Buckingham, James Hepburn, Lorraine Hepburn, Diana King, Mark Kitchen, Gillian Lightfoot, Sylvia Reading, Paul Rodgers, Rachel Rushton, Jane Scott, Maria Stevenson, Alison Wargent, Martin Wargent, Jane Williams, Ross Young.